IN DARKNESS, DELIGHT

CREATURES OF THE NIGHT

EDITED BY:

ANDREW LENNON
& EVANS LIGHT

CHARLOTTE, NC

In Darkness, Delight: Creatures of the Night

"River of Nine Tails" ©2018 by Mark Cassell
"Father" ©2018 by Richard Chizmar
"White Rabbit" ©2018 by Tim Curran
"A Survivor" ©2018 by Ray Garton
"The Newell Post" ©2018 by Eddie Generous
"Snap" ©2018 by Kev Harrison
"The Green Man of Freetown" ©2018 by Curtis M. Lawson
"Silent Scream" ©2016 by Andrew Lennon
"Valley of the Dunes" ©2018 by Adam Light
"Gertrude" ©2013 by Evans Light
"He Wears the Lake" ©2018 by Chad Lutzke
"One Thousand Words on a Tombstone: Bully Jack ©2018 by Josh Malerman
"The People in the Toilet" ©2018 by Mason Morgan
"Scales" ©2018 by Christopher Motz
"The Worms Turn"©2018 by Frank Oreto
"Human Touch" ©2018 by Glenn Rolfe
"Hinkles" ©2018 by Kristopher Rufty
"The Giant's Table" ©2018 by Mary SanGiovanni
"The Last Thing You Want to Be" ©2018 by Jeff Strand
"Infestation" ©2018 by Mikal Trimm
"The Ugly Tree" ©2018 by Gregor Xane

"Gertrude" was previously published in *Screamscapes: Tales of Terror*

Cover by Mikio Murakami.

Interior formatting by Lori Michelle of
The Author's Alley.

For more information, please visit:
www.corpuspress.com

TABLE OF CONTENTS

CREATURES OF THE NIGHT

THE PEOPLE IN
THE TOILET

Mason Morgan

CREATURES OF THE NIGHT

JIMMY WAS STANDING in his room with his legs crossed when he decided he couldn't hold it any longer. It had been five days since he last snuck outside and crouched in the garden. Five days. He'd never gone this long. It burned in his stomach, and with each passing step, he could feel it trying to sneak out. He looked at the door to his bathroom, the one with The People in the toilet, and then to the door leading to the staircase and, eventually, outside, where the sun was beginning to fall. He opted for the staircase.

It had been three years since Mom last took a wet wipe to his behind. Since then, he'd learned to fold the paper instead of crumpling it and also to put one hand over his ear and push his head against his shoulder so that both ears were muffled when he flushed. He didn't like loud noises. They scared him. Lots of things did. But nothing scared Jimmy more than The People in the toilet.

He heard them at night, slurping and sloshing behind the door, making their bad man plans, bringing with them a stench that splattered the whole room. He didn't dare leave the door open at night, and he never, ever, used the toilet for number two. And since Christmas was fast approaching, his parents always kept their door—and as such, their bathroom—locked.

Thus, the garden. He'd stashed toilet paper under some dirt near a fence post in the corner where Mom grew carrots. That's where he was headed when he felt something go wrong.

He'd almost made it all the way down the stairs when there was an inner tumbling, a belch from his tummy—not his mouth or his back, but his tummy—and then he felt it coming out. He navigated the final steps without the use of his knees. At the

1

bottom, he tried to force it up with crossed legs and a push. A warmth squished in his underwear, and he knew it was too late.

And so, onto the white carpet and in full view of his loving mother, Jimmy did a bad thing. He did a real bad thing, as evidenced by the thunder Mom made when he pulled down his shorts and squatted. The noise she made was so loud, little Thumper started barking in her kennel, a yap that barely echoed through the hallway. The thing Jimmy did was so bad, Mom cursed right in front of him. It may have been the worst thing Jimmy had ever done.

"Nothing to your father," she said as she scrubbed the carpet to a color that almost didn't look brown. "Thumper did this, do you understand?" She took him to his bathtub and washed his behind. "Do you understand me?" Her loud voice made Jimmy look away, which she noticed immediately and countered with a kiss on his forehead. "It's okay, you're okay," she said. "It's just, I thought we were through this, hun." Her eyes became big, full moons. "Why don't you use your toilet?"

The thought of speaking it aloud made him think about them, The People, and how that maybe by discussing them, he would bring them further into the world, further out of the toilet and into his bedroom, where they would take their sewage fingers and pull his covers off and he would scream and they would—

"I'm scared," he said in the smallest voice he could.

"Oh honey." She brought him closer to her chest. "You're not gonna fall in. There's nothing to be scared of."

"I'm not scared of falling in," he said. "I'm scared of The People."

Mom tilted her head.

The thick groan of the garage door sounded from behind the walls and Mom rushed out of the bathroom, down the stairs, and to the office where Thumper yapped away in her crate. She cut her thumb trying to press the metal springs together, and then

2

she took the miniature schnauzer into the kitchen, placed her in the sink, and started running the water right as The Father threw the garage door closed behind him and boomed a tremor through the walls. Mom jumped as a sensation she'd felt much too often, and for too long, slid down her.

"Motherfuckers don't know what I'm worth," The Father said. He crossed behind Mom and went for the cabinet. Clinks of glass hitting glass preceded the pouring of liquid. He lifted it to his lips. "You know, I would love to take a baseball bat to work tomorrow and bash Mr. Barber's face in." He finished the drink. "But I won't be able to, because I won't be going to work tomorrow, or any other fuckin' day." He slammed the glass onto the countertop so hard it bounced. "Why are you washin' that dog?"

Upstairs, Jimmy got out of the tub, dried off, and threw on his pajamas. He snuck down the staircase and hid behind one of the wooden banisters just in time to see The Father rip Thumper out of the sink and carry her by the neck to the carpet.

"Bad!" The Father yelled, rubbing the dog's nose in the stain. "Bad dog!" He pressed into Thumper's head with both hands. Her yelps came out in muffled sputters, the sound of them dashed against the carpet. "You'll learn, you little shit!" The Father grabbed the back of Thumper's neck and pulled her into the air. Without the insulation of the carpet, her yelps came full-force and screeched through the room. Nothing could disguise their purpose, she was crying for help.

Then The Father dropped Thumper from his chest, a height five times the size of the dog, and returned to rubbing her nose raw against the stain.

"Stop!" Jimmy yelled. He flew down the stairs and hid behind Mom's legs. "You're hurting her!"

The Father looked at Jimmy, his teeth showing through bared lips, and Jimmy saw the fake molar on his left, the golden one he

3

only saw when The Father flaunted his anger, its shimmer a signal of his rage. In Jimmy's mind, the sight of that tooth was a trigger for fear.

"Come here," The Father said.

Jimmy looked up to Mom, who was already peering down at him. "Listen to your father," she said. Her hands shook as she pressed him forward.

"You can learn something from this," The Father said. "When you break the rules, the best way to learn is hurt." He picked Thumper up and clamped his hand over her mouth to muzzle the yelps. "It's nature, how God intended. You mess with a beehive and get stung, and you ain't gonna do it again." He dropped her onto the floor and continued to thrash her nose against the carpet even as specks of red appeared. "It's how I learned, it's how your momma learned, and it's how this dog'll learn." Back into the air. Thumper's eyes were glazed with moisture. "So I'm not hurting her. I'm teaching her. Do you understand me?"

When The Father dropped Thumper again, Jimmy fell to his knees and tried to catch her, reaching only far enough to slip his hands beneath her hind legs. She spun in the air and landed on her snout, then she rolled to her side and started whimpering. Jimmy rushed to her and stroked her neck.

"Move," the Father said. "The lesson isn't over."

"I did it!" Jimmy said through tears. "It was me!"

Mom gasped. "He doesn't know what he's talking about," she said. "He just wants to protect Thumper."

The Father cocked his head and squinted. He looked confused. "You . . . "

He shifted his gaze between the stain to Jimmy.

"You did this?" Anger consumed his look of confusion, the evil in his eyes returning with new vigor. "*You did this?*"

"He's lying!" Mom said.

4

"Shut up!"

Mom stepped back and covered her mouth with her hand.

The Father crouched down to Jimmy's height. "Now why in the world would you say something like that?"

Jimmy wiped his face. "Because it's the truth!" He sniffled and pulled Thumper into his lap. "She didn't do anything!"

A vein bulged on The Father's forehead. "And why couldn't you just use your toilet?"

"Because!—" Jimmy stopped himself. Not so loud. "Because of The People."

The Father didn't move. "What?" he said.

"The People in the toilet will get me."

He blinked. Something in him went sideways. "What did you just say?"

Jimmy swallowed a glob of spit and felt it go all the way down his throat. "People are in there, I can hear them at night." He stole glances at the staircase while he spoke. "They wanna get me, get us, I know they do, so I—"

A hand came across Jimmy's cheek so hard he bit his tongue. The Father spoke slowly. "I will not let my boy grow up scared of that which is not." He undid the buckle on his belt and snaked it through the loops. "If you want to feel fear, I will show it to you." He folded the tail to the buckle and snapped it taut. "This way, you will know what is real."

"Please . . . " Mom said.

The Father raised a finger to her. "You will not doubt my father and the father before him." He turned his gaze to Jimmy, who sat crouched on bent knees and was fighting sobs. "Stand up." Jimmy rolled Thumper off his lap, the dog able to stand but visibly pained, and did as he was told. "Turn around and drop your pants."

He pulled the belt behind his head. Mom closed her eyes. Jimmy looked at her scrunched-up nose, how her skin folded in so many directions, and thought it must be how he looked, standing there, waiting for impact.

Freezing fire scalded his hide as the belt's snap popped through his ears. One seemed to reinforce the other, the pain of the hit radiating as remnants of the snap echoed off the walls. He tried to breathe but the air wouldn't come. The Father readied his belt again.

By the time he was done, Jimmy's underwear had changed color. He hopped to Mom and went slack in her arms.

"We're not done." The Father took a few breaths. "I still have to show you what's not real. Or rather, you have to show me."

Jimmy buried his face in Mom's blouse.

The Father marched them upstairs, coming up along behind them to prevent them from turning tail, the thump of his footsteps like the tick of a grandfather clock. Though their flight was only twenty-four steps, the journey stretched on and on, each second fattening into something more, something infinite and unforgettable. Jimmy couldn't feel it or know what it meant, but wide grooves of response patterns carved themselves into his brain, informing his future for years to come. The people he would befriend, the lovers he would hold. What he would consider himself.

They reached the final step and entered Jimmy's room. Batman stared back from a vinyl poster, his eyes pure white against the blue mask, that infamous scowl etched on his square face, and Jimmy wished harder than he ever had in his life that superheroes were real.

"Now," The Father said. He pointed to the door. "You're going in that bathroom and you're not coming out until there's something brown in that toilet."

"But he just—" Mom said. "You know."

"Looks like we'll be here a while, then."

"But what if he doesn't have anything in his tummy?"

"You can go make dinner."

"And bring it up? He can't eat dinner in the bathroom."

"Yes he can."

Mom picked at her blouse. "I might need help cooking."

"I'll stay here. You can handle it."

She stood there looking for a moment.

"Go on," The Father said. "Something we all like, please?"

She blinked back whatever was happening behind her eyes. "Okay," she said. She went downstairs. Jimmy watched as she left. Then he looked to The Father.

"I'm not going to wait much longer," The Father said.

Jimmy went to the door, twisted the knob, and pushed forward. The hinge creaked at each moment of rotation, the whole spin sounding like a witch's wail. Looking in from behind the doorway, he let the door swing to its stop and then clicked on the light. Fluorescent bulbs bathed the windowless room in harsh brightness, the kind meant to awaken, and he watched as the long walkway of the bathroom, sink on the right and bathtub on the left, seemed to extend, lengthening past the limits of the house's architecture. And in the corner, the toilet droned its airy whisper, the pipes behind it working just as intended. He could already sense their presence.

"Don't make me start counting."

Jimmy stared down at the threshold, where the carpet met the tile, and then he stepped over it and closed the door.

The world changed tone, the birdsong from outside replaced by the fan's constant hum. Jimmy heard it bounce off the porcelain and double in strength, rotating around him, encircling him like prey. The People were hungry. They'd been waiting.

Jimmy lifted his foot, moved it forward, and let it drop. Then he matched the distance with his other foot. He did this repeatedly, slowly inching his way toward the toilet, until he was close enough to reach the lid. He could feel them underneath, bubbling in the water, planning their attack, ready with weapons of discarded iron and bile. They were undoubtedly laughing as they pictured his demise and eventual roast on the spit, licking their lips as they savored the smell of his skin. It had been so long since they'd had a meal. So long, indeed.

The lid was silent as he lifted it with the tip of his forefinger and peeked inside. The water sat still, completely undisturbed by any movement underneath. A moment of relief came over him, and then a ripple shot across the surface.

He froze. He watched the water, waiting for them to jump out. Nothing. They knew how to toy with you. This was their game.

Another ripple expanded from the center outward in a circle, and then another, and another. Bubbles began to form on the surface, popping just as they appeared. The color drained from Jimmy's face as he watched the water inside his toilet become a miniature vortex, swaths of white foam forming around the water's edge. He stepped back and bumped his heels against the bathtub. No more room to run.

Then he heard a whisper from the whirlpool.

"*Closer,*" said a low voice. It gargled over the word like phlegm. "*Come closer.*"

Though Jimmy could not see the water from his position, he noticed the color just above the surface was changing. He edged closer, just enough to see, just a peek, just a quick glance.

Blood thicker than oil spun in the toilet and stained the bowl red. Specks of it splattered on his pajamas as it sloshed around. Jimmy watched it self-correct to a point of perfection. He could feel his breath slipping away. No amount of inner screaming got his legs to move. He peered helplessly into the hypnotic crimson flow, its cyclonic pattern a beckoning wave. Jimmy traced its movement with his eyes, looping round and round with his eyes, looping over and around and up and down and over and around and looping over —

He blinked away and broke the spell. The fear, the mental alarm, the realization of how cold he was flooded him. Why was it so cold? Tremors shook him. He turned to run, to exchange one pair of jaws for another, when the voice bubbled back up.

"Come closer now."

Jimmy hit the door, threw it open, and fell to The Father's feet with tears in his eyes. "Don't go in there!" he said. "They'll get you!"

Without words, The Father stepped over Jimmy and went into the bathroom, all the while holding a face that said he knew what to expect and was excited to watch it unfold.

But when he got to the toilet, he gave Jimmy an odd look. "What . . . " he mumbled, watching the toilet. His eyes went in circles, slowly at first but with increasing pace. He started to wobble, spinning his head as he tottered back and forth like a drunk. Then he pitched headfirst into the toilet. Jimmy opened his mouth to scream but nothing came.

Blood splashed across the room, onto the sink, the tub, the walls. The Father's feet lifted off the ground. A great grinding sound emerged, like metal in a blender, and The Father's body began to vibrate as he sank deeper into the vortex.

Jimmy rushed to The Father and grabbed his legs. He pulled to no avail. He put his foot onto the toilet and pulled harder, and then his foot slipped on the blood and he fell to the tile. He watched as The Father's knees disappeared below the bowl, then his ankles, and then finally one of The Father's loafers popped off and landed next to him.

The grinding grew to a deafening volume. It blew past the ears and went straight for the body, and as it reached its incredible peak, a fountain of bloody pulp shot from the toilet to the ceiling, splattering out like a mushroom cloud and covering every surface of the room with its sticky warmth.

The grinding quieted down and eventually stopped. The fan's

9

hum again filled the room, occasionally blotted out by the slap of gore falling from the ceiling. Pulling his hands from his eyes, Jimmy attempted to stand and slipped on the first two tries. When he gained his footing, he blocked the toilet from his peripheral vision with his hand and went to leave. That's when he heard Mom scream.

He rushed down the steps and saw her standing at the sink, frozen, one hand on her mouth and another bracing her against the countertop to support her shaking knees.

"Mom!" Jimmy shouted. "What is it?"

She shook her head and pointed at the sink. Jimmy came to her and looked.

There, sitting in a broken circle around the drain, were teeth, one of them with a golden sparkle.

HUMAN TOUCH

Glenn Rolfe

CREATURES OF THE NIGHT

ROSIE ZIPPED her leather jacket, pulled her hood up over her shoulder-length black hair, and drew her hands into the sleeves of her sweatshirt. Figures she'd get stuck out in this weather. *Shit luck* her mother always called it. Her relationship choices, Terry especially, fell in the same column. Terry stole her car and wouldn't be back until dawn at the earliest. She knew he was drinking and getting fucked up again. Every time, he promised to be better. Every time, he failed.

Headlights illuminated the rain drenched blacktop. Rosie rushed out and tried waving the vehicle down, while at the same time, hoping it wasn't some perverted spider waiting to catch its next fly.

The car swerved around her, blaring its horn, splashing cold water over her leggings.

"Fuck you, too!" she shouted. People in this town were assholes.

Hands on her hips, she gritted her teeth, as the soft rain turned angry.

"Ugh," she moaned, shaking her fists at the dark storm above.

The sound of the driver's engine vanished out of range, leaving Rosie to the wind, rain, and surrounding forest. Neither the dark nor the woods bothered her. She'd lived in Naples her whole life. This town offered a whole lotta nothin', for better or worse, for hero or foe. A kid out hunting with his father went missing once only to return alone and spouting nonsense. Rumors of inbred, murderous woods-people abounded, but Rosie'd never seen or experienced anything in her twenty years to lend credence to the outlandish tales.

She wondered if her trek to Glen's was worth the risk. Not for fear of the mythical morons walking amongst the trees, but for what it meant about her future. Part of her wished Terry would let the bottle swallow him already, or take her car and vanish without a trace. It would make everything easier.

But who would take care of him? Who would be by his side at the end?

She hated that part of her that still wanted to be that person. Walking along the road, she raised her chin and let the deluge take her tears.

There was no saving Terry from his path of self-destruction. Moving on, taking Glen up on his invite, that was her only chance.

A sound, like a dog's nails tapping across a hardwood floor, startled her. Spinning around, Rosie couldn't believe what she was seeing. There in the road, following her, no bigger than her old cat Sandy, was something that looked like a cross between an opossum and a wet racoon. It stopped and stared at her, its glowing eyes giving off a blue-tinged luminance. The light grew in intensity. Her arms crawled with gooseflesh. A strange buzzing began to sound in her ears. The hum was cut off by a voice.

She didn't know the language, yet she understood. This creature needed help. Rosie knelt and reached out. "Come here, it's okay."

The thing click-clacked its way to her, crawling up into her open arms.

"Fuck," Rosie said, craning her neck from the creature. "You reek."

The buzz in her ears sounded again.

"I'm going to take you with me to Glen's. I don't know if he'll know what to do with you, but he's a police officer—"

The light from its eyes intensified as the buzzing made her wince.

"Okay, okay," she said. "Knock it off, will ya?"

The light in its eyes dimmed, the buzzing ceased.

"All right, I won't tell anyone, but that means we'll have to go back to my place."

She opened her jacket, letting the thing crawl inside for warmth. Its nails stabbed her breasts as it settled against her.

"Good?" she said.

A quiet cooing noise, close to a purr, reached her ears.

"Yeah, you just needed a little human touch, huh?"

She zipped the jacket up halfway, snuggled her arms around the wet lump against her chest, and headed back the way she'd come.

It took about twenty minutes to get back to Terry's trailer. She opened the front door and hurried inside. She pulled back her hood and leaned against the door. She half-expected to find her car and Terry waiting for them.

She peeked inside her coat and saw the blue eyes gazing back.

"You okay in there?"

The creature sunk deeper.

Rosie unzipped the jacket and poured it out. The thing hunched to the floor, backing away, frightened or threatened, she couldn't tell.

"Hey, you're all right. This is my home," she said placing her hand to her chest. "It's warm and safe, okay?" She slipped out of her jacket, tossing it to the sofa, and sat down on the closest cushion. "Look," she said, undoing one boot, then the other. "I'll let you get comfortable while I go change into some dry clothes, deal?"

Tossing the boots next to the front door, she walked past her house guest and down the hallway.

She didn't want Terry coming home now. He'd freak out and try to kill the thing. Hopefully his toxic twin, Tom, would keep him out late.

She stripped out of her wet clothes, tossing them to the end of the bed, and grabbed a soft t-shirt and sleep shorts from her dresser. She carried the clothes into the bathroom, clicked on the light, and grabbed a towel for her damp hair. Looking in the mirror, she thought of the creature in her living room.

Why did I bring that thing home? She tried to answer the question, but felt a sudden chill crawl over her when she couldn't recall her reasoning. *What if it has rabies or something worse? Is there something worse?* She stopped and listened, but couldn't tell where the creature was. Probably right where she left it. Hunched on the floor, afraid of its own shadow.

She'd barely finished getting dressed when the unmistakable sound of her dying Plymouth rumbled into the driveway. "Shit."

"Rosie? Rosie!"

Fists clenched at her side, trying to ready herself for Terry's reaction, Rosie hurried into the living room. Terry swayed before the door, and the creature was gone.

"I can explain," she said.

"What are you talking' about?" he mumbled, stutter-stepping his way to the couch before collapsing face first onto it. He mumbled something else and then fell silent.

Where had it gone?

She dropped to her knees and peeked under the couch, her grandmother's rocking chair, and then checked behind the TV stand. Her fear from earlier raced up her spine.

She was on one knee when the screech came from behind, startling her. Rosie lost her balance and crashed into the TV stand.

"Ahhhh," Terry's muffled cry filled the room.

Rosie's eyes went wide at the sight of the thing, its claws sunk into Terry's back. The creature had changed, it was bigger. Sharp bones protruded from its long spine and the screeching grew higher in pitch until it filled her head. Rosie clamped her hands over her ears and tried to get to her feet. She was ready to cry out when it launched up to Terry's shoulder and sunk its claws into the sides of his skull. A slimy, glowing thing grew from between its legs. She saw the blue fluid dripping from it as it moved closer and closer to the back of Terry's head. Before she could make a move, the creature punctured Terry's flesh and let out a guttural moan. It began to shiver as the downward flow of blue slime reversed direction and darkened. Blood. It was taking Terry's blood.

When it finished, Terry laid silent and still.

The thing's bony spines receded into its fur. A loud squelch was followed by a soft tearing noise, accompanied the retraction of its odd penetrating organ. Craning its head, the thing gazed at her. The buzzing in her head returned, and the voice.

"I won't," she said. "I won't tell anybody about you. Please, just don't hurt me."

Its eyes closed.

Rosie crawled toward the hallway, keeping her eyes on the thing until she cleared the room. Trembling, she stood and hurried to her bedroom. She slammed the door, turned the lock, and dove onto the bed and under the covers. Tears flowed down her cheeks.

She couldn't leave. It told her as much.

The room, alive with the grey light of a new day, cold and alien, welcomed her back from the dream. Rosie raised her head from the pillow, wiped drool from her chin, and shook her head. *Holy shit, what a fucking dream.* The lump beside her assured her the strange, wet nightmare was just that, a bad fucking trip through dreamland.

"Terry?" she said. She reached over, closed her eyes, and wrapped an arm around him. He gave off heat like a furnace, and his breathing was labored. He tended to get sick easily. His drinking wreaked havoc on his immune system. She snuggled up next to him, but Terry's normal musky scent, alcohol and body odor, usually inviting and comforting, was different. Nuzzling her nose into the back of his neck, she touched cold slime. A smell like wet garbage hit her strong and swift, triggering her gag reflex.

Rosie scurried away from the horrid odor, opened her eyes, and gazed upon the source of it all. The back of Terry's neck was a mound of wet, blue slime. The hair just above had gone bleach white, his neck and shoulder glistening with a sheen of sweat.

Trembling, Rosie spilled from the sheets to the carpeted floor. The bedroom door was open, the hallway, untouched by the morning's dim light, was shaded in darkness. Her heart pounded in her chest; her thoughts scattered. It wasn't a dream.

The awful image of the wet creature and its organ plunging into Terry's head . . . she shook it away. *No, no . . .* gazing at the mess on the back of his neck, she couldn't deny the truth. Dark red blotches covered the tan sheet at his back.

He'd had been in his green army jacket when he crashed out on the couch, when the thing clawed into him, and it was still here. She stood, pulled open the top drawer of her dresser, and fumbled around for the stiletto knife she kept stashed away. Gripping the handle and popping the shiny blade, she never imagined she'd be facing an actual intruder.

She wondered if it was sleeping.

I need to get out before it wakes the fuck up.

She crept to the doorway, crossed the threshold, and started slowly down the hall (*faster than a cannonball*). The silly lyric crossed her dizzy mind, a giddy attempt to mask her fear. She pressed her bare foot to the bathroom door and pushed. Terry's clothes into a pile by the tub. The punctures on the back of his jacket were surrounded by dark, crimson stains.

What the hell did it do to him? He'd still been breathing when she awoke. He was still alive. Could she leave him? Could she abandon him here with this thing?

You don't know that it's still here.

But what if it is? What then?

Praying the creature had found its way out, Rosie continued down the hall.

She leaned her back against the wall, slowly edging forward as she came to the living room. She had a clear view of most of the kitchen. It wasn't out there. Carefully, she craned her head around the corner, scanning the living room floor, the couch *(where it latched into Terry)*, and the rocker. The hairs on her body stood as she stepped into the room for a better look. A couple splotches of dark wetness on the couch were the only things out of place.

Holding the knife between her breasts, Rosie exhaled. After scoping out the rest of the room and the kitchen beyond, certain that both, like the bathroom, were clear, she considered her next move. It struck her that she hadn't fully checked the bedroom. The suffocating feeling of dread welled up.

Run. Just get out. Go to Glen, go to the police. Anywhere but here. Get out while you can.

She couldn't leave Terry here with that thing.

She started for the hallway when the sound of their bedsprings creaking stopped her cold.

"Terry?" she said.

She looked toward the end of the hall. The floor groaned under his weight as his naked body came into view.

"Rosalita? What's happening to me?" he said, raising his hands before his dark eyes. "I can't feel my hands, I can't see right. Everything's blurry."

19

His voice sounded scratchy.

"Terry," she said. "Can you look around the room?"

"I can't fucking see."

"I know, but you need to check the floor by your side of the bed. Is there anything there?"

He shambled away from the door. Clenching the knife, she held her breath.

He moaned.

"Terry?"

A second moan was followed by the splash of vomit, and a loud thump.

"Terry?"

As she took a step down the hallway, he reemerged, grinning behind illuminated blue eyes.

Oh God, it's inside him.

Rosie screamed and bolted for the front door. She heard its heavy footfalls closing in behind her.

The dampness of the wet morning wrapped itself around her like an empty grave on a late spring evening. Rosie rushed down the driveway and ran as fast as her bare feet would carry her. The chill of the day could make her sick, but under-dressed and vulnerable, she forged ahead. She'd give her last breath to the elements before turning it over to the thing behind her.

She didn't stop until the biting cramp in her side gave her no choice. The road behind her was vacant.

Catching her breath, crouching to the slick pavement, hands on her head, Rosie tried to wrap her mind around what the fuck had happened. It was that damn thing. It had done something to her, did something to her mind, and convinced her to take it in. Made her compliant.

Jesus, what was it? Some kind of monster? An alien?

A police cruiser appeared around the bend. Rosie stood and shuffled to the side of the road.

Please be Glen, oh please.

The car rolled to a stop. She rushed to Glen as he hurried out of the car. His welcome arms were a Godsend. She shoved her face into his shoulder and wept.

"What happened?" He squeezed her close. "Are you okay?"

She didn't know where to start. She'd sound insane, but she didn't give a fuck, she didn't have time to care. She wasn't sure Terry could be saved, in fact, she felt he was gone, but that didn't mean she shouldn't try. Whatever that thing was, it needed to be stopped.

"Terry," she managed.

"What? Did he hit you?"

"No, no . . . "

"I swear to Christ, Rosie—"

She held him at arms-length. "No, Terry didn't do anything."

"Sorry, I just . . . " He hung his head. "I'm sorry. What happened?"

She told him about walking to his house, thinking she'd found a wounded animal, its strange effect on her, and then, what it had done to Terry. His glowing eyes.

"And where's Terry now? At the house?"

She nodded.

"Come on, let's get you out of this weather and warm you up."

"You'll check on Terry?"

"Of course," he said. "We'll head over now."

She let him walk her around to the passenger side. He opened the door and helped her in.

"Do you think you should call for back up?" she said.

"Do you?" he said.

All she knew was that she didn't know shit.

"Listen," Glen said. "Let's go over, you stay in the car. I'll have a look. If it looks bad, I'll call the station."

She nodded. He closed the door, came around the front of the car and climbed in.

Two minutes later, they pulled up to the trailer.

"Hold tight, okay?" Glen said.

"Be careful," she said.

He gazed into her eyes. God, she wanted to give into him. Despite her inability to deny her attraction to him or his to her, they hadn't done more than hang out and talk over coffee. She averted her eyes. She wanted to kiss him so hard, but she couldn't. Not here, not now. Whatever Terry's condition, she couldn't betray him in his driveway.

"All right, then," Glen said. He moved swiftly from the car to the steps, to the door. Gun drawn, taking in every aspect of the moment.

She hugged herself, warming her cold bones in the heated car, watching as Glen grasped the chrome knob and eased the trailer door open. Her stomach knotted.

He disappeared inside.

Visions of Terry with that thing attached to him, crawled over her mind, as she saw Glen on the floor, the creature violating him the same way . . .

She shouldered the door open, rushed the stairs, and hurried after Glen.

Thunder cracked, the flash of lightening that followed lit the living room in a strobe light-like show. Glen was at the head of the hallway. He craned his neck.

"Don't," she said. "Don't go down there. Let's just get the hell away from here."

"Just let me do a quick —"

"No, I changed my mind, it's not worth the risk."

The blue luminance lit the hallway, and Glen turned back. The boom from his gun was deafening in the trailer's tight confines.

"Glen!" she shouted, watching in horror as the Terry-thing

struck Glen's arm, knocking the gun to the floor. She watched Glen's elbow bend all the way the wrong way, and his sudden cries stabbed her to the core.

"Rosie, GET OUT!" Glen said.

She'd failed Terry, she couldn't fail him, too. She ran toward the entangled men. Glen had his good arm around the Terry-things neck, trying to fight.

She saw the gun and dove to the floor. Avoiding getting stepped on by either of them, she grabbed the weapon, and scurried farther into the hall before rising and pointing the gun in their direction.

Glen was lifted off the ground and slammed into the wall. His body going limp, he released his already weakening grasp on the Terry-thing's neck. Rosie froze. The Terry-thing bent Glen backwards by the mouth, sticking one hand around his top teeth, the other around his bottom teeth. Glen's cries rose and ceased at the horrid cracking, squelching sounds. His body convulsed as the Terry-thing tore Glen's bottom jaw from his face and flung it at her. She squeezed the trigger.

The blast tore all sound from the world. She didn't see whether her aim was true as Glen's jaw deflected off her teeth and lips. The coppery taste of blood, his or hers she couldn't tell, filled her mouth. She stumbled back, still not able to hear a thing, as she saw Glen dead on the floor, the Terry-thing standing over him holding a hand to the side of its leaking face. Dark fluid flowed over its fingers.

She couldn't even hear her own scream as she aimed and fired, pulling the trigger again and again. The creature jerked at each shot, its arms flailing as it fell, landing just past Glen in the living room.

She was still pulling the trigger, feeling the click, but not the powerful recoil. Tears flowed as her arms trembled and knees weakened. She collapsed to her knees, her ears now ringing, the smell of cordite, the scent of death, engulfing her.

"Hello?"

She wasn't sure she actually heard the voice buried beneath the ringing, as it was a hollow, distant greeting, faint as the voices found buried in the static of electronic voice phenomena.

It wasn't until she saw it was Tom, Terry's twin brother, that she knew it was real.

She could see Tom shouting *"No, what did you do?"* As he dropped down next to Terry. Terry raised his arm.

She turned the gun in her hand, ignoring the burning metal barrel, as she got up and charged ahead. Tom's shocked face gazed up at her as she threw herself atop Terry and began raining blows with the handle of the pistol to the imposter's already bloody face. Gore spattered her face and the carpet as she hammered away. Swinging as hard as she could until Tom's fist smashed into the side of her head.

Darkness caressed her as she sprawled across the floor.

When she opened her eyes, Tom stood over her, Glen's pistol in his hands.

"Tom, you don't understand . . . " Her own voice sounded miles away.

He was shouting about her killing his brother and the cop, his tear-streaked face red, the vein in his forehead bursting. He pointed one hand back toward Terry's prone body.

It was then she saw the blue-eyed creature crawling from the gaping wound in Terry's chest.

It launched itself at Tom, causing him to stumble toward her. As it latched onto his back, Tom dropped the gun and spun around the room reaching for his attacker.

Rosie grabbed the pistol. Glen had to have ammo on his belt. She hurried over to him. His dead eyes stared off into the void. She ignored his ruined mouth and focused on the belt. She found the magazine, quickly replacing the spent one.

Tom was crawling on the floor, screaming as the creature bit chucks of flesh from the back of his neck. As soon as his chest hit the floor, she knew he was dead.

She leveled the pistol at the creature responsible for all this horror. It locked its blue gaze upon her. She heard the buzzing join the ringing in her ears, pulsed behind her eyes.

"Get the fuck out of my head," she shouted as she fired.

The buzzing and throbbing ceased as the creature exploded, painting the living room wall in black and red splatter.

In the days that followed, Rosie spent countless hours at the county jail answering questions from angry officers and detectives, not to mention having to face Terry and Tom's distraught mother. Through it all, she maintained her story, eventually being cleared of any wrong doing. It was deemed impossible for her to have caused the wounds that killed Officer Glen Pekins, and determined that her discharging the officer's firearm was in self-defense.

There were still questions about what truly happened. What was her relationship with Officer Pekins? Was it a factor in the deadly scenario that played out inside the home?

Rosie had told them the truth. They refused to believe it. Instead, she found herself delivered to the Augusta Mental Health Institution. She was fine with that. She needed some time away. She couldn't look at that town, see those people, hear all the whispers . . .

When she closed her eyes that first night in her temporary home, she saw Glen with new shining blue eyes, an imposter, pretending.

She woke up screaming.

WHITE RABBIT

Tim Curran

WHEN I WOKE UP that terrible day, I saw the awful thing there on the bureau: a stuffed white rabbit. It was about two feet tall, its fur white and pristine. It was a perfectly innocuous thing essentially, yet it filled me with a weird, disjointed sense of terror. Its obsidian eyes were glassy as the surfaces of mirrors, seeming to look right at me with the most awful sense of menace.

That was silly, of course, but with its eyes glaring at me, it didn't seem as silly as it should have.

"Mason?" I called out. "Mason?"

The silence told me that he had already left for work. Was this his doing? Was this some kind of joke? If it was, I failed to see the humor in it. Or the point. Rabbits were not my thing. I neither liked them nor disliked them. They held no frame of reference, good or bad.

I swung my legs out of bed and stood up. The hardwood floor felt cold under my feet. I stood there in lounge pants and a Forever 21 tee, feeling woozy and out-of-sorts. I wondered if I was coming down with something. I had that same fuzzy sense of disorientation generally associated with viral flu.

Then whatever that feeling was passed.

Tensing, I stepped over toward the bureau. There was my jewelry box, the Horchow catalog I'd been thumbing through last night, my Galaxy S-7 . . . and that damned rabbit.

"I'm pretty sure we never owned a rabbit," I said out loud, trying to be funny, to reassure myself, and only succeeding in amplifying my burgeoning sense of unreality.

There was something else, too.

The bureau was moved. It was not even with the wall. One side was out about two inches farther than the other. It was nothing really, but I was obsessively anal about details. I preferred things uniform and ordered. Had Mason done it? I really didn't think so. He knew how such trifling details annoyed me.

I pushed the bureau back in place. The rabbit teetered, but did not fall. What bothered me the most was the rut in the carpeting. The bureau must have been in that position for some time to press a rut into the pile like that.

Impossible.

I would have noticed such a thing.

Small, insignificant details like that made me uneasy. Don't ask me to explain; I have been like that since childhood. As a girl, my report cards were filed by grade in manila envelopes and my Good Attendance awards were filed alphabetically by teacher. I wouldn't have been able to sleep last night if the bureau had not been perfectly aligned with the wall. Good God, I even organized the food on my plate fastidiously.

Breathing in and out to calm my rising anxiety, I approached the rabbit. It was just a stuffed bunny. Completely harmless, of course, yet those hollow, reflective eyes were staring holes through me. I reached out a trembling had touch to it, as much to confirm its physical reality as to break the spell of fear it held over me.

Its fur was not soft. In fact, it felt like the bristles of a hog. Tactilely, it was unpleasant, and what made it even worse was that it was warm like the body of a living thing.

I pulled my hand away with a cry.

Enough. It was just the sun coming through the window beaming on it. That's all it was. That's all it could be. These were the things I told myself as I labored over my vegan breakfast of oatmeal and blueberries.

I showered and dressed, got ready for the day in an Emporio Armani skirt suit and heels, refusing to even cast an eye at the rabbit (even though I was certain I could feel it scrutinizing me). I looked good, empowered, chic, and sexy, if I do say so myself. And that was exactly the look I was cultivating. If I landed the PacSun account, I was certain to make full partner at Broders.

"I have important things to do today," I told the moth-eaten hare, "and I don't have time for you."

It was moments later, as I checked Evernote on my phone that, again, I was struck by that odd sense of disorientation as if I was moving in one direction and reality (as I understood it) was moving in quite another. I felt dizzy and lost. I closed the app and reopened it. Nothing had changed:

8:15 Prep with Margaret
9:30 PacSun presentation—Nail it!!!
12:30 Lunch at Gregorio's

* * * * * *Don't forget your dry cleaning!

* * *Watch for him He is coming

The weight of that last note, planted me on the bed. I sat there for some time thinking, fearing that there were things I should remember, but could not. *Watch for him he is coming.* I had not written that. I knew I had not written that. I had no idea what it could even be referencing. Yet . . . there was something playing around the edges of my memory, an apprehensive sort of déjà vu that left me feeling troubled.

Something in my world had changed. I was certain of it. I just couldn't put a finger on what it was.

Life becomes incoherent now, a voice in the back of my mind whispered, and I swear I nearly screamed, because for a moment there, I thought it was the voice of the rabbit.

The day moved on and the very unreal texture of the morning was ground beneath the wheels of the progress. The PacSun presentation was a hit, as was lunch with my boss. I was feeling pretty high and refusing to think about the rabbit or my mad morning.

Mason was already home when I got there. He had that cocky little half-grin on his face that I found so unbearably sexy and so endearing.

"You landed it, didn't you?"

I smiled. "Yes, I did. How did you know? It was supposed to be a surprise."

He came over and scooped me in his arms. "Because, my little Ella, I know you. When you put your mind to something, nothing stops you. That's what I love about you: you're strictly win-win. And look at you in that skirt . . . God." He kissed me, letting it linger deliciously. "As much as I like you in it, I want to get you out of it in the worst way."

We laughed and I told him all about PacSun and how I had wowed them from start to finish. There was not a single moment of the presentation when I did not feel in control. Not a single clumsy moment or breath of dead air.

"What did Margaret say?"

"Well, she paid for lunch. That should tell you something."

"Good girl."

"How was your day?"

He scowled. "Ah, the life of a PA. I spent the morning with two colicky twins. I had a four-year old vomit on me. And . . . oh yes . . . I accidentally spilled Dr. Bella's chai tea and she called me an insufferable klutz . . . string of very un-pediatrician like expletives omitted."

The very idea made me narrow my eyes. "She's such a bitch."

"Exactly, dear. That's why I'm looking forward to quitting my job and being a kept man by my rich, successful girlfriend—faithful house-hubby, galley slave, and patron fuck-toy, that's me."

"I'll keep you busy," I told him, pulling him closer and sliding my tongue into his mouth.

"I look forward to it. But for now, I really need to shower. I think there's still vomit down my collar."

"Eww! Please do."

"Oh . . . and I think I'm taking you out to dinner. You deserve it and God knows I need it." He turned away, then turned back. "Oh, and I love you, Ella-kins."

Ella-kins. Yes, I know it's corny and perfectly ridiculous . . . yet, when he said it, I nearly melted like butter in a hot pan. I could have dripped to the floor and made an unsightly mess. But that was the effect he had upon me. Even though I was ten years older than him, I knew he belonged to me and no one else. I heard the shower running and felt overwhelmed by love. This was turning into the most spectacular day of my life . . . and to think it started with that stupid rabbit. It was laughable now. I'd ask Mason about it when he got out of the shower and the explanation would be perfectly prosaic. Probably a silly gift from one of his little patients. He'd probably left in the car yesterday and fetched it up this morning before he went in, thinking I'd get a laugh out of it. It was funny how time could change your perspective.

Still smiling about it all, I went into the bedroom and the rabbit was not on the bureau. I saw myself in the mirror, standing there, the smile etched onto my face . . . only now there was nothing happy about it. It looked positively sardonic.

I told myself either Mason had moved it or I'd hallucinated the entire business. But I accepted neither explanation. I went through the motions of looking around for it in closets, under the bed, in the spare room . . . but it just wasn't there as I knew it wouldn't be. And the reason for that, I began to think, is that this was a private, intimate sort of haunting. It was not to be shared.

I was overwhelmed with a sense of impending doom. It made me feel dizzy and dislocated. It was as if I could sense something taking shape around me, but could not identify it. I went over to where the rabbit had been, placing a hand there for no other reason than I thought I should. It felt warm, warm as the rabbit had felt under my fingers.

Ridiculous.

If this kept up, I'd be on the road to a full-blown psychosis.

I was tired, overworked, coming down from the raw-edged tension of preparing for the PacSun presentation. That's all it was. That's what I kept telling myself.

Sometimes, strict attention to trivial details can clear your mind and soothe what ails you, so I took off my earrings and put them in the jewelry box. I took off my skirt and laid it on the bed. Then I opened the drawer I kept my socks and underwear in. This is when real panic set in. I was always very meticulous about what went in which drawer and how it was organized within those confines. My underwear were always neatly folded on the right side, the socks on the left. Now they had been transposed. Frantic, I opened another drawer and another and another. I found lounge pants in the drawer reserved for tees and sweatshirts. Pajamas where my jeans usually were and—

Everything was in utter disarray.

I didn't for a moment suspect Mason. He would never do such a thing and he was completely incapable of folding clothes with my usual precision. It was quite beyond him.

I began to wonder earnestly if I was truly losing my mind. Was I doing things contrary to myself and not remembering them? This would have been bad enough for anyone, but for me

. . . dear God, it was catastrophe. I liked to keep my mind as correlated and catalogued as the rest of my life.

I forced myself into the kitchen and cracked a bottle of Strongbow hard cider. I downed nearly half of it. I was shaking so badly, I had to hold the bottle in both hands. I needed to relax and sort this out. Something was afoot, but I had to approach it logically, rationally.

The alcohol helped. Believe me, it did. Still pulling off my cider, I made my way down the hallway. Mason was out of the shower. As usual, he dispensed with vanity, leaving the bathroom door wide open. It was at this point that I would usually admire his form, but what I saw filled me with a vague sense of terror.

He was standing in front of the full length mirror, eyes glazed, mouth grinning like that of a stuffed fish. As I watched, he stepped back. Then, his arms held stiffly to either side as if he was being crucified, he began to dance with a swaying, dipping motion, moving backwards in an exacting repetitive circle. The movements were precise, almost mathematically so. It might have been comical if it wasn't for his bulging, unblinking fish eyes and that toothy, mirthless grin on his face.

I wanted to call out to him, but I didn't dare. I merely stood there, trembling fiercely, my eyes welling with tears because either I had gone mad or the world had.

Life becomes incoherent now.

Yes, that seemed to encapsulate the freakish incongruities of my life.

I stumbled off into the bedroom and sat on the bed. My mind was whirling with conflicting thoughts. I felt the same as I had that morning, only worse. Reality seemed to be flaking away and I was afraid what might be revealed beyond its confines. I looked about the room with a frightening, hallucinogenic clarity that made me clench my teeth. Everything seemed . . . disordered. I could not precisely say what it was, but things were different. Askew? Off-center? I couldn't be sure, but it was if the entire room was warped subtly, distorted in a way only my very precise, manically-ordered mind would recognize.

I recalled seeing Steven Wright a few years before with Mason and Wright had said, *I got up the other day and everything in my apartment had been replaced with an exact replica.* That was the joke, that was the rub—if they were replicas, how could you tell?

But that was the scary thing: I could tell. I could sense the transition. It was there and yet it was not. It was as if some dire mechanism was at work around me, making and re-making all that I knew. There was a crack on the ceiling shaped like a bolt of lightning. A murky darkness seemed to be oozing from it. I knew it had never been there before; it would have offended my sense of order.

Mason stuck his head in the room, dripping wet and naked. He seemed fine. "What're you doing?" he asked.

"How long has that crack been in the ceiling?"

"Since we moved in."

It was at that moment that I realized that he was part of it, too, that he had been drawn into it without even realizing it. There was a wine barrel clock on the wall that his sister had given us. It always hung next to the window. Now it was on the other side of the room near the closet.

My voice would barely come. "When did you move the clock?"

He looked from the clock to me. "I . . . what do you mean? It's always hung there."

"No, it hasn't, Mason. You know it hasn't," I said. "Just think for a minute."

"You feeling all right?" he asked. "You look a little funny."

Things become fuzzy at this point. He kept talking but I wasn't listening. No, I was staring at a large dark shadow in the corner. There was nothing there to cast it, yet it seemed to be growing darker and gaining volume until it looked like a great spreading stain.

But it couldn't have been a stain because it began to move with an undulating motion. This was where I went out cold.

The sense that everything was in some horrendous process of change and reality itself had been subverted did not lessen, it increased. For two days, I laid in bed sweating out fevers. I was never certain when I was awake or when I was asleep, what was real and what was a febrile dream. The only constant was Mason tending to me or talking on the phone in the hallway, his language sounding like some incomprehensible gibberish.

Of course, there *was* another constant—the shadow in the corner. It stood much larger than a man now, brushing the eight-foot ceiling. It had taken on an unpleasant, fearful solidity. If I watched it for any length of time, it appeared to move. I imagined more than once—or maybe I didn't imagine at all—that it made a grunting, squealing sound like a wild boar . . . yet low and distant, as if from some faraway place. But getting closer. Oh yes, closer all the time.

On the morning of the second day when Mason went back to work, the rabbit returned. It sat on the bureau as before, but it had changed. Its pelt was no longer glossy white, but a dingy gray like moldering rags. Its eyes were larger or maybe it was just the sockets themselves. It had a drawn, withered appearance like a pet that had been slowly starved to death. I noticed with alarm that a few flies lit off of it.

It was getting so I could not trust what I saw. I was not sure of anything. My head was still spinning and my thoughts confused. Yet, I was certain the rabbit was just as real as the shadow in the corner. In fact, I could smell a low stench of putrescence.

While Mason was at work, I made myself get out of bed. Whether it was my illness or what was going on around me or my subjective impression of the same, I felt more disoriented than before. The world was aberrant. I began to feel unreal, as if I had never really existed in the first place. I was losing touch. I was becoming neurotic.

I sat in the kitchen, bathing in a stream of yellow sunlight, fascinated by the motes of dust dancing in it, imagining that the world, the known universe, was but one mote surrounded by countless others.

My phone was on the table. In the twisted depths of my mind, a voice that I did not recognize kept saying, *watch for him he is coming, watch for him he is coming, watch for him he is coming,* until I thought my head might split open. I opened Evernote. It no longer said the above. That was reassuring. Then I opened the Gallery and looked through my photos. Do I dare mention what I saw? There were shots of Mason and I in Bermuda, hiking in the Adirondacks, attending his sister's wedding . . . all the usual stuff.

The only problem was they were *different* from the ones we had taken.

I mention three specifically. The first was Mason and I standing knee-deep in the crystal-blue waters of Horseshoe Bay Beach with weathered, mountainous black rocks just behind us. That much I remembered. But the titanic, seaweed-encrusted effigy rising from the surf, its arms spread as if in benediction over our heads . . . no, no, that had not been there. It was obscured by mats of yellow kelp, so what it was meant to represent is unknown. The second photo of interest was taken in the wild country above Gleasman Falls in the Adirondacks. Again, I remembered the shot . . . but not the amorphous, crooked form emerging from the forest that Mason was pointing at. The third photo I bring to your attention was a wedding shot. Mason and I, decked out in summery finery, standing near a fountain. Behind us, was a lurking figure that looked very much like the shadow I kept seeing in the corner.

As in my day-to-day life, physical reality was being altered. There were other photos which equally chilled me, but it was those taken last Christmas that scared me the worst. In each successive image, my face blurred until it was completely gone in the final shots.

Barely able to keep my knees from shaking, I went to the window and looked out over the rooftops. For one dreadful moment, I thought it was an alien cityscape of black towers and egg-like spheres, but it was only my racing imagination.

At least, that's what I told myself.

I was well enough to return to work the next day. I welcomed it. Anything to get out of that oppressive apartment and its otherworldly association. There was also the very real possibility that I was edging close to some kind of breakdown.

As I crept through traffic to Broders, I caught sight of a billboard on Fifth raised high above the bustling streets. It made me smile. It was for one of my campaigns, a perfume called Sinn, which we sold unapologetically with sex. It featured a green-eyed, raven-haired beauty looking back over her bare shoulder, holding a bottle of Sinn. She was practically smoldering, her lips full, juicy, and red as ripe strawberries. *It's not what's on the surface, it's what's underneath,* read the ad copy. That was basically the pitch I gave the suits from Christian Dior and they ate it up.

It made me feel good, positive. I was a force in this world, not some neurotic bitch steadily fading from it. I was now. I was real. You have no idea how badly I needed to feel that way. When I parked in the garage across the street and the resident religious freak on the corner handed me one of his fliers, I even smiled at his mottled, seamed face as I stuffed it into my coat pocket.

Then work. Oh, it was a madhouse, simply chaotic. I was involved in not two, but three campaigns as project manager because Bob Silverman was in the hospital following a particularly bad bicycle accident which left him in traction. It was meeting after meeting, arguing with Creative and Development, barking orders at interns and Accounts . . . endless. As stressful as it all was, it made me feel safe. I felt insulated from the madness that was beginning to be too commonplace. It even occurred to me, that given time, I might even forget about it all. Then, just after lunch—I skipped food for two vodka martinis— the pandemonium of Broders seemed to switch gears. Everything became calm and pacific. Everyone was suddenly, miraculously, on the same page and it seemed like the agency might survive another day to fight again.

I should have known something was amiss. People all across the office began to cluster in little groups, whispering and gesturing. They had a tendency to scatter or go silent when I approached, which was strange because I had good relationships with just about everyone. But now I was being marginalized, isolated from the social flow. I did not like it. In fact, it began to make my skin crawl as if I was an enemy agent in their midst and they knew it. I began to get very paranoid. People stared at me and old friends ignored me. It was as if everyone was part of something I was excluded from and knew something that I was not allowed to know.

My anxiety increased throughout the afternoon and then eclipsed shortly after five. I went to see the copywriters about a pitch for L'Oréal they were revising. I saw four faces I had never seen before.

"Where's Benji?" I asked.

The four of them looked at each other and then looked back at me.

"Who's Benji?" one of them asked.

"He's your boss if you work in this department," I said.

"We work for Kathleen. Never heard of Benji."

Under ordinary circumstances I might have demanded an explanation, but I could feel it just as I had at home: things were unraveling. Reality was frayed. What I had known for years was disintegrating. Feeling a mad sort of terror building in me, I went over to Creative. I wanted to talk to Joyce, Broder's art director. Joyce was not there. Neither was Rich or Tom or Carolyn. No one had ever heard of Joyce or the others. I stormed over to Margaret's office. She ran Broders. She was not there either. In fact, there was a supply closet where her office had once stood.

I went back to my own office.

My name was still on the door, thank God. I didn't know what to do. My paranoia was telling me there was a conspiracy at work, that my life had been synthetic, that I had maybe been brainwashed into believing that any of it had been true in the first place. I went down on my knees, shaking and sick to my stomach. Sour-smelling sweat boiled from me in rivers. I was hallucinating. That was it. That's all it could be.

I was clinging to the flimsiest rationale even though I knew it was a lie, a great seething manufactured lie.

With shaking hands, I tried to call Mason, but his number was no longer in my directory. I knew from the moment I saw him

41

performing the dance that he had been appropriated like the others. Soon, I would be alone in an alien, perverse world as reality was turned inside out.

I walked from one end of the office to the other, touching the walls and desk and bookcase, the awards and plaques I had received over the years if for no other reason than to confirm that they did in fact exist.

But in my head, a hysterical voice shrieked, *synthetic, it's all synthetic. Ella Barnes never really existed. You are a nonentity, a shadow, a ghost that is about to be erased by the intersection of something immense, something cosmic and nameless—*

I must have passed out.

When I woke much later, I was on the floor. Nearly everyone would have left, save the interns and newbies who would be sucking up the extra work of their bosses, trying to make an impression.

I checked my phone, even though I knew it was pointless.

Mason would ordinarily have called by then. He would have been worried why I was not home. But he hadn't called. He hadn't even texted. And that was because I no longer existed. Yes, I knew many things now and guessed at others that were literally beyond comprehension.

I grabbed my coat and right away, as I dug for my keys in the pocket, I found the flier the religious freak had given me. It had been balled-up, but now I straightened it, now I read the words printed upon it. It did not say HAVE YOU BEEN SAVED? as they always had in the past. No, now it read HAVE YOU BEEN OFFERED?

I walked out into the shadowy offices of Broders . . . except, they were not shadowy at all.

People were queued up, those I knew and those I did not. They ignored me. I did not exist for them. They were all staring with fixed, manic attention at some huge shaggy form that waited at the far end down where Margaret's office had been.

It was the shape from the corner of my bedroom, I realized with a hot flare of panic in my chest. I tried to focus on its appearance, to finally get a real look at it, but the harder I tried, the more it blurred and became nebulous. It was dark and shaggy with spike-like horns jutting from the top of its head. That's all I knew. That's all I was *allowed* to know.

I backed away, bumping into people who rudely shoved me aside because I was blocking their vision of what waited there. One by one, they kneeled before the beast, making obeisance to the horror. What they did then and what was offered to them, I did not want to know.

I ran for the elevators, then decided on the stairs down on to the lobby. All the way, I could hear the porcine squealing of something that stalked me, exhaling hot and sour breath against the back of my neck.

The apartment. The white rabbit, that hideous avatar of what my life had become, was on the bureau, waiting for me. Whereas before it looked withered, now it was decaying—its fur a graying pelt, threadbare and fusty, yellowed rungs of bone protruding through gaping holes. Flies crawled over it. Yet, its huge soulless black eyes looked out at me with wrath and intensity.

"Don't think I don't know what you've planned," I told it.

The apartment was equally as filthy. Dust was layered over everything, dozens of flies speckling the windows. There were jagged cracks in the ceiling and walls, that squirming darkness

43

trying to push through. My clothes were moth-eaten rags in the closet and drawers. In the kitchen, fruit in a bowl was rotted to a blue excrescence of mold.

Out of my mind, not just because of the filth and stench, but because my world, my private space, had been reduced to ruin and rot and rabid disorder, I screamed and launched myself at the rabbit. I seized its carcass in my hands and tore it into pieces, discovering that it was stuffed with graying meat and organ and hundreds of plump writhing maggots.

After that, I ran. There was little else I could do since my car was not where I left it. I wandered from street to street, moving down crowded avenues in a daze, looking up only once and seeing the billboard for Sinn. But the alluring woman was no longer there. Instead there was a crude image of the beast and beneath, HE'S COMING GIVE PRAISE.

The tall buildings that rose around me were monolithic and crooked, threatening to fall and crush me. I saw men with the blank, watery eyes of toads. And women, dear God, what seemed like hundreds of women, all of them noticeably pregnant.

Finally, my building.

When I reached our floor, I was nearly paralyzed with apprehension. Fear infested me, gibbering and giggling. In my dementia, I imagined some gap-toothed court jester with mad, rolling eyes living inside my skull like a worm in a hollow seed. This was what was left when reality as such fractured like a bone and the marrow of common sense leaked out.

I was not certain the key I clutched in my pale fingers would even fit in the lock. The idea terrified me. The penultimate absurdity. But the key fit and the lock disengaged. I turned the knob and stepped inside. Immediately, I was certain I was in the wrong apartment: the feel, the smell, the very psychic texture was all wrong. I was in an enemy camp and I knew it. Had that abomination from the office been waiting for me, I could have been no more horrified at what I saw.

The furnishings were all different and I sensed the decorative touches of another woman. But that was purely cosmetic. What really disturbed me were the framed photos on the wall. I recognized them. I recognized every one of them. I had been in them once, but now I had been replaced by a leggy, green-eyed redhead whose left shoulder and right arm were adorned with vanity tattoos. Mason was still in them, of course, and was it my imagination or did he look just a bit happier with her by his side than he had with me? Not only had sanity abandoned me and reality failed me, but love had betrayed me too.

Mason, Mason, Mason.

Was this the sort of girl he'd wanted all along? Some bronze-skinned, emerald-eyed, taut-thighed, bullet-titted whore who would go down on him in traffic or finger herself on the leather seats of his Escalade in a crowded parking lot?

Photo after photo of her wrapped around him, displaying her goodies, grinning with her enticing bee-stung lips and flashing eyes like hot jade . . . she made him happier in ways I never could.

There was a recent picture of her artfully displayed against a setting sun on a beach, her hands clutching a noticeable baby bump at her midsection.

I began to understand. The white rabbit, the white rabbit. Rabbits had long been a symbol of fertility to the ancients. Mason had wanted children, but my tipped uterus had left me barren. And now, it seemed, he had plowed a richer field.

The final insult was above the fireplace where a tasteful print of Monet's "Lady with a Parasol" had hung. It had been replaced by a bronzed plaque, some revolting pagan travesty which

45

featured a crudely-rendered face, multi-eyed, surrounded by a corona of spidery appendages that seemed to grow from it. The face was emblazoned over an inverted crescent moon that was cracked and crumbling.

I recognized it because Mason's concubine had a similar tattoo on her forearm surrounded by spiraling letters.

Terror rose inside me on leathery wings because I knew it was the symbolic representation, the holy relic of the shaggy thing that had subverted my life and distorted the very physics of my world.

My stomach turned at the idea of visiting the bedroom where Mason and his perky little fertility goddess joined nightly, probably dancing rhythmically backwards (as he had in the bathroom that day) like Medieval witches tripping on belladonna and henbane, slitting the throats of sacrificial white rabbits and bathing in their blood to ensure fertility, before consummating the deed, well-greased like rutting hogs.

I lingered in the kitchen a bit, disturbed at the variety of unnamable spices on my shelves and the quantity of well-marbled red meat in the refrigerator. I also found a quantity of ancient-looking horn-handled knives in the cutlery drawer.

I had to leave and I knew it. Good sense demanded it. That's when I realized I was not alone. I whirled around, expecting to come face to face with Mason's domesticated Circe, the fire-haired Madonna of the fields swollen with child.

But it was Mason himself.

"What . . . what are you doing here?" he asked, his rugged face and dark, sensual eyes filling my knees with water.

"Wait, just wait," I said, knowing I was a stranger to him now. "Please listen to me. I'm not a thief. Just give me a minute to explain."

But did I dare expose the architecture of my madness? Did I dare tear my wriggling insanity out by its dark roots and let him examine it by the light of day? Yes. I poured everything into it, body and soul, to stir something in him, some shred of remembrance.

" . . . before this awful thing happened, we were happy. So very happy. Don't you remember? *Can't* you remember?" I implored him and for one solitary, hopeful moment, I saw something shift in his eyes. It was all coming back to him. "Mason . . . please try to remember. Skiing in Aspen, that weekend with the Rosenbergs in Big Sur, the time we hiked Caminito del Rey . . . don't you remember? The chateau in Savoie Mont Blanc? The grape harvests?"

Whatever light had been lit behind his eyes, it was now extinguished. He was lost to me and I knew it. I felt my heart clench like a weak fist.

"Listen, lady. I don't know what your problem is or why you had to break into my place," he said, holding the flats of his hands out to stay me. "But you have to go, okay? If you leave now and don't come back, I swear I'll keep the police out of this."

I could feel hot tears spilling down my cheeks. I could barely swallow. "Oh, Mason, please. It's me . . . it's Ella."

"I don't know you. I've never seen you before. You need to go. I'm a married man. We're expecting and I don't need this kind of trouble in my life."

Everything inside me began to boil. "Why did you have to mention *her?* How the hell could you bring that whore into my house and impregnate her in my bed?"

He made excuses, as he always made excuses whenever I caught him being unfaithful. He tried everything, but I wouldn't listen. I saw the beast behind him, squealing and grunting the way *she* must have when he rode her, fertilizing her lush garden.

By then, one of the horn-handled knives was in my hand and I plunged it into his throat. The blood was much redder than I could have imagined. It was hot and meaty-smelling. At first, I

47

was repulsed by it, then oddly intrigued, and finally, excited. I remember kneeling down in a hot pool of it as Mason contorted in his death throes, catching the liquid jet of blood in my hands. How like the rabbit he looked in his agony.

I have no memory of anointing myself with Mason's blood, drawing esoteric symbols over my breasts, belly, thighs, and face.

"I have made an offering in your name," I said to the beast as it watched. "By your hand, make me fertile and rich with life so that these loins I spread for you might bear fruit."

What he gave unto me, I took into my mouth and did so willingly, gladly.

That's when she came in—the whore, the Madonna, the seed-eater, the high cunt of the fields, her belly rounded and full in its eighth month. You know what I did to her and more specifically, to the demon seed she carried. I was still dancing widdershins in the old way (as the beast instructed) over their ritually-harvested remains when the police arrived. They could not understand the significance of what I had done or how I had been called as courtesan into His house.

You, of course, know the rest. I will not speak of it again, not until the stars are right. Soon now, the shaggy savior will come down from the mountain high to claim his offerings beneath the glow of the oblong moon. And I will offer unto him the seed that grows fat and juicy in my belly.

SCALES

Christopher Motz

MICHAEL SAT on the front steps of his apartment building, scratching his foot through the thick leather hide of his work boot. It had been a minor annoyance throughout the day, but was now intense enough to get his attention. He pressed harder, but the itching had become relentless. No matter how much pressure he applied or how hard he stomped his foot on the sidewalk, the sensation remained. If he didn't know any better, he would have thought a small army of ants had set up shop between his toes.

"Son of a bitch," he muttered. "What now?"

An older woman passed, leading a small puff of white fur on a short leash. She watched Michael carefully from the corner of her eye, walking faster, dragging the little Pomeranian behind.

"What's the matter?" Michael shouted. "Never saw a guy talking to himself before? This is New York City, lady!" She was already thirty feet away, sneaking glances over her shoulder before turning the nearest corner.

Michael stood, climbed the half-dozen steps in front of his building, and entered a small, dimly lit foyer that smelled of piss, stale cigarettes, and mildew. He grabbed his mail and limped to the third floor, cursing his landlord for not maintaining the elevator. When he entered his small but tidy apartment, he noticed the mercury on his wall thermometer hovered at eighty-seven degrees.

He switched on the air conditioner and flopped down on a ratty, second-hand recliner, quickly removing his right boot to see what all the fuss was about. He peeled the sock from his sweaty skin and examined his toes. The flesh was fish-belly white and shriveled as if he'd spent too much time relaxing in the bathtub. Apart from a little redness, everything appeared

51

fine.

Michael sat back and sighed contentedly. He'd dealt with athlete's foot before, and it was a terribly unpleasant experience, to say the least. Nothing seemed to work. All the over-the-counter, anti-fungal bullshit was expensive and did absolutely nothing to relieve the itching. Eventually, he tossed out all his shoes and bought new ones and the condition mercifully faded over time.

His father had been a Vietnam veteran, and more than once harped about the importance of keeping your feet dry. A younger Michael had laughed, thinking it was silly.

I'm not joking, kid, his father had told him. *In Nam, if you didn't change your socks and keep them clean and dry, you were in for a world of hurt.*

Why? young Michael had asked.

Trench-foot! Jungle rot! Some of those poor bastards had such serious infections that the skin slid from their bones like overcooked chicken.

Michael no longer thought it was very funny after that. He stored the information away with everything else his father had passed along to him over time. It had been twenty years since that discussion, and seven since his father had died of a massive heart attack in rush hour traffic. At the time, he was just two weeks shy of retirement.

Michael rested his bare feet on the footstool and fell into a deep sleep. He wasn't scheduled to work at the construction site the following day; a little well-deserved nap was just what the doctor ordered.

When he opened his eyes, the little green numbers on his clock radio said 3:18 AM. The apartment was cool and dead quiet. Michael sat up, stretched, and gasped as pain shot through his big toe. There was a quick pinch like a nasty wasp sting that soon faded to a dull throb. He reached down and rubbed the tender skin, but the pain remained. He flipped on the lamp next to the recliner, waited for his eyes to adjust to the light, and pulled his leg into his lap so he could survey the damage.

Michael's foot smelled like old popcorn, the skin on his toes dried and cracked, his nails yellow and jagged. He poked at the skin, looking for a stinger or bite, but found nothing. There was no discoloration or swelling. His foot looked fine, or at least as good as a foot *could* look. Feet were ugly no matter what.

He stood and yawned as the stinging in his toe abated. He crossed the apartment and entered the bedroom he shared with no one. He slept in his single bed, fully-clothed, and dreamed of the moist jungle of Vietnam and the frantic search for the last bottle of foot powder on Earth.

He woke several hours later, confused and covered in sweat. Early morning sunlight flooded the apartment, and everything smelled of burning bacon.

"Learn how to cook, for Christ's sake," he grumbled. A pretty little blond had moved into the apartment next door six months ago. She was certainly something to look at and appreciate, but she couldn't cook worth a damn. At least twice a week, the entire floor would fill with the burning stink of another failed attempt.

He propped himself up against the dresser and hissed as the burning in his foot returned with a vengeance. He reached down and scratched violently, sucking in a whistling breath through his teeth.

His foot had gotten much worse.

His toes were now swollen and red. Yellow fluid had leaked from cracks in his flesh and dried into a sticky crust that flaked off in moist clumps. Michael quickly undressed and ran to the shower, scrubbing his foot with a washcloth until his skin turned pink. The burning and itching had become more than just a nuisance, now it was a constant, nagging sensation that made his skin crawl.

He grabbed a tub of aloe from beneath the bathroom sink and smeared it liberally on his foot, making sure to get the hidden spaces between his toes. He wrapped the foot in gauze and hobbled to the living room, not bothering with getting dressed. It was his apartment, after all, so who would complain if he walked around naked for the rest of the day? He switched on the television and felt his eyes getting heavy almost immediately. Six days a week at the construction site had taken its toll.

Sleeping away his day off would be a tremendous waste of time, but the body gets what the body wants.

Several hours later he awoke to an anguished scream. His own. His foot had become a stinging, burning lesson in agony. He stumbled to the bathroom and sat on the edge of the tub, fighting nausea as tears slowly ran down his cheeks. The gauze was saturated with tacky, yellow slime and spots of dark red. Carefully, he unwound the gauze, holding his breath as he exposed the skin beneath. A wet layer of flesh clung to the bandage, peeling off in a thin, bloody sheet. He dropped the soggy cloth to the floor with a plop and moaned deep in his throat. His eyes widened as he caught a glimpse of his ruined toes.

Pus leaked from deep, red cracks in his skin. Small brown scabs dotted the top of his foot, several breaking open and bleeding freely. Michael put his foot in the tub and turned on the faucet, eliciting another sharp gasp as cold water poured over the infected flesh. He bit into his lower lip to keep from screaming.

His cell phone chirped musically from the kitchen table.

Michael turned off the faucet and hopped from the bathroom on his good foot. The other dripped a combination of water and blood across the living room carpet. It throbbed with a life of its own.

Michael grabbed the phone and answered the call. "Hello?"

"Mike," a voice shouted cheerfully. It was Dean from the work site. "I know you're not going lock yourself in that nasty little apartment all night. A few of us are getting together for some drinks later. Meet us at Rumors around seven?"

"I can't," Michael replied, his voice choked with pain. "I'm a little under the weather."

"You sound like shit," Dean said. "Nothing serious I hope?"

"No, just a bug I think," he lied. "I'm going to relax, catch up on TV. Morning will be here before you know it."

"You got that right," Dean laughed. "What a way to make a living, huh?"

Michael slowly lowered his foot to the floor, exhaling a trembling breath through his pursed lips.

"I'll see you tomorrow. Drink a few for me."

"Are you sure you're okay? You really don't sound so good."

"I'll live. Have a good one, Dean."

Michael ended the call and tossed the phone on the scratched, Formica kitchen table. He fell into the chair and wiped tears from his eyes as thick fluid dribbled from his foot and pattered to the linoleum floor. The pain was excruciating. He put his head down on the table as the room spun around him.

The darkness carried him away.

The apartment was once again dark. He'd slept away the entire day. He had no idea how long he'd been out, but his ass and legs had gone numb from sleeping at such an odd angle. His lower extremities were filled with an almost-pleasant tingling. For just a second, Michael forgot about the horrible state of his foot. He stood quickly, putting all his weight on his legs, and shrieked in pain as the flesh on top of his foot grew tight and split open with an audible rip. He collapsed to the floor and writhed in agony as his skin burned with a renewed vigor. The tile grew sticky as reddish-orange muck poured from the wound in chunky clots.

His next scream was greeted by a loud thumping on the wall from the apartment next door. A second shout boomed from down the hall.

"Shut the fuck up! People are trying to sleep around here!"

"Go check your pantry for a bag of dicks," Michael shouted, "and fucking choke on them."

More angry shouts added to the chorus as Michael's vision faded. He dragged himself to the bathroom and lost consciousness.

When he came to, the apartment was once again lit with dusty shafts of sunlight. He'd lost eight hours. This was more serious than just a simple infection; this was the second time he'd passed out in as many days. He rolled over and stared at the ceiling, wondering how many calls he'd missed from his friends at work. He couldn't afford to lose this job or he'd be staying on one of their couches again. Life in the city wasn't all he'd imagined it would be.

He sat up and grimaced. His back twitched and knotted as he tried to stand, but the pain in his foot had receded. He decided he'd better call his foreman, come up with an excuse, try to save himself from the unemployment line.

The tickle in his foot brought him back to reality. He reached down to poke at the swollen flesh and pulled his hand away as if he'd been burned. His skin pulsed with a living sea of maggots. He cried out like a tortured cat and hopped to the bathtub, staring at the yellow, waxy flesh. He turned the water on full-blast and tried to wash away the tiny white worms, but they were several layers deep in the gaping gash. He held his breath and reached a finger into the red slit, scooping maggots out of the wound like a cracker full of caviar. In clumps, the writhing worms circled the drain and disappeared. He placed his foot beneath the stream of scalding water and watched as the last few maggots bubbled from the wound, along with pink bits of flesh and clotted blood.

Strangely, there was very little pain. He dried his foot, wrapped it in a clean bandage, and walked to the bedroom. Feeling much better, Michael dressed and went to the kitchen to make himself scrambled eggs for breakfast. He was ravenous. He wolfed down a half-dozen eggs, washed the dishes, and sat on the living room chair with a tall glass of orange juice. An hour later he got in touch with his foreman, explained the situation, apologized profusely, and assured him he'd be at work in the morning.

Crisis averted.

The following morning, Michael was awakened by the shrill cry of his alarm clock. Five AM was always a peaceful time in the apartment building. Screaming children were still sleeping; their obnoxious parents hadn't yet turned on their mindless talk shows at top volume; angry male voices hadn't yet begun shouting at wives too scared to shout back, and beds weren't squeaking harshly beneath the exertion of sweaty lovemaking. It was easy to forget what a microcosm of emotion existed within these walls once the sun shined its harsh light upon it.

Michael flipped the bedsheets aside and whined like a beaten dog. The bandage on his foot had come loose, and he noticed right away the maggots had returned. They squirmed from under the sides of the moist fabric, forming little piles on the mattress. He quickly pulled the bandage from his foot and hastily brushed the worms from his skin; the wound boiled with plump, white bodies. A single, fat, maggot inched its way from beneath Michael's toenail. He reached down to grab it and crush it beneath his fingers, but instead grabbed the edge of the ragged toenail, pulling upward. The nail came off easily between his fingers with a soft tearing sound, a scrap of pink flesh coming with it.

"No you don't, you little bastard," he said, grabbing the maggot from the bed sheet. He held it between his thumb and forefinger gently, watching as it whirled frantically in his grasp. "How do you like it? How does it feel to lose control?" He crushed its tiny body with a pop and wiped it on the blanket. It was then he noticed the color of his left foot had changed. It too was now an unhealthy shade of red.

An hour later, after having cleaned the wound again, Michael sat on his couch picking at the flesh around the gaping wound in his foot. Much of it had turned black. It had started stinking like rotting hamburger. The hospital was out of the question; he hadn't had insurance for several years, and all his money went into rent on his tiny apartment.

"I think it's healing, anyway," he said aloud. "No need to fear, the maggots are here." His laughter boomed throughout the empty room as he absently picked at his rotting flesh, his remaining four toenails lie scattered on the floor next to the couch.

By noon, Michel was burning with fever. The carpet was littered with thin shreds of putrefying flesh. Little red lines had begun spreading up his leg, showing the first signs of blood poisoning. He shivered and wiped sweat from his forehead, running his hands through his greasy mop of tangled hair. His legs felt pleasantly warm. Numb.

Michael grabbed his stomach, lurched forward, and vomited scrambled eggs onto the carpet. The sludgy mess was broken by thin veins of blood.

Tired. So tired.

He was awakened by loud shouts in the hall. Someone was obviously in a lot of pain, but Michael had problems of his own. The wound on his foot had opened further and a large flap of skin hung to the side like an un-zipped jacket. His toes looked elongated and had turned a frightening shade of green. The skin on his ankle and calf had turned brown and had begun to fester.

The pained scream was repeated in the hall, hurting his ears.

"Shut the fuck up, you degenerate scum," Michael shrieked. "You're not the only one with problems!" His voice scared him. It'd grown raspy and broken. His stomach rolled and burned; sour bile rose in his throat.

"Help me!" the voice shouted. "Please! It burns . . . it BUUUURNS!"

Michael stood shakily and dragged himself to the door, peering into the hall through the tiny peephole. The pale overhead light flickered, giving him a nightmarish view of the screaming man as he dragged himself across the dirty floor, leaving a shiny trail of blood behind him. The man looked up at the door with bloodshot eyes, a runner of drool hanging from his bottom lip.

"I know you're in there," he cried. "I can hear you. I can *smell* you!"

Michael stepped back from the door, shaking, holding a hand over his open mouth. He pressed his face to the cold wood and looked through the peephole again as the man dragged himself further up the hall.

His legs had been eaten down to the bone in places. Green, scaly skin had begun growing in patches over the rancid meat of his calves. His feet looked reptilian, long toes ending in pointed, gray claws. Michael jumped back with a shout and felt a warm stream of urine trickle down his leg. It hit his foot and stung like an angry swarm of hornets.

"No, no, no," he rambled. He ran to the small closet in the hall and rooted through his old toolbox. "I don't know what the fuck you have, but I'm not getting that shit. Not me. Not ever. Probably some nasty disease you're spreading all over the building. You son of a bitch. Do you hear me?" Michael wailed. "You dirty, nasty son of a bitch!"

He felt the worn wood of the handle and giggled with relief. He pulled the hatchet from the toolbox and held it up above his head like a trophy. "You get away from my door," he shouted, thrusting the hatchet in front of him. "You get away or you're getting this."

The other man's screams echoed down the hallway as Michael smiled in the dark. He pulled an old leather belt from the shelf in the closet and dragged his dripping foot behind him, leaving a trail on the carpet. He flicked on the harsh fluorescent light in the bathroom and sat on the closed toilet seat, breathing heavily, gearing up for what needed to be done.

Michael wrapped the belt around his leg just above the knee, pulling it so tight that it pinched his flesh. Almost instantly, the skin below the tourniquet began to pale. He gripped the hatchet in his left hand and closed his eyes.

"You're not getting me sick," he screamed. "No way am I

going to wind up like that."

He extended his leg and rested his rotting foot on the edge of the tub. He saw this kind of thing in movies all the time. The body was a resilient machine. It resisted death. He just needed to take care of this one little detail, and he'd have a chance.

He raised the hatchet over his head and brought it down in a vicious arc. The weapon tore into his flesh like a knife through a rare steak. Blood sprayed into the air, painting the shower curtain and raining down onto the cracked tile. His screams filled the room like an air-raid siren, piercing and constant. He felt the room spinning and knew that if he couldn't muster the energy now, he'd never get a second chance.

He raised the hatchet again and held his breath.

Michael's eyes fluttered open.

The overhead light pierced his skull. He winced and turned his head to the side to see the large pool of blood that had formed on the bathroom floor. His ragged stump throbbed in time with his heartbeat. He'd lost a lot of blood, but he was still kicking.

"Still kicking," he laughed weakly. "Not so much. Not with that leg anyway."

He turned his head, horrified, as the bottom half of his severed leg teemed with feasting worms. He could hear them crunching, chewing his flesh loudly like hungry children at an all-you-can-eat buffet. He pulled himself away from the leg, sliding easily over the blood-drenched floor. He propped himself up against the cool porcelain of the toilet and looked down at the bloody stump. It was fresh, pink, healthy. The blood had slowed to a trickle.

With some effort, Michael pulled himself upright, holding

onto the sink to keep from falling over. He reached into the medicine cabinet and grabbed a bottle of Tylenol, tossing a handful into his mouth and chewing them like candy. After a few minutes, the pain began to subside and he regained some of his energy. On one leg, he hopped into the darkened kitchen and grabbed an ice pack and a bottle of beer. He fell onto the couch, feeling more exhausted than he'd ever been in his life. The orange glow of the street lamp outside washed the room in a pleasant glow. He chuckled.

"Mark one up for the winning team," he whispered.

The room filled with the echo of a nearby gunshot as a woman screamed incoherently behind a closed door down the hall. Michael sat up and listened, panting loudly as he grabbed the arm of the couch for balance. Loud thumps trailed across the floor from the apartment above, followed by the sound of breaking glass. He looked out the window just as a body passed by on its way to the hard concrete below. It hit the sidewalk with a loud crack as a dozen men in riot gear surrounded the twitching corpse. The night came alive with automatic gunfire as three of the men walked forward and riddled the body with bullets. Blood ran into the gutter like rainwater.

Michael looked at the body and screamed. Its legs were covered in thick, black scales. A foot-long tail had grown from the base of the man's spine and hung down over his bare ass. It still twitched as the men in riot gear backed up to join the others. Michael hopped back a step and quickly closed the curtains.

"That's the guy in the hall," he shuddered. "Motherfucker turned into an alligator or some shit." He reached behind him and rubbed the smooth skin of his back, breathing a sigh of relief. "Not me. You're not going to shoot me in the street. Nope. I stopped it," he laughed. "I stopped it and I'm going to be just fine."

He heard a loud crash from below and peered through the

gap in the curtain as he watched a team of men break down the front door of the apartment building and enter with guns drawn.

Michael lunged across the room and fell to the floor in front of the bathroom door. His leg was still there where he'd left it. He slid across the floor on his stomach, pushing his leg away from him and screaming as the maggots crawled onto his arm, wiggling around in the thick hair that grew there. He brushed them off and dragged himself into the corner, shaking from fear and exhaustion as the building erupted with frenzied screams and the explosion of automatic weapons. He listened as the screams died down and the heavy footfalls of a dozen men thundered up the stairway and down the halls below him.

He closed his eyes and waited.

The door burst open as splinters rained down around him. It was getting hard to focus, but he saw the man standing there, decked out in black, aiming a large assault rifle. The man took a step back and lowered his weapon.

"Jesus Christ," he muttered. "We have one on the third floor." He talked into a small microphone in his headset and cocked his head as he waited for a response.

"Alive?" a voice crackled.

"Yes, sir."

"Infected?"

The man slowly looked over the carnage and shook his head. "I can't be certain, but he may have escaped infection, sir."

Michael held his hands above his head. He cried weakly, his breath hitching in his chest. "I'm not sick," he shrieked. "Look! I'm not sick. I did what I had to do. I stopped it."

The pool of blood spread beneath Michael as the stump of his other leg bled furiously. The hatchet rested beside him on the floor, covered in blood and chunks of raw meat. The toes on his severed foot still twitched.

"Are you seeing this, sir?" the man asked. He raised his head and focused a small helmet camera on Michael.

"Am I going to be on TV?" Michael asked.

"I think you can count on that," the man replied.

"Good God," the radio squawked. "He cut off his fucking legs?"

"Yes, sir. With a hatchet."

"Christ, give the man a medal."

Michael lowered his arms, unable to hold them up any longer. He was going to be okay, just as soon as they got him out of here and pumped him full of blood. Holy shit, was he going to have a story to tell?

"I'd follow you out," Michael said, "but as you can see, I might need a little help."

"You're going to need more than a little help, friend," the man responded.

"Can we go now? I'm not feeling so good."

"Sit tight, I'll have you out of here as soon as I get word."

The radio crackled to life again, the voice on the other end suddenly sounding tired. "Everyone get back down here. We have reports in Brooklyn and Manhattan. Team One, secure your location and meet on the ground."

"All locations, sir?" the man asked.

"Lock it down," the radio replied.

"Copy that."

Michael rubbed the tears from his cheeks and looked up at the man. His luck was about to change. He was going to be on every television in the city by morning. "I'm going to famous," he laughed.

"Brother, fame isn't always what it's cracked up to be."

Michael smiled for the camera as the man squeezed the trigger.

HE WEARS THE LAKE

Chad Lutzke

CREATURES OF THE NIGHT

I THINK IT'S probably the same for every man. There comes a time when you're at a fork in the road, and at that fork is an understanding of the world. No, a perspective. And where you're at in that moment of your life—whether you're going on 30 or well over 80—the world either works for you or it doesn't. For Mr. Overgaard, things weren't working.

This is about him.

I was practically raised at the lake house—the cabin, I like to call it. My grandparents owned it, gave it to my parents, and now I stay there by myself year round. One day I'll have a wife and we'll have kids and those kids will talk about the cabin and the lake, with stories to tell like mine. Well, maybe not like mine.

Mr. Overgaard lived on top of a hill in a small house near the cabin. He fed squirrels and birds and mourned the loss of his wife and the loss of his youth. I'd been inside that little house before. There were pictures of his wife hung throughout and a picture of himself in uniform, framed proudly above the mantle. I imagine when your knees no longer bend and you're one back strain from pissing your pants on the daily, that a picture of you in your prime is a helpful reminder that things weren't always this way. That you used to be something special. Something that caused skirts to dampen and men to cower.

The pictures of his wife were of varying ages—from her teenage years on up to just before she shrunk to a cancerous husk. We were at the cabin the summer she died. On the Fourth of July that year, Mr. Overgaard wheeled his wife out to the lake on her hospice bed to watch the fireworks show. I stayed my distance and let the two be, but I watched her. Her eyes were like two black pools pried open with childhood wonder by the multi-color explosions. Mr. Overgaard watched the show through the reflection in those pools. I think he knew they wouldn't be open for long. She died three days later.

We went to the funeral. It was the first time I'd seen a grown man cry.

Years later, the cabin was mine and I'd still peek in on Mr. Overgaard. The man as independent as can be, like a young bachelor. But with a broken heart and a pension that keeps him afloat. He tends to his lawn, keeps up the house—in and out— sweeps down the dock when the geese make a mess of it, and I've suspected even trims the evergreens along my cabin when I'm not around.

The lake is a decent size, though quaint. You can make out the houses on the other side. And with a telescope I suppose you could catch a woman undressing if that's your thing. The lake is home to a variety of wildlife, mostly geese and cranes, and frogs of course. At times, we'd even spot the occasional deer catching a drink. Just two summers ago, one strode up next to Mr. Overgaard as he sat on the dock, bent down and ate a peanut butter and jelly sandwich right out of his hand.

The lake was a sanctuary, and I know for Mr. Overgaard especially, it was a place of solitude. That man would sit on the dock for hours overlooking the still water. No pole or book in his hand, just him and the lake, and whatever thoughts the old man carried.

Occasionally I'd join him. We'd split a six-pack and I'd listen to him talk about his service in the Army, about his days working for the railroad, and about his wife. But mostly he'd talk about how great life used to be. He'd tell me the world was a better place when he was younger, that love and peace was easier to find. You didn't have to go searching for it. It found you. I believed him.

One day I had a contractor coming out to give me an estimate on replacing the dock we shared. It was getting old and sinking–
–near flush with the water—and even the slightest bit of rain submerged it for a day or two. I didn't want the old man to slip and break a hip, or worse yet end up at the bottom of the lake. But that very day I looked out and Mr. Overgaard was lying on the dock, head bobbing in the water.

I sprinted after him, chasing the geese away as they flocked around his body. I was sure he was dead. But just before I got to the end of the dock, he threw his head out of the water and looked at me, smiling.

"I'm just fine, kiddo. Taking a look is all. You'd be surprised at just how clear it is down there."

Surreal is a pretty good word for how things felt at that moment. Mr. Overgaard was well into his 80s, and lying on the dock with his head underwater was nothing I ever expected him to do, not for pleasure anyway.

He stood up—knees cracking, lungs wheezing—and asked me if I'd like to take a look. "You might like what you see," he said. "Spotted a nice-sized bluegill, biggest one I think I've ever seen. Bastard's been eluding us, it seems."

I said no thanks and told him I had a guy coming out about the dock. He frowned and said the old thing still had some life left in it and he'd like to keep it the way it was. I presented the dangers of keeping it, that either of us could fall or even bust through the wood, but he was adamant, so I canceled the appointment. I'm old enough to rightly assume age brings with it sentimentality that sometimes is the only thing keeping a man from eating a bullet, particularly after his bride has moved on.

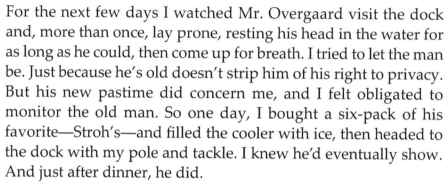

For the next few days I watched Mr. Overgaard visit the dock and, more than once, lay prone, resting his head in the water for as long as he could, then come up for breath. I tried to let the man be. Just because he's old doesn't strip him of his right to privacy. But his new pastime did concern me, and I felt obligated to monitor the old man. So one day, I bought a six-pack of his favorite—Stroh's—and filled the cooler with ice, then headed to the dock with my pole and tackle. I knew he'd eventually show. And just after dinner, he did.

"Evening, kiddo. Brought you a peel."

That's what he called his cigars, peels. I'm not sure why he called them that, but I liked the word. He handed me one.

"And I brought the beverages," I said.

He unfolded a chair and sat next to me, then opened the cooler.

"Stroh's," he said with a refreshing sigh. "Every man has his beer, kiddo. I ever tell you why this here is mine?" He held up the beer like he was proud of it, then cracked it open and took a healthy swig.

He had told me the story before, but it was a good one and I never minded hearing his stories twice, or even three times.

I lit the cigar and took a puff. There was clove in it, maybe a hint of citrus, too. I was never a fan of cigars, but the "peels" I liked. They complimented the beer, and the outdoors.

"This here was my father's beer. He first had it when he was stationed in Europe, then the war came . . . the first World War, mind you."

He took a sip.

"Before the war, the Stroh brewery was schooled in the ways of fire brewing. That's when you use a direct flame rather than steam. The higher temperatures bring out that extra bite you're tasting."

I took a sip to verify the bite.

"It's the only beer they had access to over there, and when Pops came home he smuggled a case to the states, not knowing it was already available here. Everything he brought home went straight to the attic—his uniform, his medals, even the beer. I think he wanted to forget. Well, he forgot, and that beer sat up there for fifteen years. Then one day, during the prohibition, he was up fiddling around and found the case. He was a happy man that day, like he'd found buried treasure. And I suppose he had. He was so happy, in fact, that he gave me a bottle. Not even in my teens yet and I'm flying high on twelve ounces. I knew from that day forward that Stroh's was my beer, just like it was Pop's. Course I wouldn't take up drinking until I was a man, but I knew . . . I knew."

Another sip.

"Love that story, Mr. Overgaard."

"Do me a favor, kiddo. Cut it with the 'mister' shit, you know my name. . .and don't fish off the dock no more."

"Okay, Bill . . . .but why the fishing?"

"It's beautiful under that water, son. Ain't nothing like it. Nothing up here, anyway. And when I'm under there I'm somebody else. I wear that lake like a mask."

I kept quiet, taking it in. The talk was lunacy. Or was it?

"I don't expect you to understand. Just do me a favor and don't fish off the dock."

I looked down at the dock. The wood was gray-green. The occasional wave pushed water up through a small knothole in one of the planks. Eventually it'd have to be replaced with or without Mr. Overgaard's consent.

"No problem, Bill. I'm getting a boat soon. We'll go out in it, take the peels and the Stroh's. Catch us some bluegills."

"Maybe." Mr. Overgaard raised his beer and finished it. "Love that bite."

Over the next several days, Mr. Overgaard spent more and more time on the dock with his head in the lake. I really did try to pay no mind, let him do this thing. But one day I took notice he hadn't come up for air. I ran down to the dock, convinced of his death. This time, in my panic, I slipped off the dock and into the water. I scrambled to the edge and pulled myself up. Mr. Overgaard was sitting on the dock, chuckling at my spill. His nose was plugged with tubes that ran up behind his head, his face pale and wrinkled. He had constructed a makeshift snorkel to prolong his visits under the water.

"Careful, kiddo. She gets slippery."

"This here is exactly what I'm talking about, Bill. This dock needs to go. The thing barely sits above the water. You'll be the next one to . . . "

"Let me tell you something, son. You smell that piss? That's me. I've gone through three pairs of pants in the last two days. This pissin' my pants is a whole new thing for me and it scares me to death. My time on this earth is limited . . . My body's shuttin' down, I can feel it. So, dammit, if I wanna lie here with my head in the lake to get away from it all, then that's what I'm gonna do. There ain't nothing above for me anymore. This ain't my world . . . my world died a long time ago."

Somehow, I understood. His wife was the last bit of anything that resembled love or life to him, and this violent, hate-filled world really *wasn't* his anymore. To a sweet old man who served a grateful country in a time where love really did find you, this place had become a shock to the system.

I would still make the occasional evening visit to the dock, filling the cooler with Stroh's in case he'd join me, but I decided to never bother Mr. Overgaard again regarding his time in the water.

Weeks went by and Mr. Overgaard stopped leaving the dock. He lived on it now, sustained by the water and anything else the lake provided—milfoil, lily pads, algae, small fish.

In my visits to the dock, I'd tell the occasional story of my own, or speak of my plans for the future. I don't think he ever listened. I suspected he didn't, as most of the time even his ears were submerged—an overhead mask.

The smell of Mr. Overgaard was getting harder to bear. I wanted to clean him up, for his sake really, not mine. Here was a man who had fought in a war, lived and loved and filled with more wisdom than anyone I knew, yet he lay in his own mess.

Finally, one evening as the sun fell, painting the lake orange, I lay down next to Mr. Overgaard and plunged my face into the lake. There was a quick rush of water as my ears filled, then all went silent. I opened my eyes. It was dark. A bluegill—barely visible—zig-zagged between the stalks of weeds below and something scurried in the sand, leaving behind a dusty cloud that scattered in slow motion. I held on for as long as I could, my chest pounding, my throat constricted. Then I pulled out from the water and gasped for breath.

Mr. Overgaard followed my lead and revealed his face to me, to the world. The lake was no longer a metaphorical mask but a real one.

It wasn't the snails that clogged his ears and clung to his lobes like aquatic jewelry that chilled me. Nor the algae that stained his wrinkled lips green. Or even the puffed eyelids that resembled lips now more than lids—wide, jagged slits that revealed nothing under them but empty sockets where I imagine something now lived. Something that only peeked out from its cave-like home long enough to forage for food. A cave where offspring would nest. None of that disturbed me quite as much as the smile on his face. A look of enlightenment that none of us could ever understand.

While the horror before me dripped with the same water I'd spent my childhood in, his face held contentment. A kind I wasn't sure I'd ever attain.

"Leave it all behind, kiddo." Mr. Overgaard's voice bubbled with phlegm, his breath impossibly rank. Then he dropped his head down and back into the lake.

I looked back to the cabin. The kitchen light cast a glow on the hill and slid down, spreading to an area where a swing set once stood. An area where I planned on building another for my own children someday.

While Mr. Overgaard's life neared its end, I had my own plans. Plans that gave bright hope in a dark world. Plans to keep at bay my own children's desire to get away from the life they'd been given, as they grow from blissfully ignorant to profoundly aware. To keep away the temptation to wear my own mask.

THE NEWEL POST

Eddie Generous

CREATURES OF THE NIGHT

THE CRAFTSMANSHIP was fit for a casket. Hidden beneath thick dust and stringy flea market cobwebs, the newel post became all that Samantha Tremblay saw. She had to have it.

A newel post, a totem to announce a staircase.

It had a small nubbin top above a bulbous tapering growth of Middle Eastern rhythm that budded up to the ovular column before falling into nine concentric rings, thirteen evenly spaced dots, and a second, smaller bulbous growth that tapered down toward a sharp rectangular base.

While playing hockey in the foyer, Ella and Jane had chipped and cracked the current post, rendering it ugly, inadequate. The Coyote House Bed and Breakfast had felt off since.

Samantha began the hunt weeks earlier. Flea markets, online browsing, consideration of stock designs from a company out of Hannover, Germany, and now, finally, she had perfection.

She needed to set the house rules anew. "Hey, listen to me," Samantha leered at her daughters, both fourteen. "No more hockey in here or I'll beat you blind."

The twins rolled twin sets of eyes.

Their mother was all bluster. Their father was even softer, unless it cut into his gardening time. An assistant manager of a B&B in Prescott, Arizona had a great deal of gardening to see to.

Samantha was the opposite. She spent the majority of her days dealing with the major interior operations, including the cleaning, the books, and the furnishings, leaving the rest to the girls and Nathan.

The hired carpenter was a quick hand, slowing only momentarily to deal with a sliver needled beneath his right index fingernail. "That's it," he said, popping the injured digit into his mouth.

Samantha lifted one eyebrow and downturned the other. The post was filthy with laborer prints. Sticking it home and fastening the banister and step was hardly *it*. She washed, dried, waxed, and then buffed until shoeshine fine.

"Come, come," she called out the open window behind the reception desk to her husband, Nathan, who was in the backyard digging at Bermuda grass invading the stone pathway.

Nathan came around, dusty as *The Grapes of Wrath*. "Hey, looks good. Maybe better than the old one."

"Maybe? It's perfect."

"If you say so."

"Think beyond function for once. I mean look at it." Samantha ran fingers over a smooth curve.

"Okay, it's nice."

"Fine. You've got dirt all over the carpet."

"Ella's night to vacuum." Nathan looked up.

"What? No," Ella said.

Jane was behind Ella standing beneath the mounted deer antlers at the top of the stairs. Both wore yoga capris and their house slippers—mom's rule on the footwear. "Can't flake this time. I ain't covering again."

"When have you ever . . . ?" Jane wrapped her arm over Ella's neck, headlock hold, muffling her words.

"Shut up, both of you," Samantha said.

Footfalls stomped downwards as the girls bickered. Nathan added nothing, heading to the door he'd left open. It wasn't until slippers came into view that Samantha shifted her focus from the newel post.

Thump. Clap.

The initial sound was dull. The smacking of skin on skin when a cheek met a forearm was much louder.

"Jane," Nathan said.

80

"You bitch!" Ella shouted from the floor, her lip bleeding and expanding.

Jane's expression was a mixture of angst and confusion. "I didn't do nothing!"

"You tripped me! My lip, you goddamned bitch!"

Nathan reached the fallen daughter's side and assisted her to her feet. Samantha stood just as dumbfounded as Jane. Jane's feet had been nowhere near her sister when Ella tumbled.

As punishment, Jane maneuvered the vacuum cleaner through the six-room Victorian, the toll for a crime she did not commit. Samantha had wanted to argue *the right case*, but quickly came to an obvious conclusion and remained quiet. It was a push and not a trip. Jane had done it. *Who else?*

"Coming to bed?" Nathan called from the upstairs hall.

Samantha ran her fingers over the post. "Yes, yes." Power trickled a charge, bringing with it an intense after-buzz.

"It's just a post, dear."

Samantha mouthed the words *just a post, dear,* upper lip in a fine crinkle. "You're more than that, aren't you? You're my post," she whispered.

Under the sheets, Nathan asked Samantha if the two guests in the main floor bedroom had any special requests for breakfast. She said they did not. He asked if it was still just the additional couple for the weekend. She said there was a second couple who had booked about an hour after supper. He then asked what to do about the girls. To this, she had no answer.

Samantha dreamed of a lake full of logs. She pointed to a forty-footer in a row of forty-footers, bark shining and dark in the blue water. "That one."

A bulky lumberjack in green plaid and yellow suspenders nodded and ran atop the floating logs to retrieve the chosen piece. He hefted it in classic caber toss form and flung it to the shore where it landed next to Samantha.

No longer a rough log, now the wonderful newel post. Samantha leaned to looked closer.

The lumberjack was beside her. "Summin' wrong with that'un."

Aghast, Samantha turned to face the sun shining through the bedroom window, letting the dream slip away. She flipped over to see the clock and then jerked up. After ten.

She showered, dressed, tied her hair into a ponytail, and hurried down the stairs. It was a summer Thursday, the girls had soccer, meaning nobody had the phones or the email manned. Customers are finicky and if nobody answers . . .

Samantha face-planted. It took five seconds to understand.

She'd tripped, both feet flung, as if striking a barrier simultaneously. The phone rang and she sprang for the desk.

"Coyote House, Samantha speaking, how can I help you?" Her voice was rushed and her wind short.

"Hey, just me. Ella's tumble did a little more tweaking than we figured and now she twisted it worse at practice."

Samantha turned off the front desk charm. "So, what?"

"We're late. We stopped by the pharmacy to get a tensor bandage We can't have her sitting out the tournament. That carpenter was there, too. His hand was enormous. Said *that damned post must got wormwood in it or some such thing.*"

"Wormwood, right. Idiot. So, how late?"

"Hour yet. Getting burgers and ice cream, you want any?"

She didn't, told him so, and disconnected. "Wormwood," she said, stepping around the desk, thinking of her tumble and Ella's tumble. She ran fingers over the rug. Smooth. She prodded the firm edges of the stairs. Sharp. She turned to the banister where it connected to the post and had the overwhelming urge to lick it.

So she did.

It tasted like wax, but sent a vibration that had her legs off in a hurry, to the master bathroom, to the shoebox behind the second string towels where she'd hidden certain objects she pretended not to own.

"Why you so smiley?" Ella asked, limping as she stepped through the door.

Nathan and Jane followed and behind them was a white-haired man. Samantha ignored Ella and the blush creeping up her neck. She said to the man, "Welcome to Coyote House."

"I'm a day early, any chance you've got room now?"

"Oh, we can likely work something out. Name?"

Samantha filled out the necessary information, slid the credit card through the reader, and fetched a key to *Four*. She led the man upstairs and explained supper while they walked, and when he said he was going to meet a friend downtown, she asked about the second guest he'd mentioned in booking.

"That's the one I'm meeting. I don't mean to be a randy fool, but I'm hoping to bring her back with me tonight. She's only fifty-nine." He grinned, hands in his pockets, swaying on his heels, thrusting his groin gently.

Life experience taught Samantha how to ignore the suggestive motion. "I hope that works out. Front door locks at eleven."

"She might have her own ideas, so don't wait up." He winked and Samantha turned before rolling her eyes in the very manner she'd inadvertently taught her daughters to do.

As a family, the Tremblays watched TV while digging into bowls of chili. Samantha kept an ear to the foyer in case someone walked in, called, or emerged from a room itching to ring the silver service bell.

There was a thump followed by a light groan. Samantha rose and departed the familial space unnoticed, bowl of chili in hand. When she saw the old man attempting to right himself, she set her supper on the desk and rushed to his side.

He laughed. "Lost my feet. Don't worry, made it most of the way down before I spilled."

"You tripped?"

"That I did, on that last step."

The old man did not stick around. Trip or no trip, he had a hot date. Samantha returned to her chili, took two steps toward the family room before turning around. Something was going on. Bowl on the carpet next to her, she examined the staircase. There were scratches in the wood where the post and the riser and lip of the first step met.

Reluctant to touch the post, it felt almost like cheating.

"Idiot," she whispered, knowing that when under the microscope of logic, her desire was nothing more than taking advantage of an empty home. She grabbed onto the post. Nothing surged at her core or loins, but there was a tickle, and it was different from before.

She pushed the post. Firm. It did not wiggle. She shook it. Nothing.

"Those scratches didn't come from nowhere."

The carpenter had screwed up. She'd call him after supper.

"Damned thing." The carpenter's voice had been low before, but at the mention of the newel post, his tone became a snake's hiss. "What now?"

"It's loose somehow, somewhere. You need to fix *your* work."

"Come back?" Samantha could almost hear the man's eyebrows raise with his voice. "You want . . . ? All right. Give me an hour."

Right then it made all the sense in the universe why tripping had become a regular hazard. She'd employed an idiot.

"Wormwood, pfft."

Forty minutes later, nose deep in a Kinsey Millhone, Samantha sat behind the front desk. The carpenter swung the door inward. His pallor was almost green. He was gaunt. A goodly stubble grew over his jaw, proving that it had been five o'clock a few times over. He carried a duffle bag in his left hand. Cotton bandage with oily splotches covered his right.

"I'll just get to it then," he said, eyeing the post as he kicked the door closed behind him.

Samantha nodded and looked to the book. Swirling, the letters jumbled into alphabet soup, leaving only two discernable words standing on the messy page: SAVE ME.

Quiet, unquestioning, she slipped the bookmark home and rose from the chair. She shuffled on the carpet in rubber-soled slippers over to the half-wall which split the office and staircase.

"Think I'd let you in me and you'd get away with it?"

Samantha jerked at hearing the whispered oddity and then pressed tighter to hear more.

"Might poison my skin, but I'm taking my dreams back."

It was only a second after the unzipping of the bag that Samantha saw the red head of a hatchet arc back from around the wall. Without hesitation, she leapt, words leaving her mouth like a cough. "My post!"

The carpenter was in no shape for a tussle and the hatchet, as well as the gooey bandage, came away from his hands. He slumped, tears springing. "It's evil. You got to kill it."

"Sir, you're . . . " her words trailed as she drank in the pitted gore of the man's index finger. It was puffy and yellow, tunnels like caterpillar holes in apple cores traversing the putrid flesh. She dropped the hatchet. The bandage clung to her palm, adhering with viscous pus glue. She swatted and wiped against her jeans until the bandage rolled and fell to the carpet. "You're crazy."

The carpenter tugged at his shirt. "Crazy? Crazy?" Two buttons popped and two more lost hold of their eyes, revealing a chest of thin grey hair and a series of yellowy dots, like bleached ink stains. "Look. They come at night. More and more. They come at night in my dreams and I wake up and there's more."

Nathan entered the foyer, as did the guests staying in *Two*.

"Call the ambulance," Samantha said to Nathan.

The hospital was two miles away, only a four-minute wait. The big carpenter cried, slouched against a wall, eyes firm on the post until the paramedics took him away.

In bed, Nathan asked what Samantha thought the carpenter meant by dreams of the post. She said she had no idea. He pressed on, explaining that he'd also dreamed of the post, and a fire, and two crispy daughters alongside a crispy wife.

"Really?" she said, recalling then only the tiniest bits of a lumberjack.

"Bad Juju in the air. Halloween dreaming months early."

"Stress maybe. You check the smoke detectors recently?"

"They're all working. I tested them first thing; had to after a dream like that."

She rolled over, surprised the testing hadn't woken her.

She slept lightly. Fantastical flashes came and went. Through the closed door and out in the hall, a noise pulled her halfway from dreamland.

Thump.

She did not open her eyes, fighting to fall back into respite's abyss.

Thump. Thump.

The door creaked and her mind answered enough questions to allow her eyes to remain closed. Nathan had gotten up, surely.

Thump.

The bed moved.

Something brushed her legs, sending a warm pulse, and she half-rolled, separating her thighs. "Not now," she said, closing her legs and completing the roll.

Thump.

The sound was going away, and if it had landed again, she'd slept through it.

"Mom!" Jane shook Samantha.

She opened her eyes to the mid-morning shine and a frantic daughter. "What?"

"Nothing, just saying bye!" Ella shouted from the other side of the bed. Excited soccer players.

Injured and pristine, the twins had the out-of-town tournament that could last up to three days, depending on final scores.

"Oh, and two different guests called to cancel and the people in *Two* left after breakfast." Jane led the way out of the room and down the stairs.

Money was always better with more guests, but flying solo for a couple days meant there was more work for her. One of those mixed blessings.

It was only the man with the date left and he hadn't yet returned. Samantha did as she always had, but the silence let her mind wander. The thumping up the stairs came at her and she tried to imagine Nathan getting out of bed to take the stairs, only to come up, and then . . .

Part my thighs.

That can't be right.

It was dark. She sat reading, having finished the Grafton, she'd moved onto an Amy Lukavics. The door opened and the old man stumbled in, drunk. "I still got it," he said, his stupid, half-conked gaze pouring out beneath liquor-lidded eyes. He took two steps forward, one sideways, a half step back, then another forward. "I need'a sleep."

Ass. She helped the man up to his room where he began stripping long before she closed the door. Down the stairs, she looked at the post, lowered to a crouch, and touched new grooves in the base. It made her want to take a hatchet to the carpenter himself.

Instead she rose, turned the deadbolt, got a glass of water, and went to bed.

At three in the morning, Samantha awoke to sounds coming up the staircase. Her eyes opened wide as she listened, assuming soon the door would creak open as it had the night before.

"Nathan?" she whispered, knowing it wasn't him.

Thump. Thump.

The sound drew closer and she imagined the static charges.

Thump.

Closer yet. Reality clicked.

Thump.

"Can't be. Can't be." Her words came out on a hiss. She grabbed for Nathan's pillow. "Impossible."

Thump.

Further away. Her heart hummed a drum-roll pace nonetheless.

Thump. Thump. Thump.

Down the hall. Samantha exhaled a grateful breath before gasping it right back in as screaming filled the air. "God! God! Jesus! God!"

It was the old man, his voice less drunk. A door banged open and quiet footfalls raced. Samantha listened, knowing the terrain so well that she actually saw the scene unfolding. The man squealed. A pounding returned, but different.

Thumpthump.

Falling, the man made windy noises until the first snap.

Thumpthumpthump.

Samantha launched from bed and crashed through the door. She ran to the banister at the open face of the hallway to look down on the foyer. The old man was in white boxer shorts and a white undershirt. Urine darkened the carpet beneath him. Wet brown splotches decorated the ass of his shorts. His right ear pressed tight against his right shoulder, tendons and bones bunching out at horrid angles beneath the loose neck flesh.

She had to call the police. She ran to the far end of the hallway where the visitor line sat, as there were to be no phones in the master bedroom—dad's rule on work-home balance. She picked up the handset.

It was four minutes before the police arrived: two big men, each carrying a Starbucks cup. They asked a series of questions before one branched off to talk on his cellphone beyond earshot.

"You heard thumping?"

"Someone must've come in. Someone else," Samantha said to the cop who'd stayed in the foyer. "I heard them on the stairs. Heavy steps." *Not steps, not steps at all! Thumps.*

"Heavy steps, huh?"

The other cop returned with his pad in hand. "I called the security company. You engaged the lock and the system at nine-oh-two. It did not disengage until you opened it, assumedly for the ambulance at three-ten. Nobody in or out."

"I heard thumps on the stairs," Samantha said.

"Thumps?"

"Steps."

Four eyes narrowed. The first cop said, "Now, answer me this: what are the odds a man was raving at the hospital about your B&B just before he committed suicide, on the exact night a mangled man with an odd bruise atop his head turns up in the foyer of the same B&B?"

Samantha cast a look back at the post and the stairs. More scratches, as if the thing had moved. The words *It was the post* nearly left her lips. "I don't know what to say."

"Inconvenient," the second cop said.

They left shortly after paramedics rolled the body out, but promised to be close by should she recall anything. She considered calling Nathan, but decided against it. It was late and there was nothing he could do.

She looked at the newel post.

A wide berth wasn't really possible. Samantha pressed her back to the wall as she climbed the stairs. Her gaze flashed from the stains to the scratches to the mounted antlers on the wall at the head of the staircase. Once to the top, she broke for her bedroom.

The clock face wasn't playing nice. Samantha flipped and flopped as those minute digits rose at an impossibly slow pace. At five-forty-nine, she drifted away, dreaming a voice that howled, *SAVE ME, SAVE ME, SAVE ME.*

At five-fifty-nine, she awoke.

Thump.

She sat up.

Thump.

"No."

Thump.

She leapt from bed as if on replay and ran for the phone in the hallway, not daring to check the staircase. *Somehow.*

She picked up the receiver, but put it down immediately. First the carpenter and then the man. The cops loved to pin the tail on whichever donkey *came easiest.* It was insane, the post couldn't . . .

Thump.

"They already think it's me, but it's the post! It's. My—The. Post." The phone came away from its cradle again. It didn't matter what they thought—SAVE ME—there was no proof that she'd done anything because she hadn't done anything. "I didn't," she said, loud enough that she might convince herself of it. Had she let the carpenter work with the hatchet, much of this wouldn't have happened. Everyone would be alive, maybe.

Thump.

The line rang twice before the nine-one-one operator picked up. Samantha explained the rational bits. The operator kept a level, reassuring tone, adding, "Stay on until the police arrive."

Thump.

Samantha turned to face the sound at the staircase.

Thump.

"Ma'am, are you . . . "

Thumpthumpthump.

" . . . still on the . . . "

Thump.

Samantha dropped the phone and ran towards the staircase. She stopped beneath the mounted antlers and leaned forward. "Go away!" Samantha's eyes were downcast, settled on the ground level where that damned post *belonged*. "Go away, you—"

The plain, scuffed post, the one replaced, was there at the bottom. She stared, attempting comprehension, hand resting on the banister and . . .

Her eyes fell onto the bulbous oil drop design. "No, no," she said, stumbling backwards. The fine newel post was in place at the top of the stairs, fit perfectly between the banister corners, as if it had always been there. "No!"

She broke into a sprint, made for the family bathroom. It had a heavy door and a good lock. Clicked and bolted.

Thump.

Lights, blue, red, and white, flared through the octagonal bathroom window over her shoulder.

"Oh thank you, thank you," Samantha mumbled.

Thumpbang.

The door pounded, shaking hair products and electric toothbrushes lined up around the sink like dominoes. The backs of Samantha's knees bumped the toilet as she stumbled in reverse.

Bang. Bang.

The door splintered. Samantha looked to the window and then shifted her eyes onto the door again.

Bang. Bang. Bang.

The door handle popped and fell. Samantha turned and pushed at the window glass.

Bang. Bang. Creak.

The door was open, had to be.

Samantha cried out, "Here! Here!" as she climbed through the window.

"Oh geez," one of the four cops by the two cruisers said.
Thump. Thump.
On her heels, bumping along the linoleum. So damned close.
Thump.
"Help me!" she screamed and pushed her body out further.
"Don't do it!" another cop shouted, her hands waving.
Thump. Knock.
Wood on porcelain, that had to be it. The newel post was there right under her feet.
"Please, it's here! It's getting me!" Samantha wailed, pulling further out the window, peering down into the dark forty-five feet between her and the rocky flowerbeds.
Knock. Knock.
"Lady, hold up. We're coming in."
Knock.
Samantha leaned and teetered. The words SAVE ME flashed bold and white hot before her eyes as she was falling.

Twenty-six bones. Samantha had casts on her arms, legs, and chest. This left her in a sturdy sideways U shape. She had a brace around her neck. Morphine numbed. Coherent despite the fog, she looked around as Nathan and Ella rolled her back to Coyote House.

She'd told everything. Frowning doctors gave her drugs to *even things out*. Her family looked at her like she was nuts. And maybe she was.

"Jane, we're home," Nathan said as he pushed Samantha's wheelchair. Ella walked in reverse, minding her mother's feet, as every bump felt like a car wreck.

Samantha was sullen and removed. For days she'd tried to

hold out, but rationality oozed from every word spoken to her. The newel post was just a newel post and stress had triggered something that built on the horrible coincidences around her. Nothing more.

It was good to be home.

"Jane?" The chair bounced over the steel lip that covered the separation of rug and stone by the doorway. Samantha winced and Nathan stopped. "Sorry."

"You okay, Mom?" Ella leaned in with a sorry smile.

Samantha's lower lip trembled and a scream crept up her throat as she looked past Ella to the staircase. Jane sat on the bottom step, her tongue extended to the newel post.

Snap

Kev Harrison

CREATURES OF THE NIGHT

SAMUEL CUPPED his hands over his ears, as though blocking out the scraping sound would somehow mean it wasn't really happening. He peered across the darkened room through barely-open eyes. The drawer slid slowly open, before coming to a stop.

He wrenched his hands from his ears.

Silence.

He released the lungful of air he'd been holding for he-didn't-know-how-long and sat up in bed. He forced down the duvet and twisted his body, lowering his feet to the floor. He stood up, floorboards creaking like a bullfrog mating call. He winced.

"Samuel, go to bed. You've got school tomorrow!"

Mum's room was right next door. He looked up at the drawer. His toy drawer. The one where his favorite toy of the moment lived—a robot that changed into a dinosaur. If the drawer was open when Mum came in to wake him tomorrow morning, he'd be for it. He had to close it.

He stepped forward, tiptoeing silently onto the rug, one foot before the other. He crept closer, then reached out for the brass pull and gently shoved it back. The grain of the wood made a faint scratching sound, but nothing loud enough for Mum to notice. Satisfied, he stalked back across the rug to his bed, avoiding the creaky board and diving under his duvet.

He rolled onto his side and allowed his sleepy eyelids to close.

Sleep was just beginning to wash over him when he heard the dull thud of fingertips gripping metal. Samuel spun around. He opened his eyes wide, his ears ringing with tinnitus as they strained in the silence to compensate for his poor night vision. The sound began again. Sliding, scraping, the occasional squeak as wood caught on wood. The drawer slid out until it hung down at an angle.

Samuel propped himself up on one elbow and reached for his plastic water glass on his bedside table. He took two large gulps and wiped his mouth with the back of his wrist. He reached out with the glass and missed the table's edge. The glass spun through forty-five degrees as it fell to the ground, seemingly in slow motion, the water sloshing about as if it enjoyed its newfound freedom. The corner of the glass struck wood with a clunk, followed by the splash of the remaining water dashing along the floorboard before disappearing down the cracks into the crawlspace.

Samuel took a deep breath.

A thump from next door. Another. A third, a fourth, and suddenly the thumping was a hastening rhythm, pounding along the landing beyond the left-hand wall, the muffled grumblings of Mum's tired voice the bass line to her footsteps' drums. The bedroom door swung open, a yellow crack hastily expanding until the room was awash with light, forcing his tired eyes closed.

Mum's head rotated from side to side, processing the scene in an instant, sentinel-like. She chewed at her bottom lip as she considered her opening line of attack.

"What time is it Samuel?" she said, her voice bereft of any emotion.

Samuel looked up at his glow-in-the-dark space clock and took five or six seconds to do the mental arithmetic in his mind. "Eleven forty-seven, Mum." He fixed his eyes on hers as he spoke, then thought better of it and lowered them when he'd finished.

"And what time do we close the toy drawer, until the next day?" She rested her hands on her hips.

"Nine-thirty, Mum." Samuel's voice was lifeless, he knew what was coming.

Mum spun on her heels and slammed the drawer shut. The entire chest of drawers and everything on it shook with the force of it. She turned to face Samuel and lowered herself to a crouch. "Now there'll be no toy-time tomorrow. You know that, don't you?"

She'd whispered the words, yet still managed to deliver them with no small measure of spite.

Samuel felt tears welling in his eyes. "But Mum! It wasn't me! I *did* close the drawer at nine-thirty." Then the sobbing took over. Samuel held his head in his hands and whimpered.

Mum stood. "Oh God, here we go then, the waterworks. *I didn't do it Mum!* If you didn't open the drawer, who did? Eh, boy? Mister Giraffe over here, was it?" She paced across the room to Samuel's pile of plush animals, picked up the giraffe roughly by its horns and dangled it in front of her son. "Was it him, Samuel? Getting you in trouble, is he?"

Samuel made a discontented sound between spluttered coughs.

"Well is it, boy?" She was shouting now, full volume.

Samuel smeared his tears onto the side of his face and looked up at Mum. He shook his head. "No, Mum."

She tossed the giraffe back to the pile. "Go to sleep," she said and stomped from the room, closing the door behind her.

Samuel heard the sound of fingertips rapping on the top of the chest of drawers as he pulled his duvet up to his neck. The pattern of the sound soothed him, and he was soon dragged into slumber.

There was no toy time the next day. Mum was decidedly grumpy for a Friday, complaining about tiredness and drinking coffee like the smelly man in the park drinks beer. The hours dragged on for what seemed like lifetimes to Samuel as soap opera melded into mind-numbing soap opera on the TV. Still, he sat quietly, stroking Bongo, the cat, trying to avoid getting into even more trouble.

"Nine o'clock Mum. Bedtime," Samuel cried out in an uncharacteristically cheery voice as he sprang from the sofa. He gave Mum a little wave and dashed to the stairs, bounding two at a time to the landing and into his bedroom. He changed into his pajamas in a flash and went to the bathroom to pee and brush his teeth. His space clock said four minutes past nine as he plunged under the covers and closed his eyes.

The door was open a crack, allowing a sliver of light into the room from the landing. Samuel felt its brightness cross his shut eyelids, then recede again, before coming back once more. He opened one eye and saw the door swinging back and forth, as if in a summer breeze. But it was November, and all the windows were closed.

He opened the other eye, turned onto his side and faced the door. It stilled. Invisible fingers swept along the wooden surface, sliding smoothly, their friction emitting a sound so small he couldn't be sure if it was real. Until it reached the chest of drawers. It tapped again. Hidden knuckles knocking against the surface, a hollow sound. Then the scratching, sliding of the drawer and it was open. Samuel imagined his Robosaur staring, in robot form, at the dappled ceiling.

He felt the heat rising in his throat and behind his eyes. Trails of salty tears ran in rivulets down his cheeks and over his lips to the pillow. What could he do? If he stood to close the drawer, Mum would come charging in. If he didn't, she would find it open when she woke him. Either way, he was in big trouble. The toy might even be confiscated.

He scrunched his eyes shut, sending yet more tears cascading onto his pillow. He listened. Listened so intently the silence of the room hummed. The sound of the TV from below floated up the stairs. Mum was still watching. Distracted. If he was going to get in trouble anyway, he might as well have some fun.

He shuffled down to the end of the bed and lowered a foot to the floor. He pressed down, feeling for any bending or creaking underfoot and finding none. He lowered himself from the bed and gingerly edged onto the rug and towards the drawer. He rubbed his eyes, clearing the remnants of tears from his lashes, then wiped his moist hands on his pajama bottoms.

Samuel reached forward, his fingers outstretched, groping for the toy lying there. The drawer slammed shut with such force he barely saw it. He heard the snapping of bones and the tumble of his severed fingers into the drawer before the pain had a chance to shoot up his arm. He lifted his right hand and watched as crimson liquid spurted from his open knuckles in time with his thrumming heartbeat.

He collapsed to the ground with a loud thud.

"Samuel!" called Mum. "If I have to come up there tonight!"

INFESTATION

Mikal Trimm

SOMETHING HAD BEEN nibbling on the baby again.

Seely fingered the little bites on her son's hands and feet, cursing silently. She rejected the deep-seated instinct to cry out in terror, panic-stricken and heartsick. She'd done that the first time. Now she wiped her eyes with the back of her hand and checked Donnie's breathing—deep and even. There were no signs of infection, and the redness and swelling around the bite marks was already disappearing.

She checked the rat traps in his room (none tripped) and the packets of poison (untouched). Then she sat by his crib and wept for a while, waiting for her son to wake up and be fed.

Nick had left her two months ago. He came home one night, drunk and belligerent, as usual. He lit and tossed cigarettes like Black Cats and stood outside the front door shouting obscenities at Seely, telling her how she'd never loved him, how she was probably humping every guy at the Piggly Wiggly she worked at, how she just got damned uglier every day, especially since that little bastard was born, and on and on.

Outside the trailer they shared, some underage tramp with too little clothing and too much makeup sat in Nick's truck, driver's side, gunning the engine and occasionally honking the horn. Seely heard the baby crying, and she realized she was just too tired to deal with this anymore. Too tired to deal with Nick's paranoia. Or his constant drunkenness. Or his passion for jailbait. Pick one.

"Go away, Nick." Three words, spoken in a dull monotone, and he stopped in mid-tirade.

"Huh?"

She looked into his eyes and saw nothing but confusion and, amazingly, fear. "You want to leave, go. Take the truck. Take your girlfriend. The trailer's mine. I'll leave the rest of your crap on the porch for you to pick up tomorrow."

She could pinpoint the moment when Nick realized, in some hidden portion of his mind where the brain cells still functioned, that he was being dismissed. "Hold on, bitch, you can't . . . "

Seely was already reaching beside the door as Nick began his tirade. She racked the pump on the shotgun he'd left there, insisting it was 'necessary' for protection. The ratcheting of the shell into the chamber shut Nick up again.

"The gun's mine, too," she said.

Moments later, Nick and his latest honey fishtailed in the dirt driveway. Then they were gone.

Seely hadn't seen him since, but his clothes and her TV were missing when she got home from work the next day.

"Y'all got roaches, Seely."

Seely dumped the plastic bags of marked-down groceries from the supermarket on the kitchen table, hanging her head and sighing deeply. "Hey there to you, too, Luanne."

Luanne Parsons worked the evening shift at the Gas-N-Go down the street from the trailer park. She watched Donnie when Seely worked, and Seely sat for Luanne's two-year-old daughter Fayette when Luanne pulled her shifts.

Luanne patted her shoulder. "Sorry, hon, guess I shoulda let you breathe a little, I know."

Seely started putting the groceries away, trying to ignore the gleeful edge to her friend's voice. "Lord, Luanne, we *all* got roaches."

Luanne shuddered. "I only saw a couple, Seely, but . . . "

She spread her meaty hands out as far as she could.

"Honey, they was *big*."

Luanne gathered her purse and a few pieces of peanut brittle from a candy dish on the table.

"Anyway, Donnie was a little darling today, as usual, but don't he look a little pale to you? You gotta bring him out in the sun more to soak up some light! And someone called but they didn't leave a name, and the propane guy came 'round and filled up your tanks . . . "

"Someone called?"

"Prob'ly a bill collector, honey, they don't never want to talk to anybody but the target. You want me to bring you home some Raid from the store, or you got some handy?"

Seely shook her head. "I have plenty. Thanks anyway."

As she left, Luanne called over her shoulder, "Best start using it then, sweetie. Them's some *nasty* bugs."

Seely finished putting her food away, peeling off the 'WIC Approved' stickers on the cheese by habit.

Roaches. In the South. Who'd have thought?

She looked at the bowl of peanut brittle on the table, uncovered. She pictured a big old cockroach crawling across the candy. She thought of Luanne, casually tossing the stuff down . . .

Seely dumped the bowl into the trash, trembling.

Tuscan, Alabama wasn't even big enough to be called a small town. It was a stoplight on the highway, a gathering place for people too tired, poor, or lazy to move elsewhere. Other than the necessities needed to support any center of population—a grocery, a gas station, and a Colonel Dixie's burger-and-chicken stand—Tuscan was devoid of the amenities of modern life, unless junkyards counted as a luxury. Anything else required a drive elsewhere, usually to nearby Mobile.

Seely had always hated going to Mobile. It was necessary, sometimes, but she avoided the drive whenever possible. Her car, a beaten and asthmatic old Pacer, had too many miles logged to count—the odometer had turned over ages ago, then died completely—and she never knew if the ancient rattletrap would make the thirty mile drive into the city, much less return under its own volition. And there was the tunnel to deal with, as well. In order to reach the welfare office, say, or the nearest health clinic that accepted Medicaid, she had to hit I-10 and pass through the tunnels that went under Mobile Bay.

Seely was petrified when it came to tunnels. She didn't know why. All she could think of when she was forced to drive through the concrete and tile monstrosities, her windows closed to shut out the poison cloud of exhaust fumes fogging the air, was the millions of gallons of water that loomed over her head. She was always terrified that the bay might want to reclaim the fragile tube beneath it for its own use.

She had wanted to take Donnie to the clinic a couple of weeks ago when she first saw the bites, but she'd spent so much time gathering the courage for the drive to Mobile that, by the time she finally packed up his diaper bag and bundled him out of his crib for the trip, all the marks had faded. He'd lain there unblemished in her arms, smiling and blowing bubbles. No fever, no vomiting, nothing to alert a doctor in any way. Having to go to that ratty little clinic in was bad enough—showing up there with an obviously healthy child would be even worse.

Seely wound up giving Donnie a good warm bath that first

night and dabbing him liberally with mercurochrome. He'd fallen asleep while she dried him off, and she placed him back in his crib, searching all the while for some trace of whatever had been feeding on her son.

Now, with Donnie burbling in his playpen and Fayette playing mindlessly in the kitchen with some old pots and pans, Seely clutched a can of generic bug spray, her gaze flickering into the corners and chasing every shadow.

This is silly. Roaches don't bite.

Do they?

"I don't want to be a bother, Seely."

Seely had barely opened the trailer door when Luanne started whining. It was two days after the cockroach sighting and Luanne stood there in the kitchen, looking flustered and jittery, her daughter wrapped protectively in one flabby arm. All of Fayette's belongings—toys, changes of clothes, what-have-you—were packed in plastic grocery bags on the table. Seely felt an immediate need to turn and run before the hammer fell. Instead, she shut the door quietly behind her and leaned against it, her eyes closed.

"What's the matter, Luanne?"

"I don't think I can let Fayette stay here no more. And, tell the truth, I don't really think I want to be here, either."

"Jesus, Luanne!"

Seely took a breath, tried to maintain control, but she could feel the veins in her forehead starting to throb, and she knew the leash was slipping.

"What—I mean, *why*? What'd I do to you?"

Luanne began gathering her bags, avoiding Seely's eyes.

"It ain't you, honey. It's—it's those damn *bugs*. I can hear them in the walls. They's hundreds of them, Seely, just crawling around all over the place, but they stay where you can't see 'em. Fayette won't even leave my side anymore, she's so scared they comin' to get her."

Seely wanted to scream. She wanted to grab Luanne by her limp, peroxided hair and shake some sense into her fat head. But she looked at Fayette and saw true fear in her eyes, and she thought of the bites that covered Donnie's arms and legs every morning, and she gave up. She was too tired to fight. Just like that night with Nick.

"Go on, Luanne. Get on home."

Luanne scurried out the door, roachlike in her own way, Fayette clinging to her like a parasite. "I'd take care of Donnie over at our place, Seely, you know that, but you know how Jimmie needs his sleep . . . "

Luanne's husband worked nights as a security guard in Mobile. He was not pleasant when aroused, as the fading bruises on Luanne's arms attested.

"Go home, Luanne." Seely started to close the door, but she couldn't resist one little remark. "Y'all make sure you don't wake up Jimmie, now . . . "

She shut the world out with a twitch of her wrist.

Oh, Cecelia Leigh Harden, Seely thought as she sank bonelessly to the floor, *you're really in the tunnel now . . .*

"Nick?"

"What the hell you want?"

"You know I wouldn't call you if it wasn't . . . Luanne won't watch Donnie anymore. I need you to *help out*, okay?"

Seely took deep breaths, fighting back the scream threatening to tear through her throat.

"I ain't got money, if that's what you want."

"I just need you to watch Donnie when I work, maybe, or help me pay for a sitter." *Don't scream, don't scream, don't scream.*

"I just told you I ain't got no money for you. Ain't got time, either." A sleepy voice moaned something in the background, and Nick murmured something back. "Anyway, I told you to get rid of that little bastard when you got pregnant, but you wouldn't listen. He's your problem, not mine."

"Dammit, Nick, you have some obligati—"

Click.

And then the short drive to Mobile and the long, dark nightmare of the tunnel. Seely clutched the wheel, her body knotting itself into a tight ball, nothing functioning but her eyes, her wrists, her feet. She came within sight of the gaping tunnel mouth, and in her terror almost slammed into the car in front of her.

Traffic was stopped. Seely found herself praying to two gods at the same time. *Please don't let this last, don't make me crawl through the tunnel, I can't take it. I need to get to the Human Services office and see what they can do for me, and Donnie's asleep, and I just want this over with, please, please, please . . .*

And, with another voice, she prayed to a darker god: *Don't make me go in there, I'll try again tomorrow, screw the gas money, but don't make me go in there today.*

The dark god won. A policeman walked down the line of cars, explaining that there was a wreck in the tunnel, and the wait might be a while. Then Donnie woke up in his car seat and started whining, and Seely drew a sigh of thanks.

"Sir?" The cop leaned down, struggling to hear her voice over Donnie's escalating cries. "My baby is real sick, and I need to get out of the line so I can take him to a doctor. Can you help me?"

He nodded. "Hey, I got one at home about that age. I know what it's like."

With motions and shouts, a lot of backing-and-filling, and a few illegal procedures, he managed to get Seely out of the cluster of stagnant cars and onto an exit ramp. He gave her a little salute as she pulled off the Interstate and turned toward home.

She almost lost control again as something scurried beneath the accelerator pedal and disappeared under the tattered carpet of her floorboard. She caught a flash of white, mottled and flesh-like. The Pacer careened toward the guardrails, and she wrenched the steering wheel to the left, barely avoiding a spinout into the lanes below.

Donnie started screaming, hiccupped, and put his fists to his mouth, silent once again. Seely drove onto the shoulder, choking off shouts and curses and sobs. She forced herself to open her door slowly. Once she was sure Donnie was asleep, she searched the car methodically, looking for some sign of the creature lurking in her floorboards.

Nothing. Donnie indulged in milky snores, at peace.

That night, Seely dreamed the walls were talking to her. They hissed and chattered in some indecipherable language, but the dream acted as interpreter, translating the sibilant speech into images: Nick, stumbling drunkenly from the trailer and back to his lover, followed by dark shapes that crept unseen into the tire-wells of his truck; Luanne, grabbing her things and rushing to escape from Seely's wrath, not noticing the passengers she carried out with her. Nick again, his face distorted in the Picasso way that only dreams can reproduce, saying *Kill the little bastard, he's not worth the trouble,* and Donnie, lying in his crib in a near-comatose state as dozens of ancient, chittering creatures drank up his essence while Seely watched, smiling.

Seely woke up gasping. She'd moved Donnie's crib into her bedroom after Luanne's final exit, and she hit her head on its railing when she rolled out of bed. Dizzy from the abrupt awakening and the pain from the collision, she stood shaking her head, trying to focus in the darkness.

The walls were moving.

She shook her head again, desperate to separate reality from nightmare. Nick's face flashed by, and Luanne's, and she really thought she was still asleep until she heard the noise, the nerve-scraping chittering of pestilence. She grabbed blindly for the roach spray on her nightstand, still blurry-eyed, spots of half-light swimming through her vision. Something slid along the side of her foot, and she sprayed it instinctively. The room filled with the acrid scent of insecticide, and she almost dropped the can as whatever was down there flew up in alarm, its wings stroking her thigh. She started to scream, checked it by painfully swallowing air, and forced herself to remain still.

The spots before her eyes resolved into grayish shapes, roachlike, luminescent. They wove a pattern across the bedroom, dancing from walls to ceiling to floor, leaving sickly pale slime-trails of residual light across the dresser, the bed, the crib.

The crib. They clustered around the crib, around her baby.

"Donnie!" At her shout, the shapes disappeared, and the sounds of their passing faded. The room was dark, but enough moonlight bled through the broken slats of the mini-blinds to guide her as she snatched him from the crib. She tucked the roach spray under her chin, grabbing Donnie with one arm, supporting his head with her other hand. The can of bug spray tried to slip

113

from its position, and she juggled madly for a moment, finally achieving balance—her son in the crook of one arm, and the can rested in her other palm, ready for business. She pulled Donnie's sleeping form close, amazed that the violent motion hadn't brought him instantly awake.

And she felt something, no—*something*—moving beneath his jumper.

She fought the urge to push him away, even as she swallowed a sudden rush of bile. She reached for the light switch and her hand came down on something hard and cold; it flexed its wings beneath her palm, and she fell back, tripping on a leg of the crib and falling on her bed, remembering at the last minute to cradle Donnie as she fell. His flesh seemed to writhe against her, and she knew she needed to put him down, had to let him go before she lost the little courage she still had and ran mindlessly into the night.

Donnie didn't react as she disentangled herself from him and placed him on her bed. Working as fast as she could in the dim light, she tried to unzip his jumper. Her hands shook so badly, she wound up just tearing the zipper out; it was faster that way. She could see his tiny chest rising and falling in the moonlight, and as she pulled his clothes off, she could see *them* as well.

They were bigger than she'd pictured, palm-sized, and they clustered at the joints of his arms and legs, feeding. Seely felt her knees giving way when she realized one of the roaches had attached itself to Donnie's genitals, its shell pulsating in time with his heartbeat.

No. Seely felt the anger boiling up inside her, the anger that was there the night Nick left, the anger that came again that evening with Luanne, and she reacted, as she always did, with a deadly calm. The trembling in her hands disappeared. She plucked the roaches, one by one, from her son's body, beginning with the fat bastard at his crotch. They came away without struggling, and as she pulled them off she could see long tubes protruding from them—*proboscises*, her mind provided clinically. She wrenched the roaches off and squashed them in her fist, ignoring the crunch of their carapaces, the gush of warm fluid that accompanied each death. She looked for blood spots, but all she could see were drops of whitish liquid, shining in the moonlight. She wiped the fluid off with the sleeve of her nightgown in a series of quick swipes across Donnie's chest and legs.

Once Donnie was clean, she wrapped him in a blanket from the crib, picked up the roach spray, and marched toward the bedroom door. In the wavering moonlight, the walls shifted and shimmered with a filthy grey sheen. *Doesn't matter. No matter how many there are, it just doesn't matter.* Seely felt Donnie stir, and she stopped to adjust her grip. He was squirming, and she knew he would be crying soon, hungry and confused.

Not yet, baby, not yet . . .

The shotgun flashed into her mind. Right by the front door, loaded and ready. It didn't matter that the chambers were filled with buckshot, which would do damn little against a horde of insects. *Power.* That's what it represented, what she needed now.

She hugged Donnie to her chest, ready to make the run for the front door, and the bedroom doorway vanished. The walls seemed to bulge outward, and a living curtain of roaches rushed into the space, locking themselves into place in an unassailable barricade of limbs, wings, and carapaces. They made a noise, a loud, crazed buzzing that Seely felt as a physical attack. She'd calmly constructed a battle plan in the last few seconds–the bug spray, the shotgun–only to find that the enemy was prepared, more than prepared, for her imagined tactics. Now, she could only stand and watch the shimmering veil of insects, while Donnie groggily searched for her breast. She could feel his mouth hunting wetly, trying to feed through the flimsy fabric of her nightgown.

No, not yet, baby, please . . .

Fire. Seely felt the pull of instinct. *Nothing likes fire.*

Nick had smoked like some people breathed, and he'd left cheap plastic lighters all over the trailer. Seely back-pedaled to her nightstand, set the roach-spray down, and opened the drawer, keeping her eyes on the doorway. She shuffled through the contents blindly, rejecting lipsticks and perfume samples, finally closing her hand on an unmistakable shape. She pulled the Bic out, lay Donnie over her shoulder in burping position, and grabbed the roach spray.

Snick. The lighter worked. She felt Donnie's weight on her shoulder, and headed slowly toward the bedroom door. The drapery of roaches still hung there, swaying to an unseen wind.

Seely shook the can, held the lighter up, lit it, and sprayed. The alcohol from the bug spray ignited like a flamethrower, and the false door burned away in a shower of living comets.

Seely ran through the doorway, dropping the lighter and the roach spray as Donnie shifted position. She grabbed him, holding him tightly with one arm as she snatched the shotgun with her other hand, breaking the front door open with a vicious kick. She stumbled down the cheap wooden steps, turning as she hit ground level, Donnie in one hand and the shotgun in the other.

The roaches gathered at the door, piles upon piles, and began dropping onto the rickety wooden steps below. Seely tried to ratchet the pump one-handed, failed miserably. *And what would it matter? What would you shoot?*

Nick's voice invaded her head again, uninvited, explaining why he thought a shotgun was a good idea. *You're a woman, and women can't shoot worth crap when it comes to aiming. But with a shotgun, you pull the trigger and you're bound to hit something.* Then he loaded it with buckshot. Nick the frigging genius.

Seely watched the bugs tumble toward her, slowly working

their way out of the trailer. She backed away slowly, trying to think, and all she could come up with was *fire, fire, fire.*

Then, Seely's brain cells sparking randomly at this point, something Luanne had said days earlier about the propane man popped up, and she *knew what to do.* Screw the trailer, screw Nick, screw the frigging drive to Mobile. *For Donnie.*

Seely carried her baby back to the limits of her trailer-lot, set him down behind her carefully, aimed as well as she could with a cheap no-brand shotgun, and fired.

She hit the propane tank behind the trailer on her second shot, and even from this distance the explosion knocked her back. She flew over Donnie and landed a few feet away, dazed by the fireball and the fall. She crawled back to her baby by pure mother's instinct, her eyes still trying to erase the sudden light, and she almost screamed when she found him exactly where she'd left him, still reaching for his mother.

Seely picked him up, gently, working by feel more than sight. Donnie sighed in her arms and snuggled closer. She watched her home burn, the memories of the past few years going with it, and she tried, but she could feel no sense of loss. *I've got my baby. I saved the one thing that's important.*

A sharp pain rose between her breasts. The night flexed around her as she sank limply to the ground. With the little energy she had left, she watched Donnie, his tongue now a thin, fleshy tube, begin to suckle. The moon blurred as countless insects whirred their wings, the sound like applause as it filled her ears. *Oh, Donnie, baby, not yet . . .*

Then Seely went through the tunnel.

RIVER OF NINE TAILS

Mark Cassell

"ANY IDEA WHAT killed him?" the American shouted over the chugging engine.

Elliot couldn't answer, couldn't drag his eyes away from the dead Vietnamese guide. The boat rocked as he watched the other man shuffle along the wooden seat and clamber over their rucksacks, ducking beneath the branch that had torn the canopy. In all his thirty-eight years on the planet, this was only the second dead body Elliot had seen. The first had been his wife.

"Where's the kill switch on this thing?" The other man's lip curled as he stretched over the body to reach for the engine.

Smoke belched from the long vessel's exhaust, filling the blue sky with grey clouds.

As the only passengers on the sampan, the first they'd known of any problem was when the canopy ripped, and the boat thumped the riverbank. Elliot's immediate thought had been that they were stopping despite the lack of a jetty and the captain had misjudged a landing.

The American, whose name Elliot didn't actually know, cut off the engine. He scrambled backwards, awkwardly maneuvering around the slumped body, and the silence of the Mekong Delta closed in.

"Look at that mess." The man's voice seemed even louder now. "Look!"

Elliot *was* looking.

The Vietnamese man who'd introduced himself as Captain Duc, wore brown trousers and an open shirt. Blood glistened on dark skin from where it dribbled over his chin and down his neck. Dead eyes stared through the remaining smoky wisps, seeming to fix on the relentless sun.

121

The boat tilted as the American stood, his sunglasses swaying on the cord around his neck. "It's leaking!"

Brown water lapped his sandals, splashing his socks. Blood swirled.

"Stand still!" Elliot yelled and grabbed the wooden rail. "Seriously, mate, don't move."

"I can't swim."

When Elliot relaxed his grip, he slowly stood, bracing himself against the rocking motion.

"We're in the shallows," he said, now standing straight, "we'll be absolutely fine."

Again, the other man shifted sideways. This time the sampan tilted.

"Whoa!" Elliot yelled.

Duc's body flipped to sprawl facedown, half over the side. A limp arm slapped the water.

"Jesus, what the fuck?" the American shouted.

"Keep still!"

Two ragged, near-circular holes of flesh and shirt fabric gaped beneath the dead man's shoulder blade. There were even a couple of ribs on show, splintered, grisly.

"What could've done that?" the man demanded.

Water rapidly filled the boat, now lapping their shins.

"Eels?" Elliot murmured, but doubted his words. "Piranha?"

He knew he was talking bollocks; he had no idea what the hell could've done it.

The man's chest heaved. He looked as if he was going to have a panic attack. Elliot's own breathing was fast. Beside him, extending almost parallel with the torn canopy, a low branch hooked out over the riverbank as though offering assistance.

"Come on," he said, and reached for the branch.

Water splashed as the American headed for Elliot, and the boat jerked to the left and right.

"Slowly!" Elliot shouted before he could gauge the branch's strength.

The water level rose and splashed around them, covering their knees in frothy bubbles.

"We must get off the boat!" The man flailed arms, the boat rocking. He barely managed to keep upright. The rails were submerging and the shredded canopy draped into the water. He slipped, yelled something, and leapt toward the riverbank.

Elliot looked up to the branch and allowed it to take his weight.

Behind him, he heard a splash and water drenched him. Waves rushed the mud and tree roots that lined the bank, and the boat pulled away from his dangling boots. For a moment he hung there, then hoisted himself hand over hand along the branch; awkward yet successful, he finally tiptoed the muddy bank and dropped to his knees. With his breath coming in short, hot bursts, he scrambled through reeds and slick foliage. Mud squelched.

"I'm soaked," came the voice beside him.

Mud covered the other man's clothes, mostly caking his lower-half, so much so that it looked like he wore brown trousers. His hair was flat to his scalp and water dripped from a stubbly chin. Despite the situation, Elliot almost laughed. Humor was his defense mechanism, and this was the kind of moment where it would erupt as uncontrollable laughter. Instead, he used Duc's floating body as a way of sobering him up.

It worked.

"We need to get out of here."

The American's jaw flexed as he scooped mud from his clothes, while behind him the sampan sank lower, leveling with churned blood and froth. Duc's body, a water bottle and a plastic bag drifted downstream, chased by swirling bubbles disappearing behind tall reeds where the river narrowed.

"Whatever killed him," Elliot said, "could still be in the water."

"Dude, stop stating the obvious."

"You have any idea where we are?"

"Do I look Vietnamese?"

"Mate, I'm only asking."

They stood on the riverbank and watched the waves lessen, giving way to ripples which rolled out toward the opposite bank.

"Brandon."

"Huh?" Elliot looked down at the outstretched hand. "Oh, right, yeah . . . " He clasped it. "Elliot."

Although Brandon's grip was all mud and water, it was firm, friendly. "I don't mean to be a dick."

"I get it." Elliot wiped his now-muddy hand on his shirt. "That was enough to make anyone lose their cool."

Brandon motioned to the river. "My phone was in that rucksack."

"Want to dive in and get it?"

"No chance."

"I've not had a phone since I left the UK," Elliot said, wondering when precisely he'd disconnected from the world. It hadn't been when he cancelled his phone contract, it was way before that. The months leading up to his departure blurred as though he'd sidestepped reality, so perhaps that was the reason why he felt somewhat desensitized to the insanity around him right now. He knew he should be scared shitless, wearing a similar wide-eyed what-the-fuck-just-happened expression as—

Brandon was still talking. " . . . and you're a rare one, buddy. The first traveler I've met who hasn't been glued to a cell phone. New experiences for these youngsters, and they're all attached to those things. No hope for mankind's future. Eventually everyone will live life vicariously through a screen."

Elliot glanced around them. He had no idea what to do.

Perhaps there was a small part of him that wanted to wade out into the water, search the murky depths and confront whatever it was that had killed Duc. Maybe the animal had answers about Death.

"I figure," Brandon continued, "we are both older than your typical traveler."

Elliot blinked, shivered, and focused on the man's words.

"Yeah, I guess," he murmured.

He too had met countless other travelers, most in their late-teens or early twenties. They had no idea how life could set fire to your balls. Whether boy or girl (not *man* or *woman*, they were just kids after all), they'd often exchange short conversations before they returned to a handheld device, hunched, squinting. Granted, some were searching online for information about their surroundings, local traditions, translations, and the like, yet the majority seemed fixated with that constant need for validation from peers on the other side of the globe. In the twenty-first century, there was no longer a round-the-world trip, it was more a round-the-world ego-trip. There would always be that lifeline back home for them, certainly, but there's no absolute freedom of being let off the leash, to absorb each and every experience at hand.

A lifeline . . . For Elliot, besides parents both in their seventies, he had nothing left back home. Not even a house. Not anymore.

And now he didn't even have a spare pair of pants.

Brandon pointed to the brown depths of the Mekong Delta. His voice echoed on the hot air as he yelled, "How the fuck did that man die?"

Keeping the winding length of the river to their right, the two men agreed to follow its course, where eventually, it would lead them to My Tho, the village in which they boarded the sampan. Not wanting to walk too close to the water, not knowing what lurked beneath its brown depths, they kept it just in sight.

After a long stretch of silence, Brandon asked, "What brings you out here?"

Elliot wasn't ready to answer that, especially to a travel companion whom he'd met only a few hours ago. Thoughts of Jane immediately came to him, albeit fleeting, yet enough for a familiar icy hold to grip his stomach and rise to his heart. Loss, guilt, confusion. Loneliness. He almost said, "To escape" but managed to catch himself and instead replied, "To see more of the world."

Seeming content with that answer, Brandon nodded enough to make it necessary to push his sunglasses back up the bridge of his nose.

They walked in silence again.

"The Vietnamese refer to the Mekong Delta as 'Song Cuu Long', or something like that," Brandon eventually said, "and is over two-thousand-seven-hundred miles long."

"Yep, and it starts way up in eastern Tibet."

"It does."

Elliot stopped and looked over the other man's shoulder to where he could just about see the river through swaying palm fronds.

"Apparently, Song Cuu Long means 'River of Nine Tails.'"

Elliot didn't answer, he stared at the river, thinking he'd seen something.

"Or maybe it's 'River of Nine Dragons,'" Brandon added, mistaking Elliot's attention on the river for interest in his trivia. "I can't remember now. I read it some—"

"Shhh."

The fronds steadied, making Elliot wonder if they'd moved because of the current or something else. He couldn't hear anything. He stretched his neck, not wanting to approach in case that something else was there.

"What's that?" he whispered.

Brandon turned to look, his jaw line twitching and eyes bulging behind sunglasses.

A gnarled branch broke the water's surface.

Elliot started to laugh, relax, then—

It was not a branch.

Whatever Brandon said next was snatched by a torrent of water and parting fronds. In a rush of scaly limbs and a blur of mud, what appeared to be an alligator or crocodile (Elliot had never known the difference) scrambled up the riverbank. Toward them.

The thing had the body of a crocodile yet had no mouth, just a long snout with a splintered stump where a horn once was. As the men staggered backwards, sideways, yelling and sliding in the mud themselves, Elliot failed to work out where the torso ended and where its limbs began. Limbs . . . too many . . . all along its back, thrashed and whipped away branches and foliage. Whatever the animal, this *creature*, was, it lashed out with those determined appendages—that's what they were: appendages with snapping mouths, like tentacles only with glistening circular maws filled with yellow teeth that lined the throats all the way downwards.

Even in the insanity of the moment, Elliot somehow managed to count the fucking things.

Nine.

Nine thrashing appendages, not including the four stumpy legs, each one culminating in a claw as long as his forearm.

"Run!" he shouted and sprinted up an embankment, further into the jungle.

"What the fuck is it?" Brandon's voice was too far behind.

A glance over a shoulder, and Elliot saw the man had only just made it onto the embankment. The American scrambled clumsily in the mud as though his legs disobeyed him. He got up, threw a wide-eyed glance at the lumbering animal, and ran toward Elliot. At least, he tried.

He slipped sideways and whacked the ground with a "Hummmph!"

From where Elliot stood, flanked by looming trees, he could see only the top half of the man . . .

There was a slapping sound, like a wetsuit dropped onto soft sand, and a crunch. Brandon screamed, and his head and shoulders fell from sight.

More wet sounds, more crunching . . .

Elliot went to take a step toward the poor bastard—*he had to help!*—but then saw a whipping appendage, bloody, slick and glistening in the rays of sunlight which lanced through the jungle ceiling.

More screams . . .

From somewhere far away, yet perhaps closer than Elliot thought, something like a horn blew. A piercing note, shrill. It seemed as though even the birds fell silent along with Brandon's screams. Then another note. The same, only this time sustained.

Something thumped and a branch snapped.

"You run, motherfucker!" Brandon shouted.

The horn's blast silenced at the same time as a great splash. Out on the river, water misted the air like a thousand sun-glinting crystals.

Brandon groaned, and Elliot ran to him.

Brandon was huddled in the mud and wet leaves, clutching his leg.

Elliot moved in beside him, marveling at how the man wasn't yelling. Bite marks, unsurprisingly identical to Duc's, covered his leg from thigh to ankle. One was ragged and to the bone. Blood streaked his skin, saturated his sock and dripped on the ground.

"Mate," Elliot whispered.

His first thought was a bandage for the worst of the wounds, and so immediately unbuttoned his shirt and shrugged out of it. Ripping fabric always looked easy in a movie but as he tried, he slipped and smacked his hand on the tree beside them.

Now Brandon began whining.

"You'll be fine, mate." Although Elliot wasn't entirely certain. All the shit he learnt back in school, they never taught him to deal with a man whose leg had been ravaged by a river monster with nine mouths. Algebra, long-shore drift, how Jonas Salk cured polio in 1953 . . . but what do you do when faced with a wound such as this?

The man now mumbled while Elliot succeeded in ripping the arm off the shirt. The tearing sound seemed too loud. Perhaps the creature would hear it and come back. This time for him. A squint through the foliage at the now-still Mekong water, revealed nothing.

Somewhere far away, a bird cawed.

He calmed his breathing, if only for Brandon's sake, and wrapped the fabric around the ravaged flesh.

"That's the worst of them," he said and gave it a final pull.

Brandon hissed through clenched teeth. Spit sprayed.

"Not sure what to do about these bite marks, though."

"It hurts, man!"

"Now who's stating the obvious?" Elliot looked at the remains of his shirt, not caring that he was now topless. It was wet, covered in mud with leaves and twigs sticking to it, but it would have to do. He tied it around the man's leg as best he could.

"Thanks."

"You're going to be fine," Elliot assured him. "You reckon you can walk?"

"I sure as fuck don't want to stay here."

The jungle buzzed with insects, something Elliot hadn't noticed. Now the adrenaline had lessened, and blood no longer roared in his ears, he guessed it made sense that he'd begin to notice their surroundings.

"Let's get you up," he said and offered his hand.

The buzzing sound seemed to be getting louder. Closer.

Brandon looked past Elliot's bloody hand. "Is that . . . ?" His voice was hopeful. He shifted in the mud and winced, placing both hands on the ground ready to push himself up.

"A motorbike, yeah."

"Scooter." The American still didn't grab his hand. "Two of them."

Elliot lowered his arm and followed the man's gaze to peer deeper into the jungle.

It was indeed two scooters revving, and eventually they pulled into view. Both riders were young men, one whose open shirt flapped behind him, and the other who wore a red cap. As they approached, they exchanged something in rapid Vietnamese. They pulled up in a burst of engine revs and churned mud, not too far away.

"Thank God," Brandon said, now clutching his leg again. He'd settled back down.

A cloud of petrol fumes clung to the air as the two riders regarded the travelers for a moment.

The man with the open shirt dismounted and kicked out the stand. Around his neck was what looked like a dried chili looped through a rusty metal ring and tied to a twisted leather cord. Elliot guessed it was some kind of Vietnamese superstition; back in the UK, it was a rabbit's foot for a lucky charm, so why not a chili?

The guy with the red cap stayed mounted.

"Thank God," Brandon said again as Chili-Man crouched beside him.

"You guys speak English?" Elliot asked.

Red Cap looked at him, then at Brandon.

"No?" Elliot pointed to the wounded man. "He needs help."

"Yeah, I need help," he hissed as Chili-Man prodded the makeshift bandage. "Hey, hey! Gentle! Come on . . . "

Chili-Man looked up at his companion and said something.

Elliot had so far visited Thailand and Cambodia, and while exploring, he'd made every effort to learn pleasantries: hello, goodbye, please, thank you, plus other useful words. Sometimes even phrases. Now, faced with this emergency — let alone the fact their guide had earlier been killed by a river monster — he wished he'd invested in something as simple as a phrase book. However, even if he had one, it would no doubt be at the bottom of the river.

He had to accept this insane situation they faced.

Red Cap finally dismounted from his scooter and wheeled it up against the foliage. His dark eyes fixed on Brandon, then he said something so rapidly, Elliot doubted that if he even understood even a little of the language, he'd fail to catch it. Although, perhaps he heard the words "Cuu Long."

"Hospital?" Elliot asked. "Um, medic, medicine . . . pharmaceutical . . . nurse?"

Chili-Man pulled out a hunting knife.

And thrust it into Brandon's chest.

"What the—?" Elliot's words echoed around them.

Brandon's eyes bulged, looking at the blade sliding out from the gushing wound.

Elliot stepped forward. Someone from behind — Red Cap, of course — grabbed his arms. He wrestled in the man's grip while he watched Brandon's head fall back, dead eyes locked on the branches overhead. What felt like rubber pinched his skin, binding his wrists. He struggled, uselessly.

"Get off me!"

Chili-Man approached him, slowly raising the dripping knife. Perhaps a smile twitched his lips.

"Don't do this!" Elliot yelled.

A fist swung upwards and Elliot's nose exploded in a hot wet crunch. In a blur of tears and motion, the two men forced him to his knees.

"Mnnnnnnn, mnnnnnn, mnnnph," Elliot said through a weird suffocation.

They crammed something green into his mouth, something bitter. Clamping his teeth together and trying to breathe through a broken nose was impossible. He tried to spit the stuff out, but they rubbed it over his teeth and gums. It tingled.

The pair laughed and released him.

With his arms bound, he thrashed about in the mud, spitting, choking.

"Bastards," he said, but his voice sounded strange. Perhaps . . . perhaps it was . . . because . . . his nose . . . broken . . .

Stones and twigs and leaves scratched his naked torso, yet it all felt somehow distant . . . too far . . .

And a darkness crept into his vision.

Pressing in, sideways, numbing. A coldness spread through his body, and all he could taste was that bitterness.

With an ankle each, the two men dragged him past the body of his brief and now dead companion. He slid through mud, trying to kick, to struggle, but his body didn't seem to obey.

That darkness came at him in waves.

As the drug took effect, tangled thoughts battered him. He wanted to laugh about the fact that he'd only just learned of the American's name. With his brain whirling, his face on fire, he squinted through tears and blood and that pulsing blackness, and Elliot said goodbye to Brandon. Silently though, because his lips didn't—*couldn't*—move.

By the time they had him beside the river, his arms and legs

were utterly useless. Paralyzed, it seemed, apart from his brain
. . . yet even that was as slow as the river's current which gently
lapped his boots.

They left him there.

Alone . . . to be fed to that creature . . .

Don't leave me!

Elliot listened to the two Vietnamese men return to their
motorcycles, mud squelching and twigs snapping. One engine
sputtered, revved, and then the other. Both now revving, they
rode off.

Hey!

Engines faded into the silence.

Hey!

Now he was left with only the sound of the Mekong Delta.

As he laid there, feeling the sunshine on his face in that
disconnected sort of way, the realization that Death was coming
comforted him. Perhaps he was ready . . . He'd seen Death up
close. Three times now: Twice here in Vietnam, the other back
home in the UK.

Jane . . .

Death wasn't too far away, and this time it was for him. If
there was an afterlife, he'd get to see his wife again.

Did . . . did something splash just then?

Jane.

Why was it, when Death approaches—now in the guise of the
thing that had killed Captain Duc—you begin to question if
there's some other place beyond all this?

Maybe something did splash.

This was it.

Time to die, Elliot.

And he was happy to accept.

He closed his eyes and thoughts of Jane soaked into him as
even now he knew the mud and water soaked into his clothes.

Of everything about her, all that she was . . . and—Death was coming, right now, just for him, all for him—and how he'd rushed her to hospital and . . . and not long after that how the surgeon's well-practiced apologetic gaze fixed on him, and—

Splash. The sound of a rowing boat.

Jane?

A boat.

Was he relieved? Perhaps, perhaps not. What was his life now?

A slim wooden canoe cut through the water's surface like a knife spreading smooth peanut butter on bread.

He wondered if his savior had any food on board his vessel.

Help me.

The small man with a conical hat guided the canoe toward him.

Hunger pangs—he felt *them*. Yet still he couldn't feel his legs. Or arms.

Did he want to call out? Did he actually want to be saved? Death, for Elliot, was not quite ready for him after all.

Jane, maybe I won't be joining you. Not yet.

Twilight pressed in on the darker greens which flanked his journey, the rhythmic splash and creak mesmerizing, almost hypnotic. Elliot was sprawled in the canoe, looking up at his conical-hat-wearing savior who rocked back and forth, heaving the oars up and down, splash and creak, in and out of the water. The man was perhaps in his forties, a fisherman Elliot assumed, given the tangle of net and rope that he now laid on.

He was still hungry, and the sky was darkening.

Perhaps the man was taking him to a fish farm, and he'd be

fed one of Vietnam's tasty dishes. What was the fish called? Elephant ears, of all things. Yes, that was it . . .

Definitely hungry now.

Elliot's nose was still blocked, so he breathed through his mouth. Also, just like his arms and legs, his voice failed him; he wanted to thank the man, wanted to talk about what he'd witnessed. Regardless of whether or not the man understood English, Elliot *had* to tell him.

He had no idea what the hell it was they'd shoved in his mouth, but at least the effects seemed to be wearing off. The numbness had subsided, and he felt the humidity of the evening, plus the wooden boards beneath him poking into his back. Still he couldn't move, but he guessed it wouldn't be too long before he'd regain control of his body.

This was all insane.

Occasionally, his savior would look down at him, flashing a brown-toothed smile. Mostly though, he'd glance over his shoulder to keep the canoe on course to wherever their destination was.

Stilted wooden houses lined the water's edge, their crooked jetties clawing out from the riverbank. The aroma of cooking meat teased Elliot's swollen nostrils, while the occasional local man, woman and child stared through glassless windows. At one point, where the river narrowed, a group of children sat on the riverbank and whispered among themselves. One girl, whose dress seemed too bright for her surroundings, pointed at the canoe as it sent ripples toward her bare feet. Her toes curled, and she giggled, nudging the little boy beside her. He grinned.

Elliot wanted to wave . . . but couldn't. Although his fingers did manage a pathetic twitch.

As he passed, not wanting to lose sight of them, he craned his neck—or indeed, he *tried*. Too much effort. As he returned his gaze upwards, to the first stars now piercing the ever-darkening sky, he felt the children's eyes follow him.

The canoe cut its way through the winding river, taking him deeper into the Mekong Delta. He wondered where their destination would be. The man's home? And how long until they reached it?

The sky darkened further. He had no idea how long he'd been in the canoe, nor did he have any idea how much time had passed since seeing the children. Or how long it had been since the men on scooters, and . . . bloody hell, they'd killed Brandon. And what about the river monster?

Elliot's breath quickened.

Eventually the sky turned to black and unknown constellations stretched overhead, sharp and bright.

On his twelfth birthday, Elliot had unwrapped a telescope after months of pestering his mum and dad for one. He'd already learnt every constellation in the Northern Hemisphere and wanted something to take him higher into the night's sky. With light pollution diluting the skies where he grew up in the UK, here in Vietnam, it was the blackest he'd ever seen. Beautiful. Inspiring, no less. And he saw every star, millions of them, sparkling.

Truly remarkable.

Listening to the rhythmic splash and creak of the oars, and looking up at those unknown constellations, he wondered what had made him lose interest in astronomy. He'd never thought of it before now, but he guessed it was the following teenage years that did it. He wondered whatever happened to his telescope. Perhaps it was still in his parents' attic. Also, come the age of fifteen and sixteen, he'd developed a huge interest in music and soon learnt to play guitar. Then—

"Sex, drugs and rock'n'roll," he said in a nasally voice. Chili-Man had done a fine job of busting his nose.

The Vietnamese man glanced at him.

Something shot past the man's shoulder. A fiery streak.

At first, Elliot thought it was a shooting-star, but another fired past him. This time from the other direction.

Fire. Yes, that was it.

Another, and another.

Fireflies.

So many.

Those fireflies reflected the constellations, and in seconds, more filled the sky as though they intended to stitch a canopy between him and the blackness. Thoughts of a canopy led to thoughts of the sampan and Duc. The river monster. Brandon. The hunting knife. Death. And Jane.

Always, thoughts of Jane were never far off . . .

As he watched the fireflies weave intricate patterns overhead, Elliot noticed the rhythmic splash of oars had ceased.

Something filled his mouth. Fingers. A bitterness caked his tongue.

Tingling . . .

At some point, Elliot must've lost consciousness. Or at least he'd kept floating in and out of lucidity. When he opened his eyes to squint into a sunrise, he couldn't quite make out where he was. With arms and legs awkwardly bound, pinching his skin, his muscles numb but no longer in that drugged way, it felt as though he was tied to a tree. Although, the surface was smooth: concrete, a pillar of some kind.

His head banged with the mother of all hangovers. Even worse than the one the day after Jane's funeral. Indeed, he thought *that* had been up there with one of his greats.

From somewhere close by, flies buzzed. His nose was clogged, and it felt ten times larger than it should be, yet still, the smell of damp concrete invaded his heavy head. A foul taste filled his mouth.

He was in a building, in a single room featuring several rows of pillars that reached up to a broken roof. Sunlight pushed through the overhead gaps and through the barred windows to his left and right, enough to spotlight dozens of rotted cacao husks across cracked tiles. In places, the tiles had given way to sprouting weeds and heaps of dirt. The main exit, not too far ahead of him, was nothing more than a rectangular hole in the wall which probably once framed double doors. Crumbled steps led down onto grass that stretched a short way into tall palm fronds and reeds, and then the river. Brown, still, all-too familiar.

He could not recollect how he'd got there. He remembered that bitter taste and a sickness filling his head. He remembered being wheeled into the jungle—on a cart, yes, pushed by the man he'd mistakenly thought of as his savior. He remembered seeing more Vietnamese locals, mostly adults this time, solemnly watching him. He remembered how the ride was jerky, a constant nausea repeatedly stealing him into a private darkness.

His ears were ringing, a fuzziness still pressing into his mind, thoughts colliding. It threatened to again snatch him into blackness. His chin kept bouncing back onto his chest. It was such an effort to lift his head, so he kept his eyes down, staring at the filthy tiles. What looked like rubber tubing was bound tight around his bare ankles. Close to his muddy toes, absurdly, was a grubby playing card: the three of diamonds. There was no sign of the rest of the deck.

He'd been stripped down to his underwear, and he shivered despite the humidity. Feeling incredibly vulnerable, he almost screamed, yet managed to catch it before it tumbled from dry lips. What if the monster was nearby? He didn't want to attract any attention, not wanting the monster to know where he was. He knew, however, that the monster would probably be able to smell him.

And speaking of smells . . . what the hell was that *other* stink clawing down his throat? It was putrid. He lifted his head, albeit slightly, and squinted into the shadows. Huddled in the corner, flies buzzing around them, he saw several heaped bodies. Mostly naked, each with similar wounds as he'd seen on Duc's body and Brandon's leg. He shifted to the left and right, and saw, then heard, the others in the building with him.

A sound outside, from behind, made him twist awkwardly, trying to look over his shoulder.

With his eyes now adjusting to the building's gloom, he saw he was far from alone. It appeared he was one of eight men and women, all stripped down to their underwear, all bound to a pillar. Listening to the surrounding whimpers, he was surprised he'd not noticed his company sooner. His ears were still ringing, though, so maybe that was why.

Bound to the opposite pillar, a dark-haired woman, perhaps in her fifties and wearing mismatched underwear, hung with her head down. A long stream of spit dangled from her quivering lips.

Elliot awkwardly changed position, so he could see the others, the rubber tubing pinching his wrists and ankles.

There was an unconscious man whose black skin hid beneath so much mud. He'd puked down his chest and it had spattered the broken tiles at his feet. Another man, Asian and wearing boxer shorts covered in smiley faces, was murmuring to himself, his eyes glazed. There were two women, neither any older than twenty, dressed in bikinis. Daylight streamed through an adjacent window to highlight lank hair clumped over sunburned and blistered shoulders. One was unconscious, her chin on her chest, while the other murmured, her eyes rolling behind flickering eyelids. A mumbling older man with hair thick with dry mud, glanced at him and shouted something in German (Elliot understood some of the language, but not whatever it was that came from his blood-flecked lips). Although bound to the nearest pillar, he couldn't hear what the German then began to mumble. The other captives he couldn't quite see, so didn't know whether they were male or female; he only saw their silhouettes in the gloom. However, he knew they, too, were all in a similar state of either confusion or drugged oblivion.

More shuffling from behind.

Someone else, a young guy wearing blue swimming shorts, was being dragged into the building by two men. His eyelids flickered, his lips trembled. Elliot was not surprised to recognize his captors: Chili-Man and Red Cap.

"What do you want from us?" someone screamed, the words echoing in the confines of the building. Such was the voice that shrieked, it was difficult to tell whether it was male or female.

From a ragged throat, Elliot shouted, "What is this?" and coughed.

No one answered.

A woman yelled: "Let us go!"

Again, there was no answer.

The German continued mumbling without even lifting his head.

As the two men went about tying their final captive to a pillar, another man entered the building. Vietnamese like the others, although much older, he was bare from the waist up, his skin wrinkled and saggy. He held a curved horn in both grubby hands. Hollow, etched with curious sigils and symbols, it balanced on his palms as though precious.

"No, don't," Elliot murmured. He remembered the last time he'd heard the horn being blown and it made the creature return to the river. So he could only assume this time it would summon the thing. "This is madness!"

Chili-Man and Red Cap stepped back from the newly-bound captive whose head now lolled. A long stream of spit dribbled from his chin. They walked away, footsteps echoing, and passed the older man. They nodded to him. He didn't acknowledge them as they left, and simply continued into the centre of the building.

"Don't do this!" Elliot shouted.

"Please, let me go," someone whimpered in what sounded like a French accent.

"Let us all go!" shouted someone else.

The German still mumbled.

Now holding the horn in one hand, the old man raised it to his lips, inhaled, and blew. Given the confines of the room, the note it played resonated, filling Elliot's head.

The old man blew again, long and loud.

And another, and then another.

"Stop that!" Elliot yelled.

Someone else: "Please!"

The dark-haired woman shrieked: "Noooo!"

Something splashed in the river.

Everyone hushed, apart from the mumbling German.

Elliot's heartbeat filled his head. Death was finally coming. Coming for them all.

He squinted through the exit and out toward the river. There was more splashing, and branches cracked. Palm fronds swayed. There . . . there was the mouthless snout of the creature. The ivory stump on its forehead glistened, trickling water.

Those who saw the creature screamed.

The creature lumbered up the bank, its reptilian bulk sliding through mud, and those vile appendages parting and breaking fronds. Emerging fully into the daylight, the creature paused and hung its head, nostrils flaring as though seeking something.

Us, thought Elliot, *it's following our scent, our fear.*

141

In an almost-casual way, it dragged its fat body toward the building, head low to the ground, those appendages thrashing the tall grass.

More screams echoed.

As the first paw reached the cracked paving slabs, the appendages calmed, yet still the mouths chattered. It heaved itself up the steps. Claws scraped and clicked the broken masonry. Its snout twitched, its head swayed. Even slower now, it slithered into the shadows and headed for the bodies in the corner.

The screams lessened, becoming sobs and curses and whispers of denial.

Flies scattered as the abomination slumped against the pile of dead, to nestle into the embrace of bloated limbs and rotted flesh. Curses quieted to whimpers, and Elliot swallowed his fear the best he could. Perhaps the monster wasn't going to feast on them after all. The appendages jerked, mouths closing one by one. Each coiled in on itself, some wrapping around another, tightening against the thing's scaly flank. It reminded him of Medusa's hair.

Without any sign of the horn-blower, a strange silence fell upon the captives, interrupted only by rhythmic panicked breathing and the occasional sob.

The thing didn't move, seeming content with its bed of dead bodies. Its black eyes closed, and eventually flies began to settle on its flank and unmoving appendages. The only movement now was its gently flaring nostrils. Softly breathing, its bloated stomach extended and contracted, extended and contracted. And—

The mud-streaked stomach split in a mess of blood and oozing filth, steam rising, curling into the shadows.

And three eggs, each as large as a man's head, spat out.

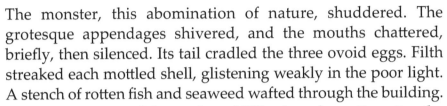

The monster, this abomination of nature, shuddered. The grotesque appendages shivered, and the mouths chattered, briefly, then silenced. Its tail cradled the three ovoid eggs. Filth streaked each mottled shell, glistening weakly in the poor light. A stench of rotten fish and seaweed wafted through the building.

Someone gagged, heaved, and Elliot heard vomit spatter the floor.

A convulsion wracked the creature's body and a front claw stretched to clutch the tiles, and then the other. Still its eyes were closed, and with steaming offal flopping out of its split gut, the creature began to drag itself away from the eggs. The tail uncoiled from around them and slid through the muck. The appendages were still intertwined close to the creature's spine and several of the mouths opened and closed. It was as though they gasped.

Screams and yells erupted. Elliot, too, added to the cacophony, his throat raw as he and his fellow captives, those lucid enough, watched the creature maneuver away from the eggs. Blood and filth smeared the tiles in its wake, claws scraping.

Elliot struggled in his bonds, bile rising in his throat. Reaching the centre of the building, the creature slowed and eventually slumped as though its legs gave out. He saw the stump at the centre of its head and knew the horn that was once there had become the tool with which to summon it.

He eyed the eggs. Why had they captured him and the others? Were they to be food for the eggs once they hatched?

A man shouted, "Let us go!"

The creature appeared to be dying, its nostrils flaring, its head twitching. As it inhaled and exhaled its final breaths, the appendages unraveled, mouths gulping air.

143

One detached with a squelch. Sentient. It slopped on the floor.

Another, and another. They left only raw holes along the creature's back, oozing pus and watery blood. In seconds, the nine appendages snaked lethargically away from the creature's now-still form. One by one, they slithered away, each in separate directions. Blind, weaving through the detritus across the floor . . .

The captives quieted, a collective intake of breath to share a blanket of silence.

Each snake-thing wriggled, seeking, teeth chattering . . .

One reached the German first. He no longer muttered. It teased his feet, and if anything, he looked more curious than fearful.

Another flopped, writhing in dirt and slime, approaching someone else further in the shadows. Elliot couldn't see who it was.

Further away in the corner, highlighted by streaming sunlight through a hole in the roof, Elliot saw one squirm toward a woman. As if with a sudden surge of life, it coiled up her leg. She shrieked. Trailing muck, the thing reached her face, teeth chattering a million miles per hour. In less than a second there was nothing left of her skin other than a ragged mess. Her scream was silenced when it shot down her throat, tail vanishing. She gagged, choked, convulsed.

So far none had approached Elliot, nor the unconscious dark-haired woman opposite, but he knew it was only a matter of time. He looked about him, searching for nearby movement.

He saw nothing. Yet.

The German didn't move as he simply allowed the snake-thing to reach his chest, its teeth grinding. His own mouth wide, he jabbed his head forward and bit down on it. He shook it from side to side, blood and muck misting the air. It thrashed in his jaws, snapping its teeth, trying to gain purchase on his chest or shoulder or neck or . . . It clamped onto his nipple and tore away a flap of skin and chunk of muscle. He yelled, releasing the thing from his mouth. It darted for the wound, ribs snapped. Blood sprayed as it punctured his heart. He contorted, and his head dropped. The snake-thing burrowed into his chest, but slowly, its tail whipping spasmodically. Then it flopped and hung from the gaping wound, evidently dead.

Another poised in front of a young woman, coiling down into itself, ready to pounce. She screamed at it, bucking and twisting. It sprung upwards and dived into her mouth. She choked, writhing. Then she was still.

Yet another did the same, this time to the Asian man. Gurgling, choking, and thrashing.

Close by, something slurped. Elliot jerked around, looking for—

A snake-thing leapt up on him, slimy, warm, wrapping its tail around his shoulder and armpit . . . then his face. It smothered him, and corkscrewed around his neck, strangling. Dots peppered his vision. Desperate to keep his mouth closed, he struggled beneath its slippery length. His nostrils hissed through busted cartilage and bone.

No choice, he gasped . . .

The thing jammed into his mouth.

His throat stretched as it forced its way downwards. Utter agony.

Darkness closed in . . . and with it, unconsciousness.

In a myriad of colors, greens and browns, and the color of Death, Elliot's vision shifted into bright light. His heart beat a monstrous rhythm in a tight chest. His sore throat felt like he'd swallowed a melon, and his stomach was bloated, aching as though he had indeed consumed one. He wanted to spew.

Then he remembered: he'd swallowed one of those fucking snake-things.

His breath started to come in sharp, short, painful bursts.

Moonlight pressed in through the barred windows and broken roof. From what he could tell, the other captives, those who remained, were slumped, unmoving. Dark filth puddled at their feet. Someone remained bound to a pillar, the man's stomach and chest ravaged like a sack of meat, sliced and gaping. A snake-thing lay folded in the bloody mess near his feet, dead. Another was on the floor a little farther away. Several were coiled, motionless in the shadows. And the eggs . . . they were still in the corner against the dead bodies.

Some of the other victims had evidently been removed from the building and it appeared there were only three people left alive, himself included. Still bound to the pillar opposite, the dark-haired woman squirmed. The whites of her eyes shone beneath fluttering eyelids.

A fiery pain exploded in Elliot's gut and snatched him back into the dark. Head spinning, the blackness welcoming. A brightness, a darkness, together it churned.

Within that peculiar half-light, half-dark, someone approached . . .

Footsteps echoed. Perhaps there were even voices.

Elliot's mind whirled, a sickness washing over him, smothered in stink. He looked around, scanned the slumped bodies in the shadows. The woman gazed at him, her jaw slack, her eyes reflecting little more than pain and confusion. Her lips parted as though about to say something, but instead belched. The stink blended with the taste in his own mouth. His stomach rumbled. His fingers tingled. A heat filled him, moved within, and a rush of nausea buzzed like insects.

Again, darkness took him back down, down, down . . .

As the buzzing sound seemed to intensify, the churning darkness melded with the light.

Someone pinched his chin, calloused fingers rasping on stubble.

"Huh?" he shook his jaw away from the fingers.

Through the darkness and flashes of sunlight, a wrinkled Vietnamese face squinted through the shadows which again threatened to take Elliot down. It was the old man from earlier, however long ago it had been when this bastard summoned the monster: the horn-blower. It was as though the man was inspecting him.

Most of the other pillars were now empty. Rope and rubber tubing coiled in puddles of clumped meat and blood and motionless snake-things. The dark-haired woman was still there. Blood and spit dribbled from her lips.

She screamed, and the sound snatched him upright.

His stomach twisted. Agony. Interchangeable, dark and light, shadows and sunshine . . . and maybe this time there was some motion.

He felt his arms and legs released, and his body slumped. His knees cracked on the floor, palms slapping the cool tiles. Two more men approached: Chili-Man and Red Cap. They lifted him, each man hooking one of Elliot's arms around their neck.

Malnourished, his head heavy after being drugged, he pathetically wrestled with them. But they effortlessly dragged him out into the daylight where the sun burned. It was as though his fists were made of rubber.

In moments they reached the riverbank.

Were they now going to let him die here?

Blinking into the sunshine, the water teased his feet as the two men left him alone. Movement from beside him, and he noticed the woman was also slumped on the riverbank, their unbound legs tangled in reeds, their bodies sprawled in mud. The sun burned his bare skin, made him itch. The sound of the men retreated back into the jungle, back toward the building.

He tried to call to them, but he only succeeded in dribbling.

The woman shivered, clutching her distended stomach.

He, too, rubbed his stomach. It looked like he was pregnant. Looking at the woman who faced away from him, for a moment he thought she was his wife . . . but images of the monster, the building, the eggs, the snake-things, consumed him. She was not his wife, she was not Jane.

Had they been freed?

Yet . . . yet inside him there was no freedom. Inside, that *thing* was there.

He moved, slid through mud, his fingers caressing something slick, curved.

An egg.

The woman shifted to face him. She belched. The stink was foul. She already held one of the eggs, but the shell was lighter than his. Just the two of them there, huddled in the reeds at the water's edge, both like expectant parents. Why was the shell of her egg lighter than the one he held? Something was wrong. Inside: no life. The egg, dead. For a moment, he remembered . . . something . . . someone . . . Jane. His Jane . . . They'd conceived. They were once close to being parents.

He pressed his face to the eggshell. It cracked as he pushed his hairy chin into the goo that oozed through segments of shell and tearing membrane. He didn't much care for the taste; he didn't much care for anything now.

Once, though, he *did* care.

Mouth open, he buried his face in the muck and slurped the gloopy contents. As he did so, he thought of Jane and the child they never had, the life they never had, and the life Jane lost. The life, the *lives*, he lost.

The woman reached out for him, her fingers raking the

blistered, crusty skin of his arm. Her mouth opened, and she murmured something, then coughed. Her body shook, then was stolen by convulsions. The egg rolled beneath her. She arched her back and turned over and crushed the egg with her bulbous stomach. Spasms wracked her body, and calmed, and then she was still.

He stared into the woman's dead eyes.

Time seemed to stretch, the sun arcing overhead, changing from hot to warm. Eventually the sun vanished. While the first stars pricked the darkening sky, he realized he clutched an egg. It nestled between his thighs. He could not remember how this last egg, this healthy egg, had got there.

His egg.

He closed his eyes, accepting the darkness.

Only this time it was a content sleep.

Waves gently lapped him. He felt different. His breathing moved like liquid, as though valves opened and closed somewhere in his throat, his nose. He slid into the mud and lowered himself into the welcoming depths of the Mekong Delta, watching his hands cup the brown water. A glance behind, and he saw the egg almost glow under the burning red of sunrise.

The woman's body, grey and sun-scorched, now hid beneath a haze of buzzing flies.

He felt a sheen of translucent skin shift over his eyeballs as he submerged. Beneath the water, he could see perfectly. He swam and marveled at the tiny bubbles tracing the scales that covered his arms.

Beneath the water, he glided. Agile. Powerful.

Along his back and shoulders there was a mild discomfort,

and he felt movement there. It was the extra appendages that were even now splitting the skin down his spine.

He would not swim out too far, nor for too long.

He couldn't.

He could not leave the nest.

Soon, he headed effortlessly back toward the egg cradled in the twists of broken fronds. His head broke the surface, water tumbling down his long face. The sun was now higher, burning orange through the reeds where the egg was barely visible. As he waded closer, he saw a crack appear in the ovoid shell.

He slid through the mud, keeping the egg in sight.

The shell cracked further, fragments peeling. A scaly muzzle tore through the thin membrane as though sniffing the air. A frail claw reached out.

The thing that was once Elliot embraced its child.

GERTRUDE

Evans Light

CREATURES OF THE NIGHT

"TELL ME ABOUT YOURSELF," I said.

Despite his condition, the man spoke with cheerful frankness, his napkin still tucked into his shirt collar like a bib. He clutched a fork tightly in his left hand, his knuckles bone white, as though he was unable to let go of it.

"I have a symbiotic twin named Gertrude," he said, matter-of-factly. "She lives in a cavity under my ribcage, next to my spleen."

He leaned forward and continued in a whisper.

"If I lie very still in bed at night, I can hear her. I think she might be crying."

He glanced around the room nervously, as though if to check for eavesdroppers.

It was hard to tell from his manner of speaking that he was injured. It would have been a natural assumption from the scene around him that the red splatter down his front was nothing more than spilled marinara.

But the half-eaten plate of food on the table in front of him held only chicken, rice and broccoli—not even a drop of red tomato sauce.

I stepped back to give the paramedic room to work. She lifted the bottom of the man's shirt, exposing the area where his stomach should have been. The abdomen was now a tattered tangle of messy flesh, looking every bit like an exploded pot pie, all the way down to the peas and carrots.

The medic gagged as she attempted to clean the area around the gaping wound, her mind undoubtedly reeling from the impossibility of the task at hand.

I covered my face with my hand to try and shield myself from the putrid smell.

"Why did you do it?" I asked the dying man.

He carefully moved the IV tube that was taped to his forearm out of the way and leaned back a bit in his chair. He took a deep breath, a faraway look of hopelessness rising in his eyes.

Shock was setting in. I knew I didn't have much time.

"*Why did you do it?*" I asked him again, more harshly this time. My voice jarred him back into reality.

"I didn't do it. She did," he said.

"Who?"

"Gertrude."

"*This* Gertrude?" I asked sarcastically, pointing to the woman opposite him, whose body was sprawled across the table. "Are you telling me she did this to herself?"

The dead woman's face was mangled and swollen and her throat torn open, as though she'd been attacked by animals with savage claws. A mass of distended blue veins bulged from the wound in her neck, like wiring from a vandalized circuit box.

He shook his head from left to right.

"That's not Gertrude," he said weakly.

"Then who is she?"

"She's my girlfriend—no, my fiancé. I asked her to marry me tonight. I even made her dinner," he said, the life in his voice melting away like an icicle in July.

"Then who the hell is Gertrude?" I demanded.

"I told you," he wheezed. "I have a symbiotic twin named Gertrude. She lives in a cavity under my ribcage, next to my spleen."

His sentence finished with a cough and a gurgle. Dark blood welled up in his mouth, spilling over his bottom lip, and dripping down his chin. Then his eyes fixed on some faraway spot over my left shoulder.

"If I lie very still in bed at night, I can hear her. I think she might be crying," he continued softly.

I watched as the last spark of life burned out in the back of his eyes.

Then, just like that, he was gone.

I motioned for the paramedic to stop fiddling with his bandages. All that was needed now was a body bag and a gurney.

Two of them, I guess.

I waited while my team marked the crime scene and taped off the front of the property so no one else would enter. With the bodies off to the morgue, we could come back tomorrow, give the scene a good combing over. No use in wasting a perfectly fine evening piddling around in a slaughterhouse, especially when the wife had a hot meal waiting for me at home.

I hoped it wasn't pot pie.

I was the last one out of the place, always am—as chief detective, it's procedure.

I flipped off the light in the hallway and headed for the front door when I stopped dead in my tracks.

There was an unusual noise, I was sure of it. I walked back to the empty hallway and listened.

There it was again.

Someone was crying.

I drew my weapon and crept down the hall towards the sound, stopping in front of the laundry room door. Whoever it was, they were in there.

Gun at the ready, I pushed the door open with my foot. Blood was smeared along the bottom half of the dryer.

I flipped on my flashlight, opened the dryer door and shined the light inside.

That's when she screamed.

I jumped back, startled, slamming into the wall on the opposite side, knocking the wind clean out of my lungs. I held the light as steady as I could, illuminating the wailing female abomination who sat inside the dryer, its naked body covered in green slime and dried blood.

It–*she*–cradled an even smaller creature that jutted out from between her ribs, a deformed beast suckling like an infant on her fleshless, oozing breast.

"He was mine!" Gertrude shrieked, her eyes hot embers in the flashlight's beam. "He was my man. She had no right to take him from me! He already had a wife, already had a child!"

She pulled the horrid thing forcibly away from her breast, and held it up in her twisted, three-fingered hand for me to see, thick pus dribbling both from her nipple and the thing's tiny mouth. It was the size of a newborn rat, but not even half as pretty.

The monster she called a child began to scream, and so did she.

And so did I.

A Survivor

Ray Garton

CREATURES OF THE NIGHT

THE FALL OF 1957 was colder and darker than usual, the coldest and darkest Betty Forrester had ever known. It only got colder and darker, until she found herself driving the pickup truck away from the farm through a black and snowy December night, crying.

It had begun in mid-October with a bite. Ed had stumbled through the back door, limping because something had bitten his right leg on the outer calf just below his knee. As she tended to his leg, Betty asked what had bitten him, and Ed said he did not know. It was small, he said, about the size of a fox, but it was not a fox.

"If you don't know what it was, then how do you know what it wasn't?" she said.

"It wasn't a fox because . . . well, I'm not positive, but I'm pretty sure it had more than four legs."

"Nothing has more than four legs," their son Robby said as he watched Betty clean the wound. "No mammals, anyway."

"This animal did," Ed said. "It had a lot of legs and became a blur when it moved. Whatever it was, it was in a big hurry and I was in its way. I think I stepped on it and it swung around and bit me. Soon as I lifted my foot, it kept going. Fast."

Betty sniffed the air for any whiff of liquor. He hadn't been drinking, so she suspected he'd let his imagination run wild in the dark.

Judging by the pensive look on Robby's face, the boy was convinced, and quite disturbed by the idea of something running loose out there with more than four legs. The boy had a fierce imagination and was quite sensitive. He preferred reading books to working on the farm, something Betty had found worrisome.

159

But Ed took it in stride. "That means he's smart," he said, "and has a better chance of making something of himself than I ever did."

"If we don't know what bit you," Betty said, "then we don't know what that bite may be doing to you."

"Don't worry, sweetheart," Ed said, smiling through his pain, "I'll go see Dr. Cartwright first thing tomorrow and have him look at it. For now, just clean it up with some alcohol and put a bandage over it, and everything'll be fine, just fine."

He was still a consistently kind and gentle man then, even-keeled and optimistic about everything.

Nothing had been "just fine" since then.

Robby noticed differences in Dad right away. He was grumpy about the shots, about the bite itself, about not being able to work (doctor's orders)—he was grumpy about everything, all the time. That was not Dad. He had always taken everything with a smile, had a positive outlook, and laughed a lot. Robby had never seen him grumpy before.

When he expressed his concern to Mom about Dad's anger, she said, "Don't be silly, honey, your father isn't angry. He's just not feeling good. Those shots are painful, his leg is sore, he can't work. He's just cranky, that's all."

It made sense to Robby. He had seen the bite on Dad's leg— a swollen mound of reddish-purple flesh with two bloody gouges about an inch and a half apart—and it had looked painful.

That fall felt more like winter. The temperature dropped faster and further than usual and the air had a snowy feeling to it well before they usually received any snowfall.

Sunday nights were the most relaxed of the week, because at

seven o'clock, *The Jack Benny Program* was on. Nobody, nothing, could make Dad laugh like Jack Benny, and the show always put him in an even better mood than usual for the rest of the night. With Dad smoking Chesterfields in his rickety old recliner and Robby on the couch, the two of them would laugh together for thirty minutes every Sunday. Dad loved to laugh.

Instead of their normal conversation, they ate in silence, as they had every night for the past week, which Robby found disturbing. It made him dread suppertime. Normally talkative, Dad said nothing throughout the meal. After supper, while Mom cleaned up in the kitchen, Robby went with Dad to the living room and they took their seats in front of the TV.

Robby had been laughing with Dad at Jack Benny for so long that now all he had to do was see the man walk on stage and he chuckled. As he watched the show, though, a smile on his face, laughing along with the studio audience, a troubling feeling grew in his chest, and at first, he was not sure why. An increasing sense of danger made his throat feel tight, and still he did not know why. As the feeling of menace grew, Robby's laughter weakened, until he stopped laughing altogether. He'd been so busy laughing at the program that he hadn't notice Dad wasn't laughing. He turned to his right, toward the recliner, and his breathing stopped.

The chair was reclined all the way and Dad was slouched low, slowly exhaling smoke from his lungs as his narrowed eyes stared directly at Robby through the milky tendrils that curled around his face. In the shifting glow of the TV set, Dad's face looked unnaturally dark.

For a moment, Robby was frozen with fear. With a small sound of fright in his throat, he bounded from the couch and ran between Dad and the TV toward the hallway. Dad unexpectedly stretched out a leg in front of him and Robby tripped, pitching forward and landing hard on the floor. As he heard the familiar sound of the recliner straightening up so Dad could stand, Robby moved fast over the floor on hands and knees, then scrambled to his feet, and lunged into the kitchen babbling: "Mom, Mom, something's wrong with Dad, he's after me!"

Startled, she spun away from the sink. "What? What's wrong?"

Robby turned and looked at the doorway through which he had just come, expecting to see Dad following him. But he was not there. From the living room, he heard the studio audience laughing on TV. To Mom, he said, "He wasn't laughing, just staring at me, and when I ran he tripped me on purpose, and—"

"You're not making sense, Robby," Mom said, drying her hands on a dishtowel. "Go to your room."

"But I'm telling you, he was looking at me like he was gonna—"

"Just go to your room and I'll talk to him." She headed out of the kitchen.

Robby did not want to be around when she started talking to him. As he left the kitchen, he heard her voice speaking quietly to Dad in the living room. In the hallway, he heard Dad shout something. As he reached the stairs, a loud, thick *smack!* came from the living room, and Mom cried out just before she fell to the floor. At least, it sounded like she had fallen to the floor.

Robby froze and listened, then turned back as Mom hurried back into the kitchen, giving him a glimpse of her bloody, swollen lower lip. He followed her in, stood and watched as she went to the sink and cleaned her wound with a rag.

"D-did he . . . hit you?"

With her back to him, she said, "I told you to go to your room."

"But he hit you, didn't he?"

"I fell. Just go to your room, Robby, I'm not going to say it again."

Her tone was firm and he knew she meant business. He went upstairs to his room and closed the door.

Dad had never hit Mom before, and he was certain that was what had happened. As far as Robby knew, Dad had never hit anyone. That was when he knew, beyond any doubt, that Dad was not merely in a bad mood because of the bite and the shots and not being able to work. He had changed.

For the first time in his life, Robby did not feel safe in his own bedroom. There was no lock on his door, but there was a straight back chair against the wall beside his dresser. He pulled the chair away from the wall and wedged the back underneath the doorknob. He still did not feel safe, but it would have to do.

After that, Robby spent most of his indoor time in his bedroom.

After that Sunday night, Dad was angry all the time. Robby avoided him as much as possible. He feared that Dad would turn on him as he had on Mom. The *smack!* of Dad's fist hitting Mom's face kept going off in Robby's head, as startling as a firecracker.

Whenever Dad went on a shouting rage through the house, bellowing angrily, knocking things over, throwing them, breaking them, Robby rushed upstairs to his room, sat on the edge of his bed, and stared at his open closet for a while, at the vague shapes in its darkness, thinking about nothing, just curling up into a ball inside himself until the shouting stopped. One such incident, on a rainy afternoon, reduced Robby to tears before he could reach his room, and he ran into Mom on the way.

"Why are you crying?" she hiss-whispered as Dad's shouting continued in the back of the house on the ground floor.

He froze in her gaze, unable to move or speak, paralyzed with fear. He could think of no safe way to respond. With effort, he squeezed out the words, "D-Dad's . . . angry. He's scuh-scaring me."

"Scaring you?" She tilted her head to one side as she propped her fists on her hips and looked down at him with an expression of bafflement. "What's the matter with you? It's your *father*, there's nothing to be scared of, he's just a little upset, that's all. He's still not feeling well, you know that. Go to your room if you don't like it, but stop exaggerating things, okay? I've got enough to deal with as it is. Look, I have to drive over to Helena Woodlow's house."

Robby stopped breathing.

"I won't be gone long," she said. "Just stay in your room and out of your father's way, you'll be fine."

"B-but, Mom—"

"It'll have to wait 'til I get back," she said, disappearing down the hall.

"Please don't go," he said, hurrying after her.

Over her shoulder, she said, "Be a *big* boy, Robby."

Once again, he returned to his room as dad continued to shout downstairs and thunder rolled overhead outside. He wedged the straight back chair under the doorknob, sat on the edge of his bed and stared for a while, then went to his bookshelf. He chose *20,000 Leagues Under the Sea*, read his favorite passages for a while, trying to ignore the fact that he needed to go to the bathroom. His bladder had been full for a while and was growing impatient.

Robby listened. All he could hear was the whisper of rainfall outside and an occasional rumble of thunder that was steadily growing more distant. The shouting had stopped. He moved the wedged chair, opened the door, and went down the hall to the bathroom. Once finished with his business there, he returned to his room, closed the door, wedged the chair against it, and took the Jules Verne book back to the shelf. He sat on the edge of the bed for a moment to listen again, staring into the darkness of his open closet.

Still no shouting. But there was a sound . . . something new and quiet enough to make Robby wonder if he was really hearing it. He listened harder as he squinted into the closet and became aware of what he was hearing at about the same moment he became aware of what he was looking at in the closet.

It was someone breathing. And in the murkiness of the closet, Robby could make out two big hands dangling from the peaks of bent knees as someone—*Dad, it's Dad, he came in here while I was in the bathroom and hid in the closet, and Mom's gone, Mom's gone*—sat in the closet and stared out at him. Between the hands on the knees, he could make out an obscure face that came into sharper focus the longer he looked at it.

It looked like his father, but something was wrong with the face, an indefinable distortion, something that made it look almost . . . thorny. Prickly. As if sharp growths of varying lengths were protruding from his face and head.

Their eyes met.

"Robby." The voice was a rasp.

"Duh-Dad?"

"I'm not well. I need help."

"Whuh . . . what can I do?" Dad's words were garbled. "What did you say?"

"Feed me."

"What, um . . . what would you like to eat?"

In an explosion of crashing sound and movement, the figure lunged from the closet's darkness and into the light where Robby could see that horrible, dark gray face, as gray hands with clawed fingers reached out, and the creature growled, "*You.*"

Robby screamed as he launched from the bed, tore the chair away from the door and threw it aside, opened the door, and ran down the hall to his parents' bedroom.

That door had a lock.

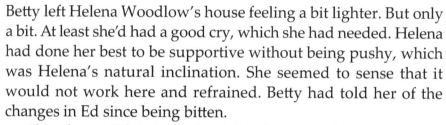

Betty left Helena Woodlow's house feeling a bit lighter. But only a bit. At least she'd had a good cry, which she had needed. Helena had done her best to be supportive without being pushy, which was Helena's natural inclination. She seemed to sense that it would not work here and refrained. Betty had told her of the changes in Ed since being bitten.

"You know Ed," she had said. "He's a gentle man. But not lately. Sometimes he's fine, like his old self. But then he'll change suddenly and become angry. Over nothing, nothing at all, just *angry*. And sometimes—I know this is going to sound crazy, but sometimes he seems . . . to change. His skin darkens, or seems to, anyway. And his face breaks out in tiny little welts. He's been keeping to himself mostly. I prefer that, to be honest. He's starting to scare Robby. I've tried to downplay everything. I'm hoping to get through this without upsetting Robby too much by simply making him think there's nothing wrong. But it's hard to do that when Ed hits me."

Helena had offered only one suggestion: "Get him back to the doctor. Right away. He needs to be looked at again."

But Betty had already suggested that to Ed and he had declined emphatically.

The visit with Helena had helped no more than she had expected, but it had been enough to steel her to go back home and make supper.

Betty knew her marriage of nearly 13 years was rapidly becoming an ugly trap with the changes in Ed. It had been two weeks since he was bitten by whatever had bitten him—she knew of no mammal that had more than four legs, and it was too big to have been any insect she knew of—but instead of getting better, Ed was getting worse. It seemed there should be *some* improvement by now, but instead, she was waking to greater dread each morning at the prospect of having to face him again. If he did not get better, if he continued to get worse and his condition was permanent—merely thinking about the possibility made Betty's throat constrict.

She simply could not be in that kind of relationship. Her childhood had been filled with chaos, anger, and violence, all centering around her alcoholic father. She and her two sisters and two brothers had taken comfort in each other during those times; without them, Betty doubted she would have come through it as well. They all had hopes of getting out of that house as soon as humanly possible. Her oldest sister had simply disappeared in the dark of night, having taken a few belongings and some clothes. They had awakened to find her gone and never saw or heard from her again. She had been only fourteen years old.

They were survivors, Betty and her sisters and brothers. That was how she thought of herself above all else—even before wife and mother, she thought of herself as a survivor.

Their mother had never taken their side or stood up for them against their father's anger and violence. They had been on their own. He had abused their mother, too, but she had not even stood up for herself. For reasons Betty never understood, Mother had chosen instead to desperately protect her marriage to a man who drunkenly beat her and repeatedly cheated on her. Sometimes after he beat one of the children, she would shout, "You're lucky you din't get worse!" It made no sense to Betty. They had come out of her body, they were *part* of her, and yet she sat back and allowed them to be terrorized and beaten by their father, almost as if she did not know them and cared nothing for them.

Betty was determined never to be anything at all like her mother. She was a survivor and *she* would shape who she became, not her parents.

She pounced on the first opportunity that arose to get out of that house: Ed. They had met at a barn dance held at Ed's father's farm, which Ed was running by then. Their courtship had been swift. Betty had pounced because she was also in love with her opportunity. He was a sweet and generous man who adored children and animals—nothing at all like either of Betty's parents. She could not believe her luck in finding such a man and she felt deeply grateful for her situation every day. She felt she had narrowly escaped a much less happy life.

They lived there on Ed's father's farm, which soon became their farm with the man's death less than a year after they were married. Robby was born in the second year of their marriage, and their family was complete. Betty had every intention of keeping it that way.

But now she wondered. The possibility of spending the rest of her life with Ed in his current state or worse made her want to tear at her collar for air. She would do anything to escape the kind of violence that had made up her childhood.

As she drove down the long gravel driveway to the house, Betty knew that if his condition did not begin to show signs of improvement, she would have to do something drastic, and that frightened her. She understood in that moment that she could not—*would not*—stay with the man who currently occupied their house, because he was not the man she had married. She was afraid of him, and her fear was steadily growing. She would take Robby and leave if necessary. She decided to pack a bag and have it ready, just in case the need arose to leave quickly.

Parking the pickup in front of the house, she killed the engine, got out, and went up the front walk to the door. Inside, as she headed for the kitchen to get to work on supper, she heard the muttering of a raspy voice. She brought herself to an abrupt halt and stood listening. When the voice spoke again, she could not understand what it said. It seemed to be coming from her left.

Turning, Betty crossed the entrance hall and passed into the living room. No one was there and neither the television nor the radio was on. She stopped and listened again. When the voice spoke once more, she turned toward the entrance to the hallway on the other side of the living room. It seemed to be coming from there.

"Robby?" Betty said, taking a step toward the hallway. There were no lights on in the hall, it was dark beyond the entrance, and she could see nothing, no one. "Ed?"

The voice spoke again, louder this time, and angry: "Goddammit, just listen to me!" Although he said more in a tone of great urgency, she could not understand him beyond those initial five words. She knew immediately that it was Ed by the peculiar way he said "Goddammit": he made it sound like it had an extra syllable. The damaged voice did not sound like Ed's, but Betty knew it was her husband.

"I can't understand you, Ed," she said. "Come out here."

She stared at the rectangle of darkness that opened on the hallway, surprised by how dark it was in there. It was a cold, cloudy, intensely gray day, and it had cast a gloom through the whole house, but she had never noticed before that the hallway ever became that dark on cloudy days. She wondered if her worry and fear were making her imagination hyperactive.

After staring at the doorway for a period of brittle, tense silence, she saw movement in that impenetrable darkness. Even though she had been looking for it, the movement startled her and she took a step back.

A figure took shape as it neared the murky edge of the darkness, but it bore no resemblance to Ed. It was too short, for one thing. Then she started again when she recognized the figure to be Ed stooped over, as if in pain.

"Ed, are . . . are you all right?"

An arm in a blue chambray sleeve extended from the

darkness and Betty gasped when she saw his trembling hand. It was dark, as if it had been burned. It turned palm-up and the forefinger beckoned her to come closer.

Betty feared her throat would close deep down in her gullet, simply seal itself off so she could no longer breathe. She found herself moving forward, but with no idea how, because her fear had killed the feeling in her legs. Suddenly feeling shockingly hot, she realized she still wore her coat. As she neared the dark doorway, the finger continued to beckon. When the hand came into better focus, she saw the small protrusions which covered it, like thorns on a rosebush.

The hand moved with such speed that it clutched the collar of her coat before she knew it had closed the distance between them. It pulled her toward the darkness as Ed's face moved forward out of it. He was, indeed, stooped forward as if he had hurt his back, but that barely registered when Betty saw his face. She opened her mouth to scream, but his other hand shot out of the darkness toward her face, which made her pull away. She imagined those sharp thorns tearing into her cheeks and lips. But when he pulled her forward and pressed his hand over her mouth, his palm was smooth.

"Listen to me," he said.

If she opened her eyes any wider, she was certain they would pop out. Ed's face was a nightmarish distortion of what it used to be. A dark, smoky gray, like his hands, it also was covered with curved, black thorns that grew out of his flesh like impossibly thick, sharp whiskers. The ridge of his brow was twice its normal size and jutted out so far that his eyes were lost in black half-circles beneath it. His voice sounded like he had been drinking ammonia.

"You need to . . . find someone for me," he said.

Betty's eyes blinked rapidly as she thought, with a heavy sadness, *He's gone insane.* But once she began to understand what he was saying, that sadness turned to more fear.

"Who?"

"Anyone. Doesn't matter who. But don't bring anybody who'll be missed. Go over to the train depot next to McCawley's orchard."

"You mean . . . the abandoned one?"

"Yes. There are always a few drunks hanging around there for shelter, especially in cold weather. Take one of the pistols. You know how to use it. If he acts up, tries anything, use it. But at least try to get him in the pickup truck first. Make sure—this is important—make sure no one sees you."

"Ed, I don't—what're you—you're not making any sense."

"I'm making *perfect* sense if you'll shut up and *listen*. I'm having a real hard time remaining calm here, Betty. Don't push me, because I don't want to hurt you, but I've only got so much control when I'm like this."

"Like . . . this? What *is* this?"

"Just listen. You bring one of those drunks back here—more, if they want to come. You could bring up to . . . three. Tell 'em you'll put them up for the night and feed them if they don't mind sleeping in the barn. Bring them to the barn, get them inside. Then you go in the house and put Robby and yourself to bed. Understand?"

"U-under—no, I *don't* understand. What are you asking me to do, Ed?"

The face moved closer. "Try not to think about it. Just do it. Because . . . because—" His voice broke and he lowered his head for a moment. When he lifted it again, she could see in the dark pits beneath the ugly ridge of his brow the sparkle of a tear. "Because if you don't, I'm going to kill and eat you and Robby as sure as we're standing here, Betty. The only reason Robby's still alive is he was smart enough to lock himself in our bedroom. The only reason you're still alive is I'm trying so hard to control myself. But it won't last, Betty, and it'll only get worse the longer

I go without . . . well, until you do this thing for me. Do you hear me? *Do you?*"

She heard him.

The following morning, after a restless night with the chair wedged against his bedroom door, Robby got up, smelled bacon and eggs, and quickly dressed, stomach growling. It was just himself and Mom at meals lately. Dad did not show himself much, and when he did, he was angry, so Robby preferred he stay away.

When he sat down at the breakfast table that morning, he saw three places set. And Mom was dashing around the kitchen with a smile on her face, something he had not seen in a while.

"Is . . . is Dad coming?"

"Of course," she said, as if he ate breakfast with them every day.

"Is he . . . still upset?"

"About what?"

Robby simply stared at her with his mouth hanging open as she brought a platter of bacon to the table. How could she say such a thing. *About what?* What did she think he was talking about? She behaved as if everything were perfectly normal, just as it had always been. Unless . . .

Had he dreamed it all? He had just woke up—had everything been a bad dream? If so, why was the chair still wedged against the knob of his bedroom door that morning?

Of course it had not been a dream. It had been going on since Dad had been bitten. He had imagined none of it. Then why had Mom been behaving as if it none of it had happened, as she was doing now?

"About everything," he said after a long silence. "You know, like he's been doing since he was bitten. All of it started with that bite."

She put a couple of fried eggs and two pieces of buttered wheat toast on his plate. "The bite is much better now and he's feeling good again. He might even be able to get back to work today. We'll see how he feels."

"He hasn't felt good about *anything* for—"

He stopped talking and froze, fork in hand, eyes on the kitchen doorway when he heard Dad in his work boots clumping down the hall. Robby's chest became tight and his throat constricted with growing panic.

Dad walked into the kitchen in his work clothes, kissed Mom on the cheek, and sat down at the table with a big grin. Mom poured his coffee as he said, "Morning, Robby. I think I'm going to try to work today, so you can just do your own chores this morning. I'm gonna see how much my leg will put up with. I want to thank you for all the help while I've been down. It's much appreciated. Looks like a cold rain out there. You ready for it?"

Robby said nothing as he stared, still motionless, fork suspended a couple of inches above his plate, marveling at the change in his father. He was his old self again. But now that Robby had seen how he behaved at his worst, he did not know if he could trust the transformation. After a long silence, he finally nodded his head once. Then Dad began chatting pleasantly with Mom.

Robby ate his breakfast and kept his head down as his parents talked. He was afraid to interact with his father. He feared that doing or saying something, anything at all, might set Dad off, so he quietly ate his breakfast, and when he was done, he lifted his head and said, "May I be excused?"

"Of course, Robby," Dad said. "If you wait 'til I finish my breakfast, I'll go out with you."

Robby nodded vaguely as he left the table.

By supper, Dad was still himself, and again at breakfast the next morning. And the next, and the next. His limp was gone and he looked healthy and vigorous, but most importantly, he seemed *himself* again, as if none of it had ever happened. As if Robby *had* dreamed it all.

But he knew he had not.

A week passed, then another, and life went on as usual, just as it had before the bite.

On Thanksgiving, a few of the farmhands brought their families for turkey supper. They played board games after the meal, sang along with songs on the radio, and it was a warm and delightful day. That was when the tension and anxiety began to leave Robby's body, when he became convinced that the trouble, whatever it had been, had passed. Their company left that evening and Robby found himself feeling comfortable and at home again.

He went to bed later and fell quickly into a dreamless sleep.

Robby sat up in bed before he was fully awake, his father's angry, shouting voice sweeping the remaining sleep from his head and bringing everything into sharp focus.

It was cold and dark. He turned on his bedside lamp and saw that his alarm clock read 1:42 AM. Hugging the covers to himself, he listened.

He heard his mother's voice speaking urgently but trying to be quiet, trying not to wake him. He looked at the lockless, vulnerable door, naked without the chair, which was in its regular place against the wall. Sweeping the covers aside, he jumped from the bed in his pajamas, lunged toward the chair, pulled it away from the wall, and wedged its back firmly beneath the doorknob.

Mom's footsteps rushed around the house: down the hall, then up the hall again, in the master bedroom, then both of them came down the hall—Mom crying as she talked fast in a hushed voice, Dad making strange, thick grunting sounds and shouting unintelligibly—and went downstairs to the kitchen. He heard the back door open. A moment later, it closed. Footsteps thumped across the wooden deck of the covered back porch, then were hushed by the lawn, and the house fell silent.

Robby puzzled over what Mom and Dad were doing. They had no plans to leave or they would have gone out the side door in the laundry room and into the garage, where the car was parked, or out the front door to the pickup truck parked in front of the house. Instead, they went out to the back yard in the middle of the night. Beyond that, enclosed in wire and some wooden fencing would be the chicken coop on the right—why would they go to the chicken coop in the middle of the night?— and to the left Mom's vegetable garden, already harvested, and the path between the two that led to the barn.

Why would they go to the barn?

Robby quickly put on his pants, shoes, and a jacket over his long-sleeve pajama top, and left his room, careful to make no noise. He was on his way down the hall to go out the back door and see what he could see, when he heard it open. He jerked to a halt and listened.

Mom's footsteps hurried through the kitchen.

He turned and rushed back to his room as fast as he could without making noise, but just as he ducked through the door, the floor popped loudly beneath his foot the way the old wooden floor often did. He silently closed the door, wedged the chair in place, and waited.

Mom came down the hall and stopped outside his door. She

remained there but did nothing for a moment—*probably listening to see if I'm awake*, Robby thought—and then hurried to the master bedroom. She returned just a moment later and passed his room, footsteps quick, keys jangling. Down the hall, past the kitchen. The front door opened, then closed.

He removed the chair and opened the door a crack to listen.

The pickup truck started and, a moment later, drove away from the house and up the long driveway between the white wooden fences.

Had he misread the clock when he woke up? He went to his nightstand and checked again: 1:54 AM now. Almost two in the morning. Where would she go at such an hour? He wondered if Dad had gone with her.

Robby knew where three flashlights were kept. He went to the kitchen, moving quietly, always listening, and found two standing upright on a shelf in the short hall that led to the back door. They probably had taken one with them out to the barn. He wondered if Dad was still out there.

He went out the back door onto the screened-in porch and peered across the back yard to the path that led to the barn. Light glowed around the barn's side door and through tiny gaps in the walls. As Robby watched, he saw a shadow move back and forth in the light.

Dad was in the barn. Then where had Mom gone?

A soggy knot developed in Robby's stomach and spread to his chest as he waited for Mom to return. He became too cold on the porch and went back indoors, slowly pacing the length of the house as he waited.

He was not sure how much time had passed—it seemed an eternity, far longer than the hours in a single night—before he finally heard the pickup rattling along the driveway, growing louder as it neared. He rushed to the front of the house, went to the large window in the living room and pulled the curtain aside.

176

Mom did not pull the pickup in front of the house as usual. Instead, she kept driving along the side to the back of the house.

Robby turned, ran to the back door, and went out on the porch again. Through the screen, he watched the pickup slowly drive all the way back to the barn. As it stopped, the floodlights mounted over the main barn door came on.

As Mom got out of the truck, Robby was shocked to see the passenger door open. A man got out and staggered around to the front of the pickup. Then a second man, heavier but equally unsteady, got out and closed the door.

The lump in his chest grew larger and made it difficult to swallow, to breathe. Something way out of the ordinary was going on and it felt wrong, although he did not know why. Maybe it was because Mom and Dad were being so secretive about it, whatever it was, as if they had something to hide.

Apparently, they did.

Mom led the two men to the barn door and opened it just a couple of feet. A soft, yellow light spilled out of the barn as the men entered. The floodlights were turned off. Mom stayed outside and closed the door behind them. She returned to the pickup, got behind the wheel, started the engine again, backed around and headed the way she had come, probably to park the truck in front of the house where it usually was kept.

She would be coming back inside the house, no doubt. Robby watched the barn a few more seconds, knowing he would have to get back into his room before Mom found that he was gone. He turned and headed back inside when he heard the first scream.

He stopped and turned to look back at the barn as the man's scream rose to a shrill, piercing wail. The second man began shrieking in short, staccato bursts. Shadows danced and leaped inside the barn as the screams went on and on.

They stopped abruptly and a deafening silence filled the dark night.

Robby ran back into the house then, ran upstairs to his room, closed the door, put the chair in place, and tore off his clothes. Wearing only his pajamas again, he jumped into the bed and pulled the covers up to his eyes as he heard Mom moving around inside the house. But he did not sleep. He briefly dozed a few times, but mostly he stared into the darkness.

He knew he was no longer safe in his own home.

One December morning, Betty made poached eggs, sausage, and hash browns for breakfast. The local news played on the radio and fat snowflakes fluttered to the ground outside. Winter had set in and Christmas was a little more than a week away. As she cooked with a remote smile on her face that successfully concealed her terror, the radio announcer said that the search for 12-year-old Nancy Clapper continued.

Even though she was a couple of years older than Robby, Nancy had come to Robby's last two birthday parties, and the Forresters knew the Clappers from church. She had been a pretty girl, and Betty wondered if Robby had a crush on her.

Hopes among those searching for the girl were not as high as they had been a few days ago. One of the many volunteer searchers had found Nancy's turquoise Emerson Pioneer transistor radio beside the road. A section of the plastic casing had broken off and blood was smeared on the gold grill. At a press conference, the sheriff stressed that the bloody radio did not mean all was lost, but added that the blood type, A-positive, was Nancy's.

Betty changed the station and found Rosemary Clooney singing "Come On-A My House," which was much more cheerful. As she cooked, Betty wished she had not thrown

Nancy's radio out of the pickup window. But she had been so stressed that day. She was always stressed when Ed sent her on a hunt, but she had been more fraught than usual then because she had never done it in the light of day. The fear of being seen by anyone, but especially by someone she knew, made Betty shaky and scattered. Fortune had favored her that afternoon when she spotted Nancy walking along the side of the road. It had made her job much easier.

Throwing the radio away had been a terrible mistake because now they had found it, and along with Nancy's blood, Betty's fingerprints were on it. Inside, just beneath her skin, she trembled with fear.

They would never find Nancy, of course, because there was so little of her left, and that had been carefully buried behind the tool shed in such a way that left no disturbed earth. The same had been done with the others, but in different places on the farm.

If only she could convince Ed to see Dr. Cartwright. Or *any* doctor. But it had gone on too long now. Since he had told her about his agonizing cravings, and what he would do if they were not satisfied, she had been going along with it all, and now she worried that the point of no return was too far behind them.

However it turned out, Betty told herself she was doing it all to protect her family. And to survive. Because that's what she was: a survivor.

Betty continued to cook, listening to the music and trying not to think about anything.

Robby came in from his morning chores to find that Mom had unpacked the Christmas decorations and put them all over the house. All that remained was the Christmas tree, its place set and waiting by the bookcase: a green metal stand surrounded by a festive red skirt with glittery fringe on the edges, and three stacks of boxed ornaments waiting to be placed on the tree.

Robby cautiously agreed to go with Dad to get the tree, as he always did. Dad drove them across the property the hill in back.

"How's your singing voice, tiger?" Dad said as he started up the hill with hacksaw in hand, Robby at his side carrying a hatchet. "Up for a little 'Jingle Bells'?" Dad started out, his voice booming through plumes of vapor as their boots crunched over the snow up the hill, and Robby joined in.

At the top, they walked among the trees until they found one that was the perfect size for the living room. Robby hacked at the trunk a few times, then Dad took over with the hacksaw, kneeling beside the tree, Robby standing beside him.

"What do you want for Christmas this year, Robby?" Dad said.

"I've got a list of books I'd like."

"Books are good. I'm looking forward to Christmas supper. A nice big meal." Dad sounded a bit winded as he continued to saw at the tree, his voice throaty and rough. "Instead of having the grandparents over, you know, it could be just the two of us. You and me."

Just the two of us? Robby thought. *What about Mom?*

"Just you and me," he went on as the tree came down. "We could eat all day on your mother, don't you think?" He put a foot flat to the ground and pushed himself upright, then turned and grinned down at Robby through the curved thorns that sprouted from his dark, rough face. His voice became wet and sloppy. "Wouldn't that be a nice Christmas, Robby? Just you and me having your mother for supper?"

Robby could not have stayed there if he had wanted to. At the sight of Dad's face, his body fled without consulting him. He ran through the snow down the hill, past the pickup truck. He did not look back to see if Dad was coming after him, he simply kept running as fast as he could, nearly tripping in the snow a few times but managing to maintain his footing as he ran. He followed the pickup truck's two tracks, trying to stay in the one on the right so it was easier to run, not wanting to slow down, not even a little.

As he ran, he tried not to think about what Dad had said about eating Mom, and he tried to prevent those words from taking shape in his mind, but he failed, and his imagination conjured an image of Mom curled into a fetal position on the dining room table, naked, dead, and cooked to a shiny pink finish, and he felt sick to his stomach with guilt for thinking such a thing as he ran and ran.

He felt a stitch in his side, but when the barn and then the house came into view, he only ran faster. A glance over his shoulder revealed nothing behind him but snow, but he continued running as if pursued, fear burning in his chest.

Robby burst through the back door shouting, "Mom! Mom! We've gotta get help! Dad's gonna hurt you! He told me!" He ran through the house looking for her, and in the hallway, she abruptly stepped out of the bathroom and brought him to a stumbling halt.

"What on earth is the matter with you?" she said in a soft, breathy voice.

Robby stopped to pant like a dog for a moment, exhausted from running and wide-eyed with terror. Finally, he said, "Dad, it's Dad, he's changed again, and he wants to eat you, he *said* so, he *told* me, he wants to eat you for Christmas and he's gonna come back soon and we've gotta get help!"

She put her arms around him and pulled him to her, saying, "Oh, Robby, I don't know what's gotten into you lately. These things you've been saying—"

He jerked out of her arms angrily, stepped back, and shouted, "Don't tell me I'm making it up because you know I'm not, you *had* to have seen him change, you know what I'm talking about, you've been bringing him *people* at night, and now he's coming for *you* and he's changed again, with thorns on his face, and I can't protect you, he's too big, I can't—"

Robby's words caught in his throat when he heard the pickup truck rattling to a stop in back of the house.

"We can hide in your room," Robby whispered, grabbing her wrist, "there's a lock on that door, he won't be able to get to us, come on, *come on*," he said, pulling her arm toward the master bedroom at the end of the hall.

When he looked at her again, he saw fear in her face, and he knew that she had been lying to him every time she had said he was imagining it. She *knew*. And now she heard his father outside—heard the pickup truck door slam, heard the tailgate rattle open—and her fear became visible on her face, but only for a moment. Then it was gone and her face was slack and expressionless.

"Did you get a tree?" she said, as if Robby had not been shouting at her. "It sounds like he's getting something out of the back of the truck."

The back door opened and Dad began singing "Jingle Bells" again, his voice thundering through the house with just a bit too much enthusiasm.

"We gotta hide," Robby pleaded.

"We're in the hall, dear!" Mom called.

Heavy footsteps clumped toward them.

Robby tore himself away from her, ran into his room, slammed the door, and shoved the chair's back up against the knob.

A moment later, Mom screamed. Robby heard her run down the hall to the master bedroom, and the heavy footsteps quickly followed her. The bedroom door slammed so hard, it seemed to shake the entire house. Dad shouted, his voice a roar, and something crashed, followed by the sound of glass shattering. Their voices went back and forth for a while, but Robby, standing at his bedroom door, could not understand what they were saying. Until Dad's voice rose clearly:

"I don't have time! I need it now!"

More quiet murmuring, then shouting, then murmuring again. An outburst from Mom: "Take him, then!"

The house fell silent and remained that way for several slow seconds.

Robby heard the master bedroom door open. Footsteps came into the hall, down to his room, and stopped outside the door. Someone knocked three times.

"Open the door, Robby," Mom said. Her voice sounded thick, as if she had been crying, but calm. She sounded safe. "Come on, Robby. Open it."

"Where's Dad?"

There was a long silence before she said, "Asleep."

Robby reluctantly pulled the chair away from the door, put it in its place against the wall, then turned the knob and pulled the door open.

Mom stood just outside the door, back straight, coat on over her dress. Robby looked down and saw the small suitcase hanging from her right hand.

"I'm sorry it had to be like this, Robby," she said, her voice trembling. "But I can't let him take me. I'm not like my mother. She was weak. That's not me. I'm not like her. I'm a survivor. Do you understand?"

Paralyzed with fear, Robby understood none of it.

"I'm sorry, Robby. Goodbye." She turned and walked down the hall toward the stairs.

And Dad stepped in to take her place, hands and face dark and covered with thorns.

Robby swung the door closed, but Dad stopped it with his arm and pushed it back open, stepping heavily into the bedroom. Saliva dribbled from his mouth, where his teeth had grown into long fangs. He kicked the door shut and tore his shirt off, body bristling with curved black barbs.

"Time to eat," Dad said as he pounced on Robby.

The boy's scream was cut short.

As she drove the pickup truck away from the farm through a black and snowy December night, the gas pedal pressed to the floor, Betty kept repeating it to herself:

"I'm nothing like my mother. I'm a survivor. I'm nothing like my mother. I'm a survivor. I'm nothing like my mother . . . "

HINKLES

Kristopher Rufty

MIKE HARPER KNEW something was off the moment he entered Matthew's bedroom. His eight-year-old son was staying the weekend at a friend's house and wouldn't be back until Sunday. His bed was empty, save Hinkles, Matthew's favorite stuffed animal. Toys were scattered here and there on the floor. Stacks of comic books were all over, a miniature city of paper and ink.

The room looked as it should be.

But it didn't *feel* right.

A few minutes ago, he'd heard a noise from the living room, a quiet thumping sound while he was watching TV. Now, as he looked around the room, he wasn't sure what he was looking for. He knew there was something he needed to find. He figured he'd know it when he saw it. Hopefully, before a knife was jutting from his neck while a masked intruder stood over his bleeding body.

Stop it. Jeez . . .

Paranoid. It was his own fault for watching Shudder all evening. When Matthew was home, which was usually, he stuck to family films and cartoons. With the little man being gone for the weekend, he went a little overboard on horror movies.

Mike searched the room, finding nothing out of place. He checked the closet, the corners, and even behind the dresser. Nothing. Heading back to the bed, he paused beside it. He put his hands on his hips. Something was different now. He scanned the room slowly, moving his head this way and that. His eyes landed on Matthew's dresser.

And his heart jumped in his throat.

Hinkles was on top, tilted to the side, his tale curling out from underneath like a fuzzy snake. Normally, this wouldn't be a big issue. He'd seen the fuzzy animal in the spot many times. But considering his son's favorite stuffed animal had just been on the bed when he came in changed things. And the fact that Mike hadn't been the one to move him made matters even worse.

He had been on the bed, hadn't he?

Yes.

He had been on top, arms and legs splayed like Matthew was about to sacrifice him before leaving for the weekend.

"Oh . . . shit . . . " Mike muttered.

The monkey's head raised to look at him.

Mike jumped back with a cry. The backs of his legs hit the foot of Matthew's bed, throwing them out from under him. He plopped on the mattress, gazing up at the dresser. The monkey stood up, moving its arms as if trying to get the feeling back in them. Its head moved from side to side, causing its neck to make soft cracking sounds.

"What's the matter, Mikey?" asked Hinkles in a deep voice that for some reason had a hint of Brooklyn in it. "You look like you've seen a ghost."

Mike screamed.

Hinkles leapt from the dresser, arms outstretched. His furry lips trembled around a mouthful of sharp teeth that hadn't been there moments ago. Mike, still screaming, flung himself to the side. He hit the floor as Hinkles bounced across the mattress.

Getting to his knees, Mike spun around. Hinkles was already on his feet. He took slow, measured steps toward the edge of the bed, his red eyes blazing. The expected questions any sane person in the situation would have flickered through Mike's mind: How was this happening? Why was this happening? How was Hinkles moving around on his own? Where'd he get those teeth? Those eyes? Those . . . claws?

Hinkles was a stuffed toy monkey, yet now resembled a fuzzy

goblin with talons protruding from the furry nubs of his hands. The tiny plaything stared at Mike, as if waiting—*daring*—for him to do something.

Mike realized this was his moment to find out all he wanted to know. The way the animal had come at his face, Mike figured it hadn't been playful roughhousing. This thing meant to cause him harm. And he was going to ask why it had to be this way.

But when he opened his mouth to speak, all that came out was: "*Yuuhhh . . .* "

Hinkles let loose a laugh that sounded like stones clacking together.

Mike shook his head. His mind had tilted, turning into a chasm of blackness that produced only shock and confusion at what was transpiring before him. He couldn't find the words he needed to say anywhere in that endless abyss.

"I like you, Mike," said Hinkles. "I really do. You love Matty probably even more than I do. But it's got to be you, old friend. You."

"Me?"

"That's what I said, isn't it?" Hinkles sat on the edge of the bed, groaning as he let his fuzzy, noodle-like legs dangle over the edge. "It's the pits, I know. But it is what it is."

If Mike became even more confused, he might suddenly forget how to comprehend even the simplest of thought patterns. "What the *hell* are you talking about! How are you . . . ?" Mike waved his hand in the air, as if the words his mouth couldn't form were hanging in the air to see.

Sighing, Hinkles shook his head.

"Do you really want me to go into specifics? Really? I'm a stuffed animal and I'm about to kill you, but you want to know why and how?"

Mike shrugged. He supposed such questions probably didn't really matter since he was going to be dead soon. Hinkles had come from a claw machine at the bowling alley. Mike had won him for Matthew when his son was four. It had been the last family day they'd had before Wilma, Matthew's mother, was killed in a car accident. How had it gone from that to the awful event happening now?

"Fine," said Hinkles. "Jesus H. I wasn't always alive. Not really. You know that old lady who ran the food court at the bowling alley?"

Mike hadn't been able to forget her. Short and rotund, she'd smelled like old chicken broth. Her skin was the color of ash and dotted with moles. Her nose was beak-shaped and tipped with a dangling skin tag that flapped like a miniature punching bag when she talked. Mike had thought it was a bizarre piercing when he'd first saw her but remembered thinking a woman her age probably wouldn't have a nose ring.

"She's a witch," said Hinkles. "And she cast a spell for Matthew, promising him that if he loved me, truly loved me, I would be his forever. Well, he loved me, all right. Especially after his mother died. He loved me so much. Loved you, too. The three of us got closer. That love of his brought me to life, for the love of Pete."

Mike's jaw began to hurt. He realized his mouth was hanging open. He closed it, smacking his dry lips. "Then why do you want to . . . you know . . . kill me?"

"I don't *want* to. I have to."

"Okay. Why do you have to?"

"You do have a lot of questions, don't you?"

Mike shrugged. "Sorry." It felt odd apologizing to a Luciferic, inanimate object come to life, but he did so without question.

"No apologies needed. I'd probably be filled with questions too, if I were in your position." Hinkles rubbed two claws together. They made scraping sounds like two knife blades. "He's getting older, as you know. And he's making friends, *real* friends.

Kids at school. He even sort of likes a girl! Can you believe it? They're so icky! It's the girl down the street, Heather."

"His babysitter? She's sixteen!"

"I know, I know. He's even watched her use the bathroom once. Hid in the shower, watching through a space between the curtains. Might have us a little perv on our hands. I hope not, but the confusion going on in that kid's head is severe."

Mike doubted it could compare to his own mind right now.

"Matty doesn't spend time with me like he used to. His love for me is . . . well, waning. And since his love is going away . . . "

"Then you're dying."

"That's right. I'm dying. His love gave me life, and the lack of it is slowly killing me." He jerked a shoulder upward in a quick shrug. "I feel so betrayed."

"You? You feel betrayed? I won you myself!"

Hinkles waved off Mike's response. "Don't take it personally."

"Don't . . . ?" Mike shook his head. Was he really arguing with this thing? "How will killing me change anything for you?"

"Because he'll only have *me*, then. He'll only be able to love me, and I'll be able to live again. With Matty. Best friends, forever."

Mike shook his head. "No. Killing me would push him further away."

"No, it wouldn't. You won me for him. Spent ten dollars in that machine just to put a smile on his face. Because of that, he'll never let me go. I'll be his connection to you. Unbreakable."

"What if killing me throws him into a deep depression? Ever think of that? He'd have to go live with my parents, and they don't exactly care for toys. Believe me, I know. I grew up with friends playing with their He-Mans and Transformers, jealous as shit! I had a Rubik's cube. A Rubik's cube! They'd probably make him throw you away."

"Even while he's mourning?"

"Yes."

"That's cold."

"It's the truth."

"Well . . . " He looked at his feet, frowning. "I guess I'll have to kill them, too."

"Great idea. Get him sent to an orphanage somewhere? Genius."

Hinkles pointed a claw at him. "Don't make fun of me."

"I'm not. I'm just trying to save my life by putting all the options on the table."

"There's only one option, Mikey. Somebody has to die so I can live."

"It's not going to be me."

"Then who's it gonna be?"

Mike didn't want *anybody* to die. He loved Matthew and would do anything for him but bartering for his life with a crazed toy-monster seemed like the perfect example of taking matters too far.

"Why don't I just make you disappear for a bit?" Mike asked.

"Are you shitting me?"

"Hear me out. He comes home and can't find you. Right? He begins to worry about you, even *misses* you. Then I find you a week or so later, and he pulls you close again and never lets go."

Hinkles seemed to consider it. His fuzzy brow wrinkled with concentration. "I don't know . . . "

"It could work."

"What if he doesn't notice I'm gone?"

"He will."

"Maybe. The way's he been so occupied with other things . . . "

"Like his babysitter, apparently."

"Right. The kid's growing up."

"Too fast."

"Yeah."

Hinkles and Mike were both quiet as that realization sunk in. Felt like a year ago, Matthew was a tiny guy running up and down the hallway in a soggy diaper. He couldn't go without his daddy's affection for longer than a few hours. Now, he was spending entire weekends with friends, not even calling him to tell him good night anymore. *And* he was peeping in on teenage girls while they pissed. So much had changed, and it terrified Mike.

He realized Hinkles wasn't looking at him. Maybe he could catch the monkey off guard. That was a big maybe. Even if he did, he wasn't sure what he would do about it. There were those claws and all those sharp teeth to worry about. The creature might be sick and dying, but he wasn't dead yet. He was still quicker than Mike could ever be.

Then another thought struck him. One that made him feel like a piece of shit. It was so wrong that he didn't even want to consider it a moment longer. But the idea took shape in his mind, forming so vividly that it was impossible to forget about it.

Pretty soon, he was convinced that it was the way to go.

"What are you thinking, Mikey?" Hinkles stared down at him.

"I have an idea."

Heather's car was alone in the driveway. Mike figured it would be. Her parents used Fridays for date night. They were usually gone until late so that gave Hinkles and him plenty of time to get inside and . . . do what had to be done. They'd parked across the street and had been observing the house for ten minutes. Didn't look as if anything was going on over there.

"You sure you can do this?"

Mike looked over at Hinkles in the passenger seat. The seatbelt strap made a black bar on his small chest. His eyes peered up at him, two orbs glowing crimson. He nodded. "It's her or me, right?"

Hinkles nodded. "Right."

"Then, yes, I can go through with it."

What scared Mike the most was how truthful that statement really was. He felt no guilt about trading Heather's life for his own. Plus, if the sight of her was causing his son to commit disgusting acts of voyeurism, then she needed to go.

"No other kids over here tonight?" Hinkles asked.

"Heather's kind of a loner. No."

"She behaves?"

"Seems to."

"Good."

"Does it matter?"

Hinkles shrugged. "It won't in a few minutes."

Mike nodded. "Let's get this over with."

He cradled the stuffed animal in one arm as he crossed the street. Though it was a residential street, Heather's house had plenty of trees and shrub walls for privacy. It was just a little after nine, and the neighborhood seemed to already be down for the night. Being seen by a neighbor probably wasn't going to happen, but he still was careful as he made his way to the backyard.

Faint light glowed in the downstairs windows. There were blinds hanging over the glass, but they hadn't been shut. Mike stepped up to a window and peered inside. The kitchen was empty, the only light coming from the shroud above the stove. Nobody seemed to be moving around in there.

Mike hurried around to the back and climbed up onto the deck. He figured it was a smarter idea to enter back here. There were two ways in—a pair of patio doors and a single door further down. He tried the patio doors first.

They opened just fine.

Hinkles chuckled. "Stupid girl."

"You're getting off on this, aren't you?"

"A little."

Mike rolled his eyes. Though he wasn't regretting his decision, he wasn't exactly relishing the idea of letting a teenager be murdered. He was thankful Hinkles had agreed to do all the work. All Mike had to do was make sure she didn't get away. Should be a piece of cake.

They moved through the bottom floor of the house, checking the rooms downstairs. Heather wasn't down here. As if to confirm that, a thump came from upstairs. The ceiling creaked from somebody walking upstairs.

Mike and Hinkles looked at each other, nodded once, and went to the stairs. Though they tried to be quiet, each step seemed to squeak or groan. Mike half expected to find Heather waiting on them with a shotgun when they reached the top. Though she was nowhere around, the muffled sounds of lousy, modern pop music came from behind the first door in the hallway.

While a woman whined about drunk-texting somebody, Mike approached the door. He leaned in close, putting his ear to it. He listened. He couldn't hear anything other than the music. For all he knew, she might not even be in there.

He looked around from where he stood, his eyes searching every doorway he could see. The bathroom was across the hall, the door hanging partway open. It was dark inside. She had to be in this room in front of him. On the other side of the door. Probably on her bed, playing on her phone or watching TV. Doing typical teenage-girl shit.

And she had no clue she was about to die.

What the hell am I doing?

Creeping around somebody's house like a madman from a

slasher movie with his witch-conjured sidekick ready to give a poor girl an early demise. How was this real life? It would be almost funny if it weren't so serious.

He couldn't do this. There had to be another way.

He was prepared to share this epiphany with his partner when the bedroom door swung open. Heather, wearing a pair of athletic shorts and a long t-shirt, was on her way out. Her eyes met Mike's and she jumped back with a shriek. "Mr. Harper! What are you doing here!?!"

Mike held out his hands. "Sorry, Heather. This isn't what it looks like!"

"How did you get in? How did . . . ?" Heather's eyes moved to the left and flicked down. She saw Hinkles, sitting on his forearm like a ventriloquist's dummy. Her words rose in pitch and intensity, turning to hysterical screeches.

"Sorry, Heather," said Hinkles. "It's exactly what it looks like."

Heather's mouth stretched wider as a relentless assault of screams poured out. Hinkles hurled himself from Mike's arm, latching onto the girl's face. His arms and legs hugged around her head, locking in the curls of her blond hair.

Heather stumbled back, arms flailing. The door slammed shut as Mike started to enter.

"Hinkles!" he yelled. He reached for the door. His hand paused at the knob. Maybe he should wait. She was a big girl. Not physically, of course. But she was grown enough to handle herself. She was pretty, sure. Short. But strong-willed. She'd be fine.

Mike gulped. He never realized before how big of a wimp he truly was.

Things crashed and shattered from the other side of the door. Heather continued to scream as if she were crying into her pillow. They grew louder, closing in on the door. It banged in its frame.

Mike jumped back with a cry. The door shook and thudded with such force that he wouldn't have been surprised if it broke away from the hinges. Blood began to spill out from the crack at the bottom, spreading in a dark puddle on the wood floor.

The door went still.

Heather's screams had gone quiet.

Other than another horrendous song from Heather's playlist, the room was silent.

Mike stared at the door, waiting. It didn't open. "Huh-Hinkles?" Gone was the absurdity and ridiculousness of his situation. Gone was the shock and utter confusion. All he felt was a sick fear that caused his muscles to stiffen. He couldn't move, couldn't look away. He could barely breathe. "Hinkles?"

The doorknob slowly turned. Mike was shocked when Heather staggered out, her eyes wide and blank, mouth slacked open. Her hair was a tangled mess of yellow and red. Scratches and gashes made bloody patterns on her cheeks. Her shirt was torn and shredded, hanging off her shoulders like torn drapes. Her shorts were gone. Her thighs were raked in meaty slices that spewed blood over her knees.

And hanging from her hand was Hinkle's head, a tail of gooey gore clinging to a stuffing-shaped spine. It looked as if she'd torn it from his body during the bloody battle.

"Holy shit," Mike gasped. "Hinkles?"

The monkey's eyes no longer glowed red. Though he'd been talking more than he ever should have been before, there would be no words coming from him anytime soon.

"I . . . killed it . . . " said Heather in a monotone voice. Her eyes didn't blink, remained wide and focused on nothing as she shuffled like a zombie toward the stairs. "I . . . killed . . . "

He watched her approach the stairs, watched her right foot step outward as if the floor would still be under it when it came down.

"Heather?" Mike reached for her. He wasn't close enough.

Heather toppled forward.

"Shit!"

Mike ran to the top of the stairs and gazed down. Heather tumbled down the stairs, silent except for the cracking sounds her bones made as they snapped. She landed in a pommeled heap on the floor below.

Hinkles' severed head rolled away from her.

Though she'd fought for her life and survived Hinkles' feral attack, she was dead now.

Mike stared down at her for a long time. Then he ran into her room, grimacing at the gaudy splashes of red covering her walls. He was careful not to step in any of the puddles and sprays on the floor, walking like he was crossing a minefield to collect Hinkles' headless body from the floor by her bed.

He hurried down the stairs, hopping over splashes of blood along the way. He jumped over Heather's twisted form, landing on the other side of her. He snatched up Hinkles' head and ran out the back door.

Back at home, he buried Hinkles in the woods behind his house. The supernatural spark that had filled him with life was gone. All that remained was a dingy shell and blood-soaked stuffing.

Afterward, he took a shower. Clean and feeling better, he burned his clothes in the fireplace. He figured that was probably being overly cautious, but he didn't care. He noticed *Trilogy of Terror* was playing on TV. For a couple minutes, he watched as the possessed doll tried its best to kill Karen Black. Then he shut it off. He'd probably never be able to watch that movie again, which was a shame. He'd loved it since he was a kid. He went to his movie collection and dug out the Blu Ray. Then he threw it in the fire with his clothes.

He sat down on the couch with a cold beer and tried to figure out what he would say to Matthew when news broke about Heather. To make matters worse, he knew his son would want Hinkles for support.

But he was gone, too.

THE UGLY TREE

Gregor Xane

CREATURES OF THE NIGHT

LANA TOUCHES the mole over her left eyebrow and thinks of it as the navel of her face.

Her mark.

She blinks, clears her head. Her fingertips graze her sculpted eyebrow, then wipe away a stream of tears. Terror is an ugly expression, and she won't let it show. She has a strong bond with her face. Absolute control over its contortions. She appears calm and collected, despite the tears, and the vomit burning the back of her throat.

The video display inset in her bedroom mirror shows a live stream of the front drive of her gated home. A black sedan rolls to a stop two stories below. If she turns and looks out the window, she'll see the real thing, waiting there like a hungry spider.

Four men in dark suits exit the car. The doors shut behind them automatically, like flower petals closing at dusk. Their faces don't register on the security display. They look like ghostly quadruplets in designer sunglasses. Their skin glows and blurs, glitches, threatening to disintegrate and scatter to the winds like dandelion fluff.

Lana knows if she looks out the window, she'll see perfectly normal faces, each one distinct. But she doesn't look. Their fuzzy heads are fun to watch. A neat effect.

An alert flashes in the mirror. She taps it with a finger, and her executive assistant's face appears. Venice isn't smiling. "I can't turn them away again."

"I know."

"Deadroom?"

"Yeah. They're not house guests."

"Very good."

"And don't offer them any refreshments."

"My pleasure."

Lana slips into her heels. She steps into the hallway. When she arrives at the elevator, an electronic eye scans her. The door opens in recognition.

She waits inside with her arms crossed over her chest, ignoring her reflection in the mirrored chamber as it sinks into the earth.

The door opens with a soft beep, and she exits into a narrow tunnel, a tube baked from exotic plastics and volcanic sands. She walks through circles of light. Male voices and deep murmurs spiral down the tunnel, circling the curved walls like blood round a drain, swirling, a disorienting vortex of indecipherable speech. She imagines herself creeping toward a flock of hooded cultists speaking in tongues.

A retractable metal shelf outside the deadroom holds four mobile devices, red warning lights flashing. If she touches any of them, she'll receive a debilitating shock.

She enters the deadroom. The door slides down behind her, sealing her in with four dangerous men. They sit in leather salon chairs, legs crossed at the knee, gloved hands hanging loose on the armrests. All sit with a relaxed confidence belonging only to those who know they are above the law.

Lana doesn't greet them, doesn't meet their eyes. She walks past, sits on a metal stool behind a black metal table, and avoids seeing her face in its cold, reflective surface.

She finds Mr. Gaines staring. She nods and steals a glance at his companions. Their faces don't show it, but she knows they're killers. She can picture these three as boys in boarding school uniforms, little angels with mischievous smiles. They aren't smiling now though. This is serious business.

Gaines is serious business. His face is different from the frat boys', strikingly asymmetrical, a face that'd be compelling on the big screen. It's hard, and wide, like a crudely cut stone idol from an old Saturday matinee, something with a chamber hidden inside. She imagines her fingertips exploring it for hours, looking for the secret pressure point that will release its secrets.

Gaines smiles.

She winces.

His teeth are all white, all straight, but too narrow. He speaks her name, asks her how she's been. His voice is deep and rich, with the timbre of a soap opera villain. His words twist with an exotic blend of foreign accents. "You look well," he says. "Better than last time."

Lana controls her memories, her face. She doesn't let her lips draw tight. She won't allow her jaw to clench. She speaks like a clinician dealing with a patient she secretly despises. "If you don't mind, I'd like to move this along. I'm tired." She glances down at the black leather case next to his chair and swallows. "I've got an early flight to catch."

"You need your beauty rest," Gaines says, no longer smiling. "You must look your best at the premiere."

Lana taps a lacquered fingernail on the slick tabletop.

Gaines winks and hoists his black bag onto his lap. He presses his thumb into a sensor and unlocks the fastener. He withdraws a black leather folio, unzips it, stands, takes three steps toward Lana, and places it on the table. He flips a few pages, flips them back, then turns the folio around and presents a document to Lana for her review.

She tucks a strand of hair behind an ear and stares down at the seal stamped on the cover page, a tree with an odd number of limbs. The blank spaces between the branches form a dozen tormented faces. She brushes the image aside, crinkling the page.

"Careful," Gaines says.

Lana issues a derisive sniff and scans the document. It's short.

Only five pages. When she finishes, she shoves it back at Gaines, almost slamming it into his crotch.

Gaines doesn't flinch.

"No," Lana says.

"Do you need to read it again?" Gaines asks.

"This is sick."

Gaines nods. "Corrosive."

"Why?"

"You know I cannot answer that."

"I can't do this anymore."

"You will." Gaines zips the portfolio closed as if underlining his statement.

Lana covers her face with her palms, presses her thumbs into her cheekbones, massages a developing headache. "What are the alternatives?"

"You know the alternative."

"Can it be quick?"

"No." Gaines steps away and slips the folio back into the leather bag. He whispers something in an alien tongue as he reaches down deep into the bag to retrieve the threat. He clicks his tongue, chitters, and hisses a lullaby to a thing Lana doesn't want to see.

"You don't have to show me again."

"But I do. You need to see her. You need a reminder."

Lana continues to hide behind her hands. She listens to Gaines turn toward her, the hush of his expensive overcoat brushing against his tailored suit, the creak of his leather gloves as he grips the small wooden crate she's seen a dozen times before, an antique cage with wire mesh on all six sides. She tries to imagine it's empty this time, just a box filled with a thousand intersecting shadows, but she hears a vibrating trill, low and soft. The sound hits her between the eyebrows and travels down her nose like a nervous tick. Her palms become wet with tears.

Gaines places the box on the table with a gentle click.

"Don't bring it any closer."

"Look at her."

"No. I'll do whatever you want."

"You will look at her and *then* you will do whatever we want."

"Kill me."

"You know it will not be that easy, Lana. All I ask for is a little peek. A brief glimpse. A quick reminder."

"I can't."

"You can. You have seen her before."

"I can already feel them pulling toward her. Put it away."

"No."

Lana runs her fingers through her hair, eyes squeezed shut. She can't control her face. A rare moment. Her beauty is lost.

"Open your eyes, Lana."

Lana opens her eyes and stares at a black silk tie, leather gloves, and cuff links bearing the same seal from the folio, that ugly tree.

Lana turns her head, left, just slightly, her eyes swivel, and she sees what's inside the cage.

Her eyes meet the thing's multifaceted eyes, and she sees thousands of tiny faces staring back at her. All are Lana's face, swirling in a dizzying kaleidoscopic which threatens to hypnotize her.

She's seen it before. The threat. It has three sets of vestigial wings that buzz on its back, blurring into a shimmering pattern, like a lightning storm. Golden hair covers its segmented body. Its abdomen is bulbous and ridged, splotched with emerald, ruby, and an oily yellow.

It looks like an insect, but it can't be, because it has an uneven number of legs. Its seventh limb, which looks like the rest, except that it is shiny black, not a dull gray, is called 'the fiddle' because the creature's other legs use it for stridulating, producing a sound like a needle scraping over a vinyl record. But there is a counter tone that is even more maddening. It barely registers, but Lana can feel it clawing at the backs of her teeth, like mewling baby rats trying to scrape their way out of her mouth.

She turns away, puts her hands to her face, and feels her skin shift and bubble beneath her fingertips, as if hundreds of teeny round seeds are rolling around just under the surface.

She knows what these things are. They're the males, performing a mating dance in response to the music the female of their species plays inside her cage.

"Stop," Lana says. "Please."

"That is the magic word." Gaines sweeps a black silk cloth over the creature's cage, making a show of it, like a world-class illusionist.

The unholy chirruping stops. The things crawling inside Lana's face break into a frenzy as they search for their mate, causing a searing pain she equates with having acid thrown into her face. But this torture only lasts a few seconds before the males become dormant again, receding from the surface of her flesh, leaving it smooth and taut and glowing with health and good breeding.

Her hands fall from her face, and she sees her eyes reflected in the table, big and round, brimming with tears, dark and . . .

"Beautiful," Gaines says, lifting her chin with two fingers of a cold, gloved hand. Their eyes meet. "So beautiful."

THREE YEARS AGO

Price doesn't fuck like a normal man. Lana knows there has to be some specialized training behind his abilities in the bedroom. She suspects he's an intelligence operative, a weapon used to extract secrets from foreign diplomats and the bored housewives of billionaires. She's a puzzle box he solves with ease every time.

She's lain bare, exhausted, covered only in sweat, on sheets that probably cost more than her yearly earnings at the restaurant where she serves as a hostess. Every night putting on an audition for its rich and famous clientele, serving up charm, poise, and her beautiful face.

Price's fingers trace her jawline, her lips, her cheekbones. His face hovers in the darkness, just a shadow with a deep, sexy voice. He speaks and she shivers. "I think we have a role for you now."

"Who's we?"

He moves his hand down between her legs. "It's a small part."

"Mmmm."

"In a major production."

"When's the audition?"

"No audition."

"I get it." Her hand moves down to join his. "This is the audition."

Price smiles. A helicopter searchlight sweeps the room, revealing bright, white teeth. A body like marble. Walls filled with artwork worth millions. Nudes. Hunts. Dark forests. Visions of hell. Gods ripping infants to pieces.

"You remember that lunch we had with Gaines last week?"

"Yeah."

"That was your interview. Of sorts."

"Oh. I didn't care much for him."

"No one does. But he gets deals made."

"What is he?"

"He's an arborist."

Lana laughs. "Seriously."

"I am serious. He also manages talent."

"What agency is he with?"

"He works with all the big ones. Howard. Sunset. Meyer."

"Wow."

"And this isn't just a walk-on part, Lana."

"Really?"

"But you'll have to do some nudity."

"I'm not"

"You'll have a love scene with" Price leans in, whispers the name in her ear.

She gasps. "You're kidding me?"

"Well, it's more of a sex scene."

"Fuck."

"Exactly."

"You're playing with me, right?"

That helicopter searchlight sweeps the room again. His smile is even bigger. "Not the way you think."

Lana grabs him by the scruff of his neck, pulls him down for a kiss, wiping that smile off his face. She kisses him long and deep. His fingers work with hers, quickening, and she comes, bites his lips, arches at his side, exhales through her nostrils like a wild horse fighting the saddle.

After she catches her breath, she playfully bites his neck, his shoulder, his chest, and asks, "When does filming start?"

"Next month."

"Tomorrow's next month."

"Shit. You're right. Then I guess it's next week. But there's something you've got to do first."

"I hope you don't mean *someone*."

"No, it's not like that."

"Good."

"There is an initiation you'll have to get through. A rite of passage type thing we've all been through."

"I don't know. Sounds like a lot to ask for a small movie role."

"That's just for starters. Think of it more like an investment in your career. What we're talking about is a support system. You won't have any trouble getting work after this."

"It sounds like I'll be joining a cult."

"No one is asking you to join a cult."

"Then some kind of secret society?"

"Not exactly. More like a secretive system."

"A system for what?"

"Guiding public policy, perception."

"Why me?"

"You've got talents. Those talents could be leveraged for a greater purpose."

"What purpose?"

"That I can't say."

"Why not?"

"That information isn't for the uninitiated."

"What would I be asked to do?"

"Champion specific causes. Promote policies. Advocate. Influence. Persuade."

"I'm not sure I'm comfortable with that."

"With what? Playing a role? Isn't that what you've dedicated your life to?"

"This sounds different. This sounds like lying to people."

"Isn't that what acting is? Convincing people you're someone you're not?"

"Yeah, on a movie set."

Price laughs. "You really think any big-time actor isn't acting when they're not on set? You believe they're showing their true selves on the late night talk shows? You really think all of that isn't a construction?"

"I'm not a big-time actor."

"You can be. Chances are you will be."

"What's this organization called?"

"Nice try."

"What?"

"Were you looking to do a web search?"

"Maybe."

Price laughs again. "It doesn't have a name."

"I find that hard to believe."

"I know. This whole proposition seems absurd. It seemed like that to me, too. But I took a leap of faith because I had a feeling the game was rigged and I wanted to be on the side of those rigging it for once in my life."

"And did you get what you wanted?"

"Yes."

"And what was that?"

"You're looking at it. Living in it. For now."

"That sounds like a threat."

"No, Lana. I'm making you a promise. I'm promising you the world."

"But at what cost?"

"I told you. Lies. Manipulation. Pretending to be something you're not. Subterfuge. Espionage."

"I'm not going to have to perform human sacrifices?"

"No human sacrifices."

"You're not going to turn me into an adrenochrome junkie, are you?"

"Where'd you hear about that crazy shit?"

"Internet."

"No. No adrenochrome. No child sacrifices. No black magic. That kind of shit goes on, sure. But not in this organization. I promise."

"Promise?"

"Yes."

"The world?"

"And all its worldly pleasures."

And at this moment, naked in his arms, his warm flesh pressed against hers, she seals the deal with a kiss.

Lana meets Price at a club called Root. She's never heard of it, and it isn't in the best neighborhood. It's an exclusive establishment, and her name is on the list, as promised. She walks through the bar area, alongside the dance floor, and under an archway which leads to the restrooms and the kitchen. Down the hallway, there is a fourth door. It's unmarked. And unlocked. She opens it, as she's been instructed, and steps cautiously down a flight of stairs covered in shifting mosaic tiles which threaten to catch her high heels and send her toppling down to a concrete floor and a broken neck. She grips the railing and descends into the darkness. The club music fades as she goes, and an unsettling silence takes its place. The stairwell curves to the left and ends at a claustrophobic landing and a single, locked door.

She presses a buzzer to the right of the door and waits. She looks up into the eye of a camera mounted near the ceiling and fights the urge to wave.

The door clicks open with a hiss and stands slightly ajar. No one pulls it wide to greet her. She pushes it open and finds a dimly lit hallway, clean, cool air, and the faint hint of household disinfectant.

She steps inside. Her heels barely register on the composite flooring. When she approaches a turn in the hallway, the door closes behind her, sounding like a master whispering a command to his dog, snapping his fingers for emphasis.

Hiss. Click.

Her neck and shoulders tense. She holds her breath and turns the corner.

A gurney blocks her way. Two people, a man and a woman in surgical masks, latex gloves, and scrubs emblazoned with a round emblem she can't quite make out, stand behind the gurney, fingertips tented on its cushioned surface, poised, ready to pounce.

A door opens on the right side of the hallway, casting the surgeons in a pale glow. A shadow slides across the floor and takes the shape of a man. Price steps into the hallway.

He hugs her, offers soft pleasantries, makes comforting noises.

Price isn't an actor. This isn't convincing. She wants to break free from him and run, but she leans into him, kisses his neck, his face, his lips, and asks for more calming words she won't believe.

She has to do this.

She has to play her part.

Price takes her by the hand and leads her to the gurney, motioning for her to sit.

She does.

He indicates that she should lie down.

She does.

He tells her not to worry as the surgeons buckle the restraints over her chest, binding her arms to her sides, and her legs together.

She knows she should struggle to free herself, but she remains still. She doesn't say a word when the male surgeon withdraws a syringe and taps a vein in the crook of her arm. Her blood freezes.

And she can't say a word after the injection. She moves her mouth, begs Price to make them unstrap her, but no sound comes out.

The overhead lights grow too bright, and she floats away.

Lana finds herself in a darkened chamber, spotlight aimed down at her face. She wants to turn her head away, but she can't. A brace holds her head in place, vice-like. Her mouth is propped open with plastic struts, and she screams until her throat hurts, but no one comes to comfort her. Price promised he'd be there for her through everything, but he never appears.

The male surgeon floats into view. He holds a scalpel up to the light and twists it in his fingers, turning it, admiring it.

The female surgeon appears. She holds a long tube in one hand and a white cloth in the other.

The scalpel descends, traces Lana's jawline. The tube hisses to life and follows the blade, suctioning away Lana's blood.

They've given her nothing for the pain. She screams, vibrates with agony, but she can't deter the surgeons from their work.

The blade cuts along her hairline, slips under her upper lip, her bottom lip, circles her nostrils. The female surgeon holds Lana's eyelids open while the male surgeon works the blade underneath.

Lana is strapped to a wheelchair. Darkness all around. She sits in a circle of light, in a dark chamber of unknown size. It feels like her face is on fire. She can move her jaw again, and she cries out for help. Demands explanations. Begs and bargains, but every word she speaks sounds wrong. She sounds like a stroke victim, or like a deaf person who's learned to speak without ever hearing words.

When she explores with her tongue, she discovers why she isn't able to form words correctly. She has no lips. Her tongue travels exposed teeth, and she recalls a scene from a pirate film she loved as a kid, a fat worm crawling out of a skeleton's mouth.

Tears stream from her naked eyeballs. Then, as if in mockery of those tears, a latex-gloved hand appears and sprays a fine mist into her eyes.

This same hand returns to spray her face with something that smells like medicine. And two gloved hands mount a device on her head that suspends a black rectangle in front of her face on a gooseneck extender. She imagines she looks like an anglerfish, teeth exposed, eyes bugged out, bait dangling before her in dark, abysmal waters.

The black rectangle flips around to reveal a mirror. And she's left alone to stare into what was left behind after they flayed her face.

She smells butter.

No.

She sniffs. It's a butter-flavored cooking spray.

The mirror is pushed aside. Thankfully. She can't bear to look into that visage of angry red anymore. That monster isn't her.

Three figures in black robes, hoods pulled up to cast their faces in shadow, sit at a round table facing her.

That latex-gloved hand returns and sprays her eyes again. When they clear, that same gloved hand holds a frying pan, angled so that Lana can see what's inside.

Lana sees, within a halo of sliced peppers and onions, her face. It looks like a flimsy Halloween mask, mouth agape with shock, hollow eye sockets staring up at her. The nose is like some wilted, exotic vegetable.

The gloved hand holds still until Lana realizes what she's looking at, then whisks the pan away.

It hurts when she screams, and the sound that comes out is nothing like she expects. Her throat is raw and closed up. She sounds like a hungry vulture crying out to protect its carrion morsel from its siblings.

Her head fills with the most awful noises. Snapping,

bubbling, hissing, sizzling. And her nose fills with a scent from childhood, one connected to fond memories of her mother.

Fried baloney.

Lana dry heaves.

She struggles against her restraints as three plates are set before the monks.

She curses at them with the throat of an angry vulture as their knives and forks clink against their plates, as they lift scraps of her face to their lips, as they chew and swallow her beauty, her strength, every mask she has presented to the world, and her very sense of self.

Lana wakes in a grand garden. Heat lamps shine down from a grid of steel crossbeams. Industrial fans circulate air. Greenery all around. Budding flowers. Trembling fronds. Butterflies. Buzzing insects. And the sound of trickling waterfalls. The air tastes like spring after a cool rainstorm.

She sits in a different wheelchair. It's made of wood, and it feels like an old comfortable rocker. She isn't tied down anymore. She's wearing a plush bathrobe, hands resting in her lap. Unnaturally relaxed. She's been injected with something, but doesn't care.

The female surgeon wheels Lana through a maze of foliage, and they arrive at a clearing devoted to a solitary tree cordoned off by brass stanchions and velvet ropes. The tree's crown is broad and imposing. The uppermost branches flirt with the hot lights some thirty feet above.

She has no idea what kind of tree she is looking at. She knows nothing about plants or flowers and couldn't have named anything she passed on her way to this clearing, but she knows instinctively that this tree is a rarity. Possibly a hybrid. Overly cultivated. Pruned and shaped until its branches curl and twist, like something from one of her dad's psychedelic rock album covers. Looking at it makes her fear an acid flashback. She can taste the ghost of strychnine on her tongue. Her teeth grind. Her jaw clenches.

She rolls forward and sees the bark moving, swirling, like black static on an old TV set.

The chair rolls closer still, stops a foot away from the velvet ropes, and she sees that the bark isn't animated. What she's seeing are hundreds of thousands of tiny insects crawling over one another. They cover the trunk, the branches, tumble off onto the soil below, into a swirling mass of insects scrambling over roots and rocks and gravel. These insects are black, tiny, like bloated fleas. They form hypnotizing patterns as they dance and swarm and exalt under a grating chirruping that Lana can feel in her molars.

Hanging from the vines of this ugly tree are great pale leaves which resemble weeping human faces. Black eye sockets and gaping, toothless mouths. The faces hang at the ends of their tendrils at all angles, upside down, sideways, looking down at her with strange, frightening expressions, trapped souls calling for her to set them free.

A naked boy runs from behind a rustling bush and climbs up the tree with quick, jerky movements. Lana thinks the boy at first has dark skin but soon sees he is covered with pinprick scars. His hairless scalp. His eyelids. His genitals.

Thousands of insects crawl up his body as he climbs the trunk and reaches high for a feminine face dangling at the end of a yellowing tendril, hanging at an odd angle from a spot on the left side of its brow.

The insects coat his arm, like jelly moving uphill. They file into the face he holds in his grasp, tunnel through the empty eye sockets, the open mouth.

The boy slides down the tree trunk, blinded by insects, careful not to inhale any of the bugs. When his feet hit the dirt, he looks like a statue made of a million fleas in tight formation. He steps to the edge of the potting soil and holds up the face he's plucked from the tree. The female surgeon, now wearing an open black robe over her white scrubs, stands ready with a plastic tray.

The boy returns to the bushes.

The female surgeon presents the tray to Lana. It fits neatly into slots on the arms of her wheelchair.

The surgeon ties off her robe, pulls the hood up over her head, concealing her face in shadow, and points to the gift bridged across Lana's lap.

The leaf looks like Lana's face reflected up at her from a bowl of milk.

The surgeon monk, with slender, nimble fingers, takes up the face and drapes it over Lana's bloodied visage. It flows over her contours and melts into place like hot wax.

Lana is a knot of involuntary muscle spasms, lockjaw, and hyperventilation. She seizes. The surgeon monk rams a rubber stick between Lana's teeth. A needle jabs into her thigh. Her leg goes cold, and a moment later, that cold travels her body and shuts off all the caring.

She lives in the movement of her own slowing breath. Calming. Her blinking eyelids are now a luxury.

She can blink again.

Once Lana settles into her rolling chair, the surgeon monk presents her with a handheld mirror, nothing special, fingerprints smearing its surface.

But Lana barely notices.

She only has eyes for the face now returned to her.

Her face.

With a new black mole above her left eyebrow.

On a face this beautiful, it seems an affectation, a cosmetic application, a little black lie. But Lana doesn't care.

Hell.

She likes it.

It only looks like a lie.

SILENT SCREAM

Andrew Lennon

STOMPING THROUGH THE TRAIL, wet mud splashing up her legs and covering her socks, Melody sighed and exhaled a loud frustrated huff. She waited a moment for someone to ask what was wrong, and when no response came, she huffed again.

"Okay, what is it?" Mark asked, waiting for the moaning to begin.

"Well, look at me." Melody threw her arms up in an exaggerated gesture.

"What?" Mark looked her up and down. "You mean because you've got a little bit of mud on you?"

Melody paced back and forth, mud splashing with each step.

"Look, it's not just the mud. I'm dripping wet, I don't even know if it's from the rain or the sweat. It's disgusting, a girl isn't even supposed to sweat."

Mark laughed at her.

"What are you laughing at?"

"A girl isn't even supposed to sweat," he mimicked. "Are you serious? We're on a hike. It's normal to build up a bit of a sweat. It's good for you. And I'm not being funny, but we're not exactly overexerting ourselves, are we? We've fallen a long way behind the others. If we don't get a move on then we're going to get left behind, and probably lost."

"*Fine!*" Melody snapped, and marched ahead of Mark. "I don't know who ever thought walking through the middle of nowhere was fun anyway?"

Mark laughed and shook his head as he watched Melody march off. He held back for a moment so he could take advantage, and get a good look at her in those tight hiking shorts. Even covered in mud and sweat, Melody was hot.

Mark was going to use this hiking trip to finally try and make his move on her. That's assuming she was still talking to him by the time they set up camp. He had a feeling she was going to be sulking soon enough after breaking a nail or getting her shoes dirty or something. Yes, she was hot, but that didn't mean she wasn't annoying. As she rounded the corner out of sight, Mark started to pick up the pace a bit to catch up with her.

He started to jog a little bit; he didn't want to fall behind completely on his own. God knows he wasn't the best at orienteering, and there was no chance he'd find his way out on his own. Hitting a raised root, he stumbled, falling forwards. Mark managed to put his hands out and break his fall but for a moment, it knocked the wind out of him.

Climbing to his knees to get back up again, he noticed something on the floor in front of him. It was fluorescent green; it looked like a nail that had been dipped in paint. When he picked it up, he could feel that it certainly wasn't any kind of metal, nor plastic. He'd never seen anything like it before. It just looked so out of place, perhaps it had fallen out of someone's bag.

"*Arrgggghhhhhh!*" A scream sounded from further up the trail.

"*Melody!*" Mark sprinted toward the sound of the screaming; he rounded the corner, pushing leaves and branches out of the way. In front of him stood Melody, her hands raised to her face, either side of her wide screaming mouth.

"Melody, *what is it?* What's wrong?" Mark asked in a panic.

Debbie and Keith came running into the clearing from the other side of the trail. They had already covered quite a bit of distance ahead of the other two, but sprinted back at the sounds of the screams.

"*What the hell is it?*" Keith asked.

"*Melody!*" Debbie screamed while retrieving a pistol from her rucksack. "Did something attack you?"

Melody hysterical screaming continued for a second until she was able to get one word out. "Spider."

The three companions stood, jaws dropped, staring at the hysterical woman.

"Are you *fuckin' kidding* me?" Keith asked.

"There's a spider . . . on me," Melody began to hyperventilate.

Mark approached Melody and grabbed her by the shoulders. He started to shake her until she looked him in the eyes.

"You need to calm down," he said. "Where's this spider?"

"It . . . it was on my shoulder."

He looked at her shoulders, then he walked all the way around her, checking her back, her hair, everything. Mark laughed. "Well, it looks like your screaming scared it away."

"It's not *funny!*" Melody snapped.

"I thought you were being attacked by a bear or something, Melody. *Jesus Christ*, do you have any idea exactly how many insects are in these forests? That was probably the hundredth spider on you today, just the first one you noticed." Debbie put her gun back in her bag.

"Please, don't say that." Melody's face was a picture of sheer panic. "I hate spiders."

"Did you think someone came and cleaned the forest for you before we arrived?" Keith asked in his best sarcastic voice. "Seriously, Mark. You need to sort your girl out, man."

"I'm *not* his girl," Melody spat, and with that she stormed ahead.

"Keith, come on, man." Mark looked at his friend.

"Sorry." Keith held his hands up in the air in defence. "I thought by how far behind you guys had fallen that you'd already sealed the deal."

"Forget it you two." Debbie called. "Let's go catch her up before she spots a snake or something, and the shit really hits the fan."

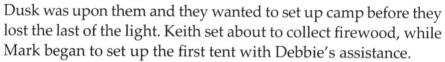

Dusk was upon them and they wanted to set up camp before they lost the last of the light. Keith set about to collect firewood, while Mark began to set up the first tent with Debbie's assistance.

"We need to make sure that the soil is tough enough to hold the pegs," Mark said. "Sometimes the wind can really pick up speed while travelling through these trees. We don't want to wake up and find that the tent is flying away from us."

"What about here?" Melody asked.

Mark looked to the woman standing in the middle of four trees about half a metre apart from each other.

"Yes, the soil there will be okay, Melody," Mark said, "but you realise that we need enough space to actually fit the tent, right?"

"Oh, yeah," Melody replied in her dizzy way.

"Why don't you help Keith collect some firewood?"

"Okay." She started rummaging on the ground collected small pieces of wood.

"She is really, really dumb," Debbie whispered. "I honestly don't understand what you see in her."

Mark glanced at Melody, who was bent over while collected the firewood from the floor. Her arse shaped to perfection, the cheeks just barely tucked into her shorts, less than an inch away from escaping. Mark licked his lips.

"Yeah, I don't get it either."

Mark found a large clearing in the trees. Ironically, it was just behind the spot that Melody had previously mentioned.

"Debbie, this spot is perfect; we'll be able to fit both tents in here, with the fire in the middle," Mark called.

"Sounds good to me," Debbie answered. "Let's get 'em set up." She threw her bag to the floor.

It didn't take them long to set up the tents. Both Mark and Debbie had been camping countless times, so it came as second nature to them. Shortly after they had finished, Keith returned with arms full of firewood. Melody followed closely behind him, with a hand full of sticks. Debbie looked at Melody and rolled her eyes.

"Well done, Keith. That should do us for the night," Debbie said. "Set them up in a little triangle on the floor."

"Oh, and he can do that spinny thing with my pieces to start the fire," Melody said, filled with enthusiasm.

"Or we could just use this?" Keith smiled and held his Zippo in the air.

"Oh, okay, well it's not as cool, but I guess that could work."

Before long, the fire was crackling and spitting embers. The four campers sat around it, embracing the warmth. Darkness hadn't so much as crept up on them, but rather swept a blanket across the sky. One minute it was light, the next it was gone. Melody gazed upwards.

"The stars are so bright out here," she said.

"Yeah, it's beautiful, isn't it? I didn't think we would be able to see them through the trees, but it looks like we've got a good spot." Mark put his arm around Melody and pulled her closer to him. She liked it when he did that, it made her feel warm, safe.

"So, what do we have to eat?" Keith asked.

"The only thing you should ever cook over a camp fire," Mark answered. "Sausages, and for dessert, marshmallows."

"We really are living the dream, aren't we?" Keith laughed.

"Can't beat the view in the starlight café, my friend."

As always when having fun, the night passed by far too quickly. The group was beginning to feel drunk after consuming several cans of beer. Choosing not to leave litter and piles of cans lying round the forest, they had decided to keep their litter in bags that they had brought along with them. Seeing the three plastic bags full with beer cans, they decided it was probably a sign that it was time for bed.

"Right, I think I'm gonna call it a night," Mark announced. He looked to Melody. "You comin'?"

"Not yet, but let's see what you can do." Melody giggled.

"Oh God, I think I'm gonna throw up," Debbie said.

"Night, boys and girls," Keith said. "Come on, Debbie. I suppose I'll let you sleep in the tent with me."

"Oh, you suppose." Debbie laughed. "You have no idea how many men would want to share a tent with me."

"Oh yeah, I'm really lucky. Yay." Keith whined in a tired tone.

"Night everyone," Melody called.

Before they left for the trip, Melody had told Mark about how scared she was at the thought of sleeping outside in the wilderness, alone. He, of course, comforted her and explained that she wouldn't be alone, he would be sharing the tent with her.

Now they were here in the tent, Mark had kissed her goodnight and tucked himself into his sleeping bag. Melody lay on her back staring to the roof of the tent. She heard something crack outside.

Nothing to worry about, she thought, *they had left the fire burning*.

It was probably just spitting embers again.

But what if it wasn't? What if that was the sound of someone creeping up to them, ready to burst into their tent at any moment, or slash it open with a knife?

"Mark," she whispered.

He snored in return. He must have fallen into a drunken sleep almost instantly.

"*Mark!*" she shouted his name this time.

"Woah, what it is?" he sat up in fright.

"I'm scared, I can't sleep. Can I get in your bag with you?"

"Hang on," Mark sighed, half asleep as he crawled out of the bag. "Actually, I think we can connect these bags together and make a double duvet."

A smile spread wide across Melody's face. "That would be perfect."

"It might be a little bit cold; we won't be lying on anything. Although I suppose I could throw our coats under us."

"Oh don't worry; I'm sure we can keep each other warm,' Melody said, suggestively.

It was too dark for Mark to see her facial expression, but he was hoping that her tone meant he was going to be getting lucky as soon as he had sorted the blanket out.

Struggling to see, he fumbled with the zippers from the two bags, Melody shined the light from her phone on them, in an attempt to try and help. Eventually he connected the two and zipped the bags up. As he said, it had created a large double duvet.

"Right, let's just spread our clothes on the floor a little bit so we're not just sleeping straight on the ground sheet. That'll make us feel a little bit warmer."

As suggested, the two spread their clothes around evenly to try to cover the space on the floor. It wasn't the most comfortable, but it was certainly nicer than sleeping on the cold ground sheet.

"This is perfect, thank you. Night," Melody said, and gave Mark a quick peck on the lips.

"Night."

Mark sighed quietly, guessing that quick peck on the lips was a subtle way of saying he wasn't getting any tonight. He rolled over so his back was facing Melody, and tried getting himself comfortable. She snuggled into his back, the warmth and the feel of her breasts pressing against his back felt amazing. He wanted to turn around and kiss her, but he couldn't find the courage. Gradually, sleep began to consume him.

Melody lay awake, her arm wrapped around Mark's chest. She could hear the change in his breathing; he had fallen asleep now. She felt a little a bit annoyed, since she was sure that he was going to make a move on her tonight. After hinting over and over again, she thought that surely he would seize the opportunity while they were lying in bed together. Now, he was asleep.

I know what'll wake him.

Melody gently stroked her hand up and down Mark's stomach. He started shuffling a little bit, but was still asleep. She moved her hand further down, pausing at the waistband of his boxers. She hesitated for a moment.

Did he want this? Maybe he would wake up and freak out.

No, this was it, she was going for it. She slid her hand into his boxers and wrapped her fingers around his penis. It was still limp in his drunken sleep. Slowly she began to slide her hand up and down. She could feel his shaft hardening in her grip. He began to groan. Still, she slid up and down, gradually increasing the pace.

"Melody?" Mark asked, still mostly asleep.

'Shhhhh," she whispered. "Just relax."

She gently pulled on his shoulder so he turned to lie on his back. Melody lowered herself beneath the makeshift duvet. She slowly lowered Mark's boxers, his penis sprung upright as it escaped the waistband.

"Well, you're awake now," she giggled. "At least down here, anyway."

She took him whole in her mouth, twirling her tongue around his shaft while she held him in her warm, moist grip.

"Oh my *God!*" Mark called out.

Melody giggled, and almost choked. She removed him from her mouth.

"You like that?" she asked.

"Jesus Christ, don't stop." He pushed his hips up as if to direct himself back into her mouth.

Melody slid her hand back up and down quicker this time, and then followed the action with her mouth. Mark was moaning and groaning above her. She was getting moist herself, just at the thought of how much pleasure she was giving him.

She shuffled back up the quilt so she was now face to face with him.

"Hi," she said.

"Hi," Mark gasped.

Melody sat up and removed her shirt, Mark couldn't see very well due to the lack of light, but what he could see looked perfect to him: Melody's perfect perky breasts silhouetted on the wall of the tent. She leaned forward as Mark grabbed them and took her nipples in his mouth. She moaned as he sucked, and he slowly rotated his thumb around as he licked them. Melody moaned more. Slowly, she lowered herself and allowed him to enter her. She was so wet, warm, and tight.

"Oh God, that feels good," Mark sighed.

Melody started to gradually slide up and down on Mark's shaft, he kept pulling her closer and taking her nipples into his mouth. She started to increase the pace, faster and faster as she began to bounce on him. Slapping noises filling the tent as her arse hit his thighs.

"Oh, God. Oh, God, I'm gonna come," Melody panted.

"Shhh, they'll hear you," Mark laughed.

"*Oh my God!*" she screamed.

She flopped forwards onto Mark's chest. He wrapped his arms around her.

"You didn't finish did you?" she asked.

"No but . . . "

"Shhh, it's okay. I'll take care of it."

231

She lowered herself back down and took him once again in her mouth.

"Oh my God," Mark whispered.

"Mmmmmmm," was the only response.

Debbie lay on her back, grinding her teeth while listening to the sound of Mark and Melody pleasuring each other. She thought back to a camping trip a few years ago. Back then, it was her who filled the forest with screams of pleasure. She remembered waking up with Mark's head between her thighs, his tongue flicking rapidly, making her tremble with delight, but that was a lifetime ago. Now they were just 'friends'. They had both agreed to never discuss that night again, with anyone else, or between themselves. It was a drunken mistake and better best forgotten.

Except to Debbie, it wasn't a mistake. It was everything she had ever wanted. It was Mark. Now she had to lie in silence and listen to someone else enjoying him.

"Well, at least one of us is having fun," she sighed.

She glanced over to Keith; he was lying flat on his back. He let out a very quiet snore. Debbie smiled; she thought it was cute.

"Let's give you a little bit of fun."

Debbie quietly crawled over to Keith. She unzipped his sleeping bag slowly, trying not to make a sound. Keith muttered something in his sleep, but Debbie couldn't understand him. She just ignored it. She climbed on top of Keith so her legs straddled him and then she leaned forwards. She began to kiss his neck.

"Huh, what's going on?" Keith asked.

"Shhhh," Debbie whispered, and kissed him on the lips.

"What the fuck are you doing!" he shouted and shoved her onto the ground.

"What's the matter?" Debbie asked, confused.

"What are you *playing* at?"

"I just thought we could have a little bit of fun."

"Why the hell would I want to do that?" Keith laughed.

"If you're not interested, then fine." Debbie sighed. "You don't need to laugh at me."

"Look, Debbie. I'm sorry." Keith calmed down now; he was rubbing Debbie's arms. "You're a lovely girl, but . . . "

"But you're not interested, I get it."

"No, it's not that. It's . . . "

"What?"

"Debbie, I'm gay."

Debbie shoved Keith's hand away from her arm, and scurried back from him.

"You're what?" she snapped. "Is this some kind of fucking joke?"

"No." Keith said. "Why would it be a joke? And being honest, I thought you knew. I've never exactly kept it a secret."

"Oh my God," Debbie laughed. "I really am fucking stupid."

She climbed to her feet and started to unzip the tent.

"Where are you going?"

"Out."

"Don't be stupid, it's the middle of the night, Debbie."

"Fuck off, Keith. Go back to sleep."

"Fine, whatever."

Keith got back into his sleeping bag and zipped it up again. He turned to the side and got himself comfortable. He heard Debbie zip the tent up from outside.

"Drama queen." He sighed to himself. "She'll be back in a minute."

Debbie circled the fire; she was happy to see it was still burning. It was a cold night and the warmth of the fire made her feel better.

"Oh, Debbie," she sighed. "What are we going to do with you?"

She let out a small giggle at the thought of how insane she must look now. Sitting in the middle of the forest on her own, talking to herself. It's just as well no one was watching her.

At that thought, she heard a rustling coming from one of the bushes. She turned to see what it was, but it was too dark. All she could see was the light from the fire shining to on the leaves. She held her breath and cocked her ear a bit, as though that would help her to hear something.

SNAP.

This came from another bush. Debbie had heard enough, there was something out there and it was circling her. She rushed to Mark's tent. Instinctively, she wanted the person that made her feel safe. That was Mark, and she didn't care if he had another girl in his tent. Pulling up the zip as quick as she could to gain entry, she could hear whatever the thing was rushing towards her. She turned to look.

Mark smiled as he felt legs straddle him once more. Melody was certainly the hottest girl he had ever been with, and this girl had one hell of an appetite on her. He wasn't sure if he was going to be able to manage to go again.

After the amount of alcohol he had consumed, he was surprised that he was able to go the first time, but with a body like Melody's, he thought, *she could even give the dead a rise.*

"You ready for round two?" he smiled, and opened his eyes.

234

Debbie's face was an inch away from his own. Her mouth gaped wide open as though she were screaming, but there was no sound. Her eyes were wide open with terror.

"*Debbie?*" Mark shouted.

Before he knew what was going on, Debbie had disappeared. She flew backwards out of the tent; again not a sound came from her. Mark rushed out of the tent. Debbie was nowhere to be seen. In fact, nothing looked wrong at all. The other tent was still zipped up as normal, and the fire was still burning. Everywhere was silent. Even the forest was sleeping.

"Man, that was some fucked up dream," Mark said to himself. "It seemed so real."

The quantity of beer that Mark had consumed suddenly began to rush up on him. He needed to empty his bladder and quickly. He jogged over to a bush that was just outside of their camping circle. Having his manhood hanging in the darkness made him feel on edge. *What if there was a something out there, waiting to attack him. What if it bit him?*

Something rustled in the bush beside him, causing him to turn in a panic and in doing so, urinate onto his own feet.

"Oh for God's sake," he snapped.

Looking toward the fire, he saw a small bat fly quickly through the circle. He had obviously disturbed it with his toilet trip. When he had finished, he walked back to the fire and grabbed one of the water bottles that they left nearby. He poured the water on his feet and then held them up near the fire to dry them off. After a few minutes, he decided that he was dry enough to return to bed, which was just as well because the cold was really starting to settle in. He wanted to get back in bed next to Melody. Just the thought of her warmed him up.

He unzipped the tent and crawled in. Melody sat up, holding the sleeping bag up to her neck.

"Where have you been?" she asked.

"I just had to go to the little boy's room."

"Well, hurry up and shut the door, I can feel the cold coming in."

"Yeah, it's freezing out there," Mark said as he zipped the door closed.

Melody let go of the sleeping bag. It fell down to her stomach and left her bare, perfect breasts exposed. Mark looked and smiled.

"I suppose I better warm you up then, hadn't I?" Melody gave a cheeky smile.

Melody was once again mounted on top of Mark. He had tried to keep her quiet, but her moans of pleasure echoed throughout the forest.

"Shhh," he laughed.

"Ah, fuck 'em. I want them to hear that I'm having a good time."

Melody continued to move back and forth. Mark lay on his back, wondering how long he was going to be able to keep this up for.

"Mark?" Keith called, from outside the tent.

"Shhh," Mark said to Melody. "Yeah . . . what is it?"

"Have you seen Debbie? She took off a while back, and she's still missing."

"Hang on."

Mark grabbed his clothes and put them on. He zipped open the door part way, leaving it closed enough for Melody to get dressed without being seen.

"What do you mean she took off?" he asked.

"Well, we had a little bit of an argument and she stormed off."

"What did you argue about?"

"She, erm . . . " Keith giggled. "She tried to have sex with me."

"*What?*" Mark said a little bit too loud. "Dude, doesn't she know that you're gay?"

"Well, she does now. Shit, I thought everyone knew. I've never hidden it."

Melody appeared from the tent door.

"What's going on?" she asked.

"Well . . . " Mark began to speak when a loud crack came from above them. A log about two metres wide crashed to the ground just a few feet away from them. Mark and Melody turned to look at Keith, who was highly animated, throwing his arms about, and his mouth was open as though he were yelling something, but no sound came from him. He was silent.

His eyes wide in terror, he pointed to his throat, in the centre of his neck, small splinters stuck out forming a circular shape.

"Keith," Mark asked. "What's wrong? What the hell is *going on?*"

A grunt came from beside Mark, and before he had time to react, something rushed passed him and carried Keith away, like he weighed nothing more than a mere rag doll. Mark didn't have chance to get a very good look at it, but he knew that whatever it was, it was big and green.

"We have to go, *right now!*" Mark called.

"Okay, I'll just grab my . . . "

"Forget your stuff, Melody. Run."

Mark grabbed Melody's hand and they started to sprint through the trees. He wasn't entirely sure of which direction he was headed, or where it led. All he knew was that he had to get as far away from that thing as he could. If it could carry Keith away so easily, then they weren't going to put up much of a fight.

His thoughts trailed back to his dream last night, when Debbie was screaming in his face, well, trying to scream No sound escaped her lips, just like Keith, before he was taken away. It wasn't a dream, whatever that thing is; it was taking their voice, and disabling their vocal chords.

Stopping them from crying for help.

Running as fast as he could, his hand gripping Melody's tight, and pulled her along. Mark could hear movement in the trees above him. He knew that whatever this thing was, it was tracking them down.

"We need to get out of here and find help."

No response came, Melody's pace began to lag, and she started to slow him down. Mark turned back to look at her, she was still trying to run with him, but her eyes were wide in panic. She was pointing to her neck. The same circle of splinters was embedded in her flesh. The thing was here.

"Oh shit," Mark exclaimed. "Oh shit, oh shit."

He stopped running and tried to pull the things from Melody's neck, but they appeared to be barbed and hooked in deep. He couldn't pull them free without tearing the skin.

Melody's mouth was moving frantically, but no sound came from it.

"Just calm down," Mark said. "I'll get these things . . . "

Melody smacked him in the face to get his attention. She pointed behind him.

Mark began to turn; a cold shiver of fear ran down his spine. He knew from the look on Melody's face that whatever this thing was, it was stood right behind him.

Once he had turned around, he looked up to the creature. It was like something straight out of a science fiction movie. Bigger than Mark had originally thought, this thing stood about seven feet tall, resembling what can only be described as a reptile. The face looked similar to that of a lizard, its eyes glowing red. Muscles seemed to be bursting from every limb and every inch of its abdomen. It began to raise an arm. Mark could see a circle of spikes slowly start to protrude from this thing's wrist.

"That's where they're coming from," he whispered.

Bracing himself for the moment that the spikes fired at him, and silenced him for good, Mark shut his eyes tight and flinched. He heard a thud and took a peek: the giant creature lay motionless in front of him on the floor. Thick red blood poured from the back of its head. Behind the creature stood a man. His clothes were old and ragged, he was very skinny, and he looked as though he'd been barely surviving out here in the wilderness for quite some time.

Mark's jaw dropped, he turned and hugged Melody in an embrace of joy.

Facing his saviour once again, Mark rushed to him and grabbed him in a big bear hug.

"You killed it. You saved our lives," Mark cried. "That thing was huge, how the hell were you able to stop it?"

The saviour held up a large stick, on the end of it was a rock, sharpened into a weapon. It resembled something tribal, primitive. Mark noted the creature's blood on the end of the weapon. The saviour began to draw something in the dirt below.

Mark and Melody approached, confused, still in shock. Melody was pulling at Mark's arm in a panic, still gesturing to her throat and her silence.

"Just, wait a second, Melody." He turned to the man. "What is it?" he asked.

Upon inspection Mark could see that the man was writing in the dirt, Mark gave him space until he had finished.

Once done the man stepped back, he gestured to his throat and then pointed to his writing in the dirt. It read, "It couldn't hear me coming."

FATHER

Richard Chizmar

THEY STAND AT the glass partition, side by side, arms at their sides, hands touching, staring at the man they refuse to call father. They study him, eyes unblinking. They appear as if they are trying not to smile.

The two men look like they could be twins—with their dark, curly hair, high cheekbones, and emerald eyes—but they are not. Twenty-two months separate their births.

The older son steps forward, presses his forehead against the cool glass, like an innocent adolescent anxious to spy the first fluttering flakes of a forecasted snowstorm outside his bedroom window. But neither of these men was ever young of heart or innocent of mind. Such things did not exist in their home.

The younger man remains in place. After a moment, he crosses his hands as if in prayer and says, "Do you remember the first time?"

"Like it was yesterday."

"All of our yesterdays."

The older son leans back from the glass and nods. "I was nine, you were seven . . . "

" . . . and we were at the beach house," his brother finishes.

"Mother remained at home in the city, presumably attending to some important business errand, but we both know He planned it that way. He wanted us to himself that weekend."

"We arrived on Friday evening and after we unpacked and had dinner—I remember we ate at the Bayside Inn; best crab cakes and lobster bisque on the coast—He surprised us by allowing us to play on the beach until sunset. I tried to build a sand castle, but the surf was too rough and kept washing it away. You collected seashells."

"I still have one of those shells. Hidden in my sock drawer."

"Celeste showed up the next morning, looking as perplexed as we were."

"We had three rotating housekeepers on duty in the city, but none of them had ever worked at the beach house. He used a local service for that."

"He told us to go into the playroom and not come out until He'd had a chance to speak with Celeste."

"We thought He was going to fire her. She had missed her bus the week before and come in ten minutes late. He'd been furious."

"But it was so much worse than that."

"The playroom at the beach house was one of the few pleasant memories I had of that time."

The younger son's lips twitch into something resembling a smile. It's a painful expression he doesn't often wear. "All those books and puzzles."

"The movie posters on the walls. And the miniature horses by the big bay window. What did we name them again?"

"Mine was Spirit. Yours was Thunder. I remember we would have races."

A snap of fingers. "That's right."

"The racetrack and the train set were my favorites. I would pretend I lived in one of the tiny houses which lined the tracks and fished off the little stone bridge."

"What about the stuffed dinosaurs? They were as big as we were."

A shake of the head. "I'd forgotten all about them."

"I noticed the cameras first. One tucked up high on the bookshelf, another smaller one attached to the ceiling in the corner, its red light blinking in the shadows."

"It wasn't until later that we learned He had hidden a half dozen cameras throughout the room."

244

"Before we could even investigate He brought in Celeste and explained the Game."

"She was smiling and nodding along with Him as he told us, but her eyes were puffy and shiny as if she had just finished crying."

"And she kept glancing over her shoulder at the open door."

"At first you didn't believe Him. You told Him so and He just laughed. But I knew He was serious. He never joked about His work."

"She screamed the first time I swung the hammer. And then she started praying."

"There was so much blood. Her foot was ruined."

"But she never said another word after that. Not when we switched to the pliers or the razor. She just made that grunting sound, almost like an animal."

"And she cried the whole time. I remember the silent tears on her blood-spattered cheeks. Like make-up running in the rain. And her eyes . . . I think her eyes were the worst."

"That look of betrayal."

"He didn't even stay in the room with us. Just barked out His instructions, left His tools, told us what would happen to mother if either of us disobeyed, and locked the door behind Him."

"We never had a choice, did we?"

A long moment of silence. Then: "Celeste was a tough lady."

"Yes. She was."

"I'm sure she was paid handsomely for her . . . efforts . . . and never had to clean another house in her lifetime."

"Would have been difficult with all that damage to her hands and feet."

"Indeed."

"I haven't thought of her in years."

"I have."

"When it was over, He came back into the room and shooed

us away. I remember we ran down to the beach and washed ourselves in the Atlantic."

"We couldn't stop crying."

"But at some point, the crying turned into laughter. We laughed and laughed, as if we had gone mad, and splashed each other in the waves."

"I wonder why that was."

"When we got back to the house later that afternoon, Celeste was gone."

"And the playroom was locked up tight. Not that I wanted to venture inside."

"Haven't stepped foot in that room since that day."

"I haven't either."

"Later he took us to dinner and talked about the meteor shower expected that night. He sat there and picked at his seafood pasta and acted like nothing had even happened."

"And he talked about the Red Sox game—do you remember that?—which was odd. He had never talked about sports before. At least with the two of us."

"Do you think he was nervous?"

"Doubtful."

"What then?"

"Probably bored . . . "

A slow, thoughtful nod, eyes pointed at the ground. " . . . and thinking about his next project."

"I know we promised each other not to . . . many times . . . but if there ever existed a day to admit such a thing, today is the day: I'm sorry, but I watched the video once."

A gasp. "Excuse me?"

"I stumbled upon it online one night when I couldn't sleep. I was drunk and angry. I couldn't believe my eyes when I read the description."

"And you actually watched it."

"Not all of it, but . . . enough."

"And?"

"It was heinous. I vomited in my office trashcan and turned it off. I haven't been tempted since."

"I've never been tempted. Not even once."

"Then you are most fortunate."

The two sons turn to each other, faces pale beneath their raven hair. Their eyes, identical bottomless pools of green, look sad and lost and angry.

But there are no tears.

Not for the man they refuse to call father.

And not for themselves.

VALLEY OF THE DUNES

Adam Light

"WHAT YOU SHOULD DO," said Larry, pointing a nicotine-stained finger at the ocean, "is pick a place on the horizon, and focus on it. Tune out the distracting noises around you, and suppress the arguing voices inside your own head for once. Listen to the surf as it meets the shore while you stare at the point where the sky meets the water. As everything else fades into the background, you will begin to understand just how insignificant your problems are in the grand scheme of things. It is a humbling feeling, and a truly liberating experience. I know it, because I learned how to do it a long time ago. It's the closest I've ever come to successfully meditating. Once I realized how fleeting everything really is, my stress level dropped straight through the floor."

Tanya nodded at Larry approvingly, only half-listening, while she daydreamed about swimming out as far as she could and then going even further to escape his incessant babbling. He was a great guy until he opened his mouth. He was good looking, but overtly obsessed with himself, thought he was the authority on every topic. He had been cool at first, but it had not taken long for her to discover he was the type she usually avoided.

She watched his lively gestures with a cool detachment she hoped he didn't notice, as his ravings became more pronounced, volume swelling as his monologue gained gravitas. While Larry's animated energy and passion may have been positive characteristics, he was too nihilistic to be very interesting. A feeling spread through her, sharp and bitter like a sudden winter squall whipping through a snow-blanketed aspen forest. It was the feeling she got when she knew she was going to be forced into breaking off another relationship. More and more lately, she was tasked with ending these things. She was becoming a professional break-up artist. Why did she always have to do it? Was that the important question? Did it matter?

Simple, she told herself. You swim through the schools of colorful fish, oblivious to the sea of possibility around you, and zero in on the camouflaged losers that blend in almost perfectly with the normal ones. Then there were the ones that at first seem like they are down-to-earth and have their shit together until they show their true colors, proving to be mentally or verbally abusive, insecure douche bags, sociopaths, or plain creepy assholes. Either way, they never wanted to go away. They all fell tails over nose for her.

She longed for just one of them to say, "It isn't you, it's me," or "I never want to see you again. Please don't call." It was depressing, always being the bad guy. Still, she did derive a certain modicum of satisfaction from ending the relationships, if she was telling the truth. She could not pretend that she didn't enjoy the process in her own twisted way. There were plenty of fish in the ocean, but the one she was looking for felt like it was about to become the one that got away, so at the very least she could balance the scales with the pleasure of ending things.

Larry had taken this relationship to the point of no return, so it was him, not her. He would never go away on his own, and she knew it.

She had already met someone else, anyway. She was going out with Todd Reynolds on Friday night, maybe he would be different. It was the first time she'd made two dates so close together. Though she knew juggling men was wrong, it was an activity that she had recently realized was not beneath her.

She was pushing thirty and her urge to settle down, start a family and feel comfortable in life for a change was beginning to alter her in various and surprising ways. A couple of years ago, dating two men simultaneously would've made her feel slutty.

Nancy, a coworker at the bank, was constantly dating, and the rotation of prospective mates was a complex narrative Tanya had once tried to keep up with but had finally stopped trying. Tanya was dead certain Nancy had doubled, even tripled down on her dates for the weekend at times.

She had once thought Nancy to be a loose, easy woman, but now she felt she understood the girl's motivations. How often did one meet the person of their dreams or fall in love on the first date? One had to spread oneself around to meet the optimum number of potential partners if one ever hoped to meet stringent expectations.

By Friday, she knew Larry would be nothing but a fading memory and she'd be on to the next in an endless procession of lousy potential mates.

Shit happens, she thought, but felt remorseful already. She really liked Larry.

Minus the endless philosophizing.

And his smoking habit.

That was the worst thing. Every other minor annoyance paled in comparison to the man stinking like an ashtray twenty-four-seven. She had convinced him to start chewing gum and wearing cologne, but those steps did little to mask the foul bouquet that accompanied him everywhere he went.

The sun was sinking close to the waterline, the ocean lit up as brilliant rays colored the surface, a million golden shimmers of light dazzling her eyes, making her look away, right into Larry's tirade.

"So, you're a lot like me, I think," he was saying, "in ways not a lot of people tend to be alike. In fact, I've never felt that anyone was so like me and my way of thinking before I met you. It's true. I can see your 'fuck the world' mentality because you wear it like a smoking jacket, for Christ's sake."

He shook his head and laughed, a not too unpleasant display of his good looks, sadly the very thing that had attracted her to him in the first place, but not enough upon which to build a meaningful relationship with another person.

"Let's go out into the water and give the sunset the finger." He suggested, still laughing a little, but unfortunately, dead serious about the suggestion. He knew how to ruin a good thing, she didn't deny him that much.

"If you want us to go act like imbeciles, I'm down." She replied, hoping he would change his mind, but knew it was the last stupid act in which she'd partake with Larry.

The beach had been mildly bustling up until the last half hour. Now, they were alone save a couple strolling lazily along the surf line, the young man kicking wet sand with his toes with nearly every step, his girl elbow-locked to him, gazing admiringly as the sun set behind him.

A real postcard moment, she thought.

She couldn't wait for them to move far enough along that they were no longer likely to hear her and Larry going about their shenanigans.

A pang of regret hit as she followed Larry down to the water. He wasn't all that bad. He liked to act stupid, and he was perpetually pontificating about how everyone is just a dream within someone else's head, or how the universe hated everyone, and was eventually going to suck the whole mess into oblivion a billion light years away, through a black hole or whatever, but he wasn't the worst guy she'd ever dated. Regardless, their time together was dropping as quickly as the sun, the ocean preparing to eat it for the night. Smaller and smaller.

The doomed couple, as she now considered the two of them,

splashed around and made lewd gestures at the last sliver of sun before the darkness enwrapped them and Tanya grew chilly. Tired of the antics, she made her way back to dry land, Larry close on her heels.

The young couple she'd seen walking earlier was long gone. As the tide came in, it erased their footprints, taking with it all traces the two had ever existed. Tanya was happy they were gone.

She was tired, and hungry.

She hated to end it with Larry, but she was reluctant to squander any more of her precious time in his company.

"Larry?"

She batted her eyelashes in his direction.

He noticed, and shot her a toothy grin, giving his features a lupine appearance for a moment.

No moon shone above. Though a dazzling array of stars adorned the black heavens, the beach was blanketed with a dead void. Even the barrier dunes, only twenty or thirty yards away, were hard to pick out behind their spot on the sand.

"Yes, Tanya?" Larry asked in return.

"I have something I want to tell you."

"Okay." His smile grew even wider this time. In the gloom, it looked as though something had crawled onto his face and stretched out for a nap.

She took a breath and readied herself for the spiel, but he interrupted before she could begin.

"Before you say anything," he blurted, "I want to tell you something, too."

He looked away towards the ocean, heard more than seen now, its constant rhythm a surcease for Tanya's mind as Larry began prattling again.

When he looked at her again, his eyes were moist. She could tell, even if she could barely see his features. "I've been thinking about you and me, I guess. You see, I think you and I are great together, Tanya, and I'm ready to ratchet our relationship up to the next level."

Before she could process this, he added "Move in with me, Tanya."

Once he said it, she saw him visibly relax, and suddenly realized he'd been rather tense throughout the day. Now she knew why. Though his proclamation was touching, his idea of where the two of them were heading couldn't have been further from reality.

She felt bad, but she smiled at him anyway. Beamed at him, really. Opened her eyes as wide as she could and positively grinned from ear to ear. In the dark, she wanted to be sure he knew what he was seeing. It was terrible, but she was overcome with the feeling that making him think she was excited about his idea was the right move.

His reaction was nothing short of what she anticipated from him. His posture changed. He swelled with accomplishment, his confidence increasing until he nearly toppled over backward with the magnitude of it.

It was all too much. Tanya erupted with laughter, so contagious Larry found himself swept away in his own giddy excitement, unwittingly misunderstanding the nature of her mirth.

When they both settled down enough to allow for an attempt at communication, Larry's voice was conspiratorial. "Do you feel like going back in the dunes for a little while?"

Without a second to think about it, she grabbed Larry's hand and hauled him after her as she took off for the privacy of the dunes.

His hand was warm, damp, and his grip faltered after their momentum took them halfway up the first dune and then flagged, requiring more endurance than he possessed. Before Larry could drop and slide back down the side of the dune, she tugged him, harder than she meant. Her effort jerked his body along behind her. He managed to get his feet back to where they belonged as they crested the barrier dune and descended without pause down the other side into the pitch-black darkness of the valley between the dunes.

The perfect place to enjoy some privacy, she thought.

Out of breath from exertion, Larry bent over to grab his knees, trying to get his wind back. Tanya came up close to him, rubbing his back for a moment to show solidarity. Soon enough, Larry was himself again. As soon as he was fully composed he began the act of losing his composure again. His hands fumbled at her swimming top, and one of his knees worked her legs apart enough to position itself between them.

Tanya gently grabbed Larry's chin and pulled his face close to hers, until their noses were kissing. "Larry, you're perfect for me," she whispered.

His eagerness was all too evident. He nodded enthusiastically before going in for a kiss. She allowed his mouth to do its thing the first time. He tried again and she held up one of her hands to halt him. "Easy, big fella."

He backed off and through the murk she felt him staring impatiently at her. "I wasn't finished, Larry. I said you're perfect for me, and I meant it. In this moment, we live in the same space and time. We are one, Larry. Can you feel that? Isn't it beautiful?"

He was growing ever more restless, and demonstrated that fact by placing a hand on her breast, massaging it roughly. He was getting overheated.

She decided that she had to do what was required of her now. Damn, it was bittersweet, ending things.

"Larry," she said, "I want to devour your heart and mind with my love. Do you want my love to devour you?"

"Yes!" He was emphatic.

"Good. I never thought this would go any further than here, but this is perfect. Don't you think?"

"What are you talking about?" His tone was pleasant, but she sensed irritation. He was absolutely sweating sexual tension. It was intoxicating.

"This place, silly. I love it here. It's perfect for this. I mean, for what's about to *go down*."

He grinned, and his tone was lascivious when he replied. "And please do tell me what, or who, *is* about to go down around here. You or me first?"

With a practiced twitch of her neck muscles, and the aid of a sultry moan, she unhinged her jaws. "I'm breaking up with you, Larry," she said.

"Okay, whatever, get your ass over here." he chuckled. Then he made his move, grabbing her, drawing her into him, wrapping his arms around her with a smothering embrace.

Damn, she thought. *Guy's trying to fucking absorb me.*

The way he'd positioned her couldn't have been better. Larry was about six inches shorter than Tanya, and his cranium was almost perfectly aligned with her chin.

"It isn't you, it's me," she moaned in his ear, pushing his head down ever so slightly, correcting the angle. She opened her mouth to its full capacity, revealing her special teeth as she took the first bite. It perfectly removed the top of Larry's skull, leaving his warm brain shockingly exposed, but intact.

She held Larry up at arm's length from her, and appraised him. His face was drawn, gaunt, mouth working like it was filled with words so devastating that their very utterance would shift the planet on its axis. Suddenly, his face was sheeted in crimson as his heart pumped with deadly force in that dark valley. The blood that had circulated for so long within Larry's body was now set free to flow where it would, to soak into the sand and evaporate. Though not easy to make out in the dim light, the look

258

of horror etched onto Larry's drawn face was one she would remember for years to come, one of the best she'd ever created.

She pitied him in that moment, though he warranted none and the moment passed quickly enough. He was the lucky one, after all. The dating scene was a nightmare, and he was better off removed from its unrelenting repetitiveness. At any rate, he wasn't very good at it.

Had he really thought she'd move in with him after a handful of dates? That kind of move was never going to work, and if it ever did, the poor desperate girl who fell for it would end up miserable.

Larry's mouth finally stopped moving, and she shook herself free from her reverie to get down to business. She needed to hurry, so Larry wouldn't get cold before she consumed him.

An hour later, Tanya emerged from the darkness of the dunes, walked back to her car and drove the five miles to her apartment. Although relatively clean after taking a second dip in the ocean, she was still salty and needed a shower. She was exhausted, lethargic, but utterly fulfilled. Larry may not have been the best boyfriend, but he made an incredible meal.

Later in bed, she turned on her cell phone and a voice mail notification pinged. It was Todd Reynolds, calling about their upcoming date. He wondered how she felt about taking a stroll on the beach after the restaurant. The weather this weekend was supposed to be perfect.

Tanya thought about the valley of the dunes and smiled. Despite how engorged she currently was, she felt herself getting hungry again already.

THE GREEN MAN OF FREETOWN

Curtis M. Lawson

CREATURES OF THE NIGHT

"I DON'T CARE what they charged him with. He's a murderer. He killed my little girl! He killed my grandson!"

The scathing accusations of his father-in-law are just static mumbles to Charlie Jacobs. They barely exist, same as the iron shackles around his ankles and wrists.

"He's a murderer, and you shouldn't ever let him out!"

Charlie is in another place and another time. Wholesome smells like storm-born ozone, and wildflowers replace the rancid piss, sweat, and disease that permeates even into the rooms outside of general population.

"Thank you, Mr. Reilly," someone from the parole board says, politely informing the grieving old man that he's said enough. He doesn't argue, but begins to weep.

Charlie gazes down at the cement floor. It is hidden beneath memories of bare, muddy earth. His name is called and he looks up. Even when he tries to be in the here and now, the cramped dimensions of the hearing room are lost to sylvan walls of maples and oaks.

"Do you have anything to say to the parole board, Mr. Jacobs?"

Scripted words, bullshit platitudes that his lawyer wrote, roll off Charlie's tongue. The tears that run down his face are genuine, however. They fall into the blood and mud at his feet.

He spews more insincerities. Lies about the grace of god and incidental confessions of humility. A trail of gore, diluted by the torrential rain, leads off into the darkness between the trees. Something moves in those heavy shadows—a monster, or a ghost.

The prison chaplain is the next to speak. He testifies about

263

Charlie's character, his dedication to biblical study, and his record of good behavior.

Charlie squints, trying to make out the creature hidden behind the veil of shadow and rainfall. Something stumbles out from the darkness. It's his wife, Amber, but broken and ruined. Her face is painted with mud, blood, and bruises, her blonde hair streaked with crimson.

"If granted parole, Mr. Jacobs, do you have a plan for reintegrating into society?"

His son cries out for him from beyond the tree line. A hand with scaled, waxen skin reaches out from the shadows and grabs Amber by the hair. "This isn't how it happened," she says in a monotone voice at odds with her expression of abject terror.

"I do, sir." Charlie says aloud. "I have a plan".

A green highway sign declares that Freetown State Park is two exits away. This stretch of road should be familiar to Charlie, but it isn't. In the light of day, beneath a cloudless, powder blue sky, it looks benign. Fresh blacktop and crisp, white lines stretch on to the horizon. There's no roadkill smeared across the lanes. Not even so much as the blown-out corpse of a tire on the side of the road.

When he last took this drive it had been dark as the devil's soul. Charcoal clouds had obscured the moon and cried black rain tears over the asphalt.

He looks in the rearview and ponders how much older he looks now. The last six years took a toll on him. His eyes are vacant, framed by crow's feet. His beard is more white than blonde, the same as his hair. Scars he earned on the inside mar his face.

Another four miles pass and Charlie buzzes by exit 38. Some pop song he's never heard, something that came out while he was behind bars, plays on the radio, but he doesn't hear it. He's humming "The Sweater Song", out of tune and out of time with the number coming from the speakers. It was what they had listened to last time. They sang it loud and discordant, with joyous abandon. An anthem of resistance against the darkness and the storm.

Charlie flinches as the highway merges with a small bridge. Below the bridge and to either side, forest stretches out for miles. The paint on the guardrails is inconsistent. Faded mint with spots of orange rust gives way to John Deere green, then back to mint. Tears obscure his vision as he drives across. In the time it takes him to blink them away, he's over the bridge, and further down the highway than the three of them had ever made it.

Charlie's car is parked several miles back. It took almost an hour of hiking along trails, and then another through untamed forest to find his way to this clearing. He looks up at the highway overpass that bridges the canyon. The sinking sensation of freefall makes him nauseous as he looks up at the steel framework.

Shaking off sickness and vertigo, Charlie turns his attention to the ground. The soil is dry and thirsty. Rich colors fill up the landscape—dark brown earth, jade foliage, and flowers of the deepest scarlet and azure.

Despite the familiar bridge above, he second guesses if he's found the right place. He finds proof in the hard-packed earth, however. Jagged stumps of broken saplings. Half buried shards of safety glass. Bits of broken plastic, all translucent, tail light red.

A tarnished hood ornament—a rust and chrome ram's head jutting out of the dirt, like a sphinx lost to the desert sands.

Charlie crouches down and rubs the ram's horns, the same way Ash would before every car ride.

"Have you seen my boy?" Charlie asks the hood ornament.

It does not respond.

"He's here somewhere. I need to find him."

The chrome idol rests stoically, and Charlie sighs. He prayed the ram would break its silence. He needs an ally.

The forest was full of devils, despite the illusion of serenity it presently wore. Charlie had researched the place in depth during his trial and his stay in prison. Stories abounded in regards to Freetown. Ghosts of angry natives and murdered settlers wandered between the trees. Sirens called men and women to suicide. Witches lived in caves and hollows.

Charlie falls to his knees before the rusted, chrome totem. He begs it for guidance.

"I know you saw what happened," he breathes. "Whatever stole my son, just tell me where it took him."

His only answer is the call of birds and the buzz of insects.

Charlie falls onto his back and screams at the clear, taunting sky. His fist bangs against the hard the earth and comes up bloody. He looks at his hand, then the ground. Broken glass surrounds an outcropping of golden, funnel shaped mushrooms.

Charlie picks one and examines it. It gives off a sweet, subtle smell like apricot. Like his wife's perfume.

He stands and notices more patches of the same mushrooms. They form a sparse trail into the tree line. The world turns dark and wet in the blink of an eye and the trail of mushrooms is replaced with a stream of watered-down blood, then everything is bright and dry again.

The gaze of the ram's head is set in the direction of the golden fungi, and Charlie knows which way he has to go. He thanks the hood ornament aloud, bites into the mushroom in his hand, and follows the others into the trees.

The mushroom doesn't taste like it smells. Not like apricots, nor like his wife. It has a subtle, peppery flavor, along with a hint of copper from his own blood drizzled over it. Charlie wonders if he should be eating it, or if it will make the other mushrooms angry. Will they shuffle around, leading him away from the truth?

He shrugs off the absurd thought and continues along the mushroom trail for miles. He grimaces at every tree root or rock which interrupts the path. Did Amber's skull smash against these protrusions as she was dragged? Was Ash's flesh lacerated by unflinching stone and uncaring wood?

"Don't leave us," Amber mumbles, and Charlie isn't sure if her words are being whispered in his ear or in his memory. Up ahead the golden trail of fungus stops. Charlie half expects to see his wife waiting at the end, even though she is years dead. Instead he catches familiar bits of geography. He's never been this far in the Freetown woods, but he recognizes certain landmarks from courtroom pictures. The fieldstone foundation of a long abandoned cabin. A rusted bootleggers still half buried in the dirt. The dead husk of a tree with an inverted cross carved in the bark.

"This is where they found you," Charlie mumbles, as he drops to his knees and runs his fingers along a rust-colored stain on the foundation. The dim light filtering through the lush canopy above vanishes. The bird songs and insect buzzing of summer gives way to the patter of raindrops, and Charlie feels the rain running down his cheeks. It's warmer than it should be, but he gives it no thought.

On the ground before him lays Amber. Mud and rain mix with the blood in her shredded belly. Brackish water pools out of her open mouth, like a broken, morbid fountain. The blue of

267

her eyes, normally so startling in their richness, seem dull juxtaposed against the crimson of burst blood vessels.

Yards away, a song plays in the trees. It's "The Sweater Song", but slow and uneven in pitch, like a warped record played at half speed. Charlie stares into the tree line, and he sees a figure in coarse, earth-tone robes. Beside the robed figure is a little boy in Ash's clothes. His back is turned to Charlie and he stands deathly still.

The thing in the robes places a hand on Ash's shoulder, but it is no human appendage. The fingers are a rich green, and covered in overlapping scales. No, not scales, Charlie thinks. It's even further removed from man than that. More like the bracts of an artichoke. Its face is hidden by storm and by the shadows of its hood, but golden whiskers, like stalks of barley, poke through the shadows. Charlie can't see its eyes, but he knows it stares at him, challenging him.

A gurgling sound comes from Amber's corpse. A bubble forms in the water in her mouth. It pops and releases a word into the air.

"This . . ."

Another bubble forms and pops.

"Isn't . . ."

Charlie looks back into the tree line. The robed figure is gone, and so is Ash. The warped music still plays in the forest ahead, though.

Pop.

"How . . ."

Charlie jumps to his feet, his heart in his throat.

Pop.

"It . . ."

He doesn't give his wife another glance, nor the opportunity to finish saying her piece. The light of the real, present day world nearly blinds him as the darkness retreats into his mind and soul.

Charlie can't see the robed monster through the flora, but branches whip and leaves tremble in its wake. He follows into the woods, and his mind fractures.

He is in simultaneously in two different places and two different times. Unrelenting sheets of water assault his windshield as he drives through the ghosts of night and storm, all the while he gives chase through daylight summertime forest of the present. He and his family sing along with Rivers Cuomo on the radio, while a mockery of the same music echoes through the trees. The smell of beer, cigarettes, and vanilla air freshener fill his senses in one reality, while the scents of pine and dead leaves dominate the other.

He's aware of both. Experiencing both moments as one.

The grade of the earth steepens ahead of him, and Charlie rushes recklessly downward. In another place and time he presses down heavier on a gas pedal. Amber tells him to slow down. Her words carry from the past into the present, but he heeds them in neither. A moment later his foot catches on a tree root and his tires lose traction on the bridge.

Charlie tumbles down the hill, collecting bruises and laceration. The thirsty soil sups upon his spilled blood.

The Ram crashes through the guard rail. An airbag explodes out from the steering column and breaks Charlie's nose as the vehicle careens into the canyon below.

He rolls to a stop at the bottom of the hill in the summertime forest. Nothing feels broken, but he's lost his wind and can't stand.

In the noontide storm, he is met with an explosion of glass, and omnipresent pain. The radio is still playing, indifferent to Amber's pained moaning. But Ash . . . Ash is too quiet.

Unable to stand, or even breathe, Charlie sees the monster clad in burlap robes. It's crouched over his son, holding him down with dendritic appendages. Slurping and ripping sounds echo off the trees, not lost beneath a warped, droning song decrying that the singer has come undone.

Charlie cuts the engine and the song dies. He calls to his son in the backseat while pushing away the deflating airbag, but Ash doesn't respond. He doesn't even whimper, or cry. Looking behind him, he sees the back window next to Ash smashed, and the boy's face is a scarlet mask.

Breath returns to his lungs, and Charlie screams for the monster to get away from his boy. It looks up at Charlie, giving the man a clear view of his son. The child's features are shredded and torn beneath a crimson wash. His beautiful little boy is barely recognizable.

"I need to go get help," Charlie mutters, struggling to open the driver's side door. Amber begs him, between labored breaths, not to leave them. Her voice holds something greater than desperation. The severity of her tone frightens him to his bones.

The monster throws back its coarse, tan hood. What lies beneath is more flora than fauna—a mockery of Charlie's own face, sculpted from hops and nettles, with a beard of golden barley. Blood drips down its chin and covers its lush, green hands.

Charlie drags them both out of the wreckage. Amber screams in pain as he clumsily pulls her from the passenger side door and lays her in the mud. Ash is quiet and still.

"You killed my family!" Charlie screams at his floral doppelgänger. "This isn't how it happened," the thing replies, in a slurred voice. Even from yards away, Charlie can smell the scent of blood and fermentation on its breath. His thoughts get fuzzy and a subtle vertigo sets in.

The mud gives way under Charlie's feet as he scrambles up the incline of the canyon. The steep walls shrug him off, indifferent to his desperation. His buzz is gone, but his motor skills are a wreck, whether from trauma or drink he isn't sure.

He screams for help as blood loss and exhaustion knock him to the ground. Cradled by the wet earth and blanketed by the storm, he reluctantly drifts into unconsciousness.

"This isn't how it happened," Charlie mumbles into the mud of six years past and at the monster before him in the here and now.

"Oh, but it is, Charlie," the Green Man replies.

"No! You dragged them away and murdered them!" There are tears running down his cheeks as he cries out the accusation.

"You killed them, Charlie, and coyotes dragged them away while you slept it off."

Charlie mumbles, "no," over and over again, shaking his head as if the gesture will make the word true.

Coldness washes over his body and he finds himself alone, a bottle pressed to his lips. He sits at the bottom of a hill, in a patch of golden mushrooms with his back to an ash tree. A face stares at him from the label on his bottle—a Celtic Green Man with a grim expression.

Through the trees he hears Amber and Ash, both begging him not to leave. He swigs down the rest of his beer, smashes the bottle against the ground, then leans back and lets the cold buzz overtake him.

"I'll never leave you again."

With a terrible calm he grips the neck of the broken bottle and plunges its jagged edge into his own throat. He falls over, next to the shattered glass. From the beer's paper label the Green Man watches Charlie die, its severe gaze softening as his blood sates the soil.

The Worms Turn

Frank Oreto

CREATURES OF THE NIGHT

"HE WAS COMPLETELY NAKED. I know he has a privacy fence and it's his property. Still, it was a bit of a shock." After the divorce, Nell had sworn she'd never talk to Ted again. *But voicemail doesn't quite count, does it?* Except of course it did. Ted would listen eventually. Maybe play it for his new girlfriend, Kelli or Kerry, whatever she was called.

"Get a load of this. The ex has finally gone around the bend."

But no one could blame me, Nell thought. *You had to call someone when your neighbor turns out to be a monster. And he seemed so nice.*

Mr. Harrah had stood there, naked as the day he was born. Nell just knew he would gaze up at the bathroom window and catch her staring. The thought made her breath catch in her chest, but she couldn't look away. Instead of turning his head, Mr. Harrah opened his mouth wide and vomited out a shower of worms.

The worms, thousands of them, not only came out of Mr. Harrah, they were Mr. Harrah. His flesh parted in long thin tendrils, crawling over each other. Nell stood there a good five minutes watching what had been her solid looking neighbor dissolve into a writhing mass. The worms roiled in a low heap under the moonlight and then disappeared into the dark soil.

"He has the most beautiful plants in his yard," Nell said into the phone. "That's why I was looking down over the fence. You know worms are quite good for—" *You're babbling, Nell,* she told herself. The voicemail cut off with a sharp little chirp. Nell hit redial and waited through three rings and Ted saying, "We can't come to the phone right now." Was that a woman giggling in the background? When the tone sounded, Nell found she had nothing left to say.

Some things she hadn't mentioned. Like how she had only just stepped from the shower when she first saw Mr. Harrah. And how their shared nudity had made her stomach feel full of warm honey, that is, until he'd changed. No, some details you did not share with your ex-husband.

"But why call Ted at all?" She asked herself. *Habit?* After fifteen years of marriage, it would make sense, but she suspected something darker. Ted had been a bully and a tyrant. It was his decision she shouldn't get a job, and that children for a woman as fragile as Nell were out of the question. But she'd gone along with it. Grown to depend on him making decisions, so she didn't have to.

When Ted left, Nell had been terrified, believing herself to be the hothouse flower he'd wanted. But instead of withering, she'd flourished. Finding work, first as office manager at a local architecture firm, then parlaying her—'useless' according to Ted—English degree into a more lucrative position ghostwriting the firm's business proposals. She had friends now, and colleagues who valued her opinion. "You panicked that's all. So, you ran back to the one person who would be happy to tell you what to do." For a moment a wave of self-disgust rivaled Nell's fear. She shook her head. Nothing could make her go back to living that way. Not even a monster next door.

Nell sat in her kitchen. A practical place, neat and orderly. A good place to think. What next, the police? *Hello, I need to report that my neighbor is what . . . a were-worm? He has a lovely garden, but the whole worm thing scares the shit out of me. Could you pop over and talk to him?* They'd have her committed.

Nell's skin prickled into gooseflesh. What if Mr. Harrah had seen her? What if he came over to shut her up? She ran to the front door and turned the deadbolt, for all the good it would do. In her imagination, a sea of worms already crashed against the house in pink fleshy waves. Long sinuous shapes pushed themselves through hidden gaps in the construction. *Do worms have teeth?*

"He never looked up," Nell said aloud. "He was too busy . . . coming apart."

The doorbell rang.

Nell's hand shot to her mouth, stifling a scream.

There was a pause then the sound of knuckles rapping wood.

"Ms. Phillips. It's George Harrah from next door." The knuckles rapped again.

Nell counted to five, drawing a deep silent breath with each number.

"Ms. Phillips, I can see your shadow on the curtain."

Shit. "It's late, Mr. Harrah, What can I do for you?"

"I wanted to apologize. Um, for the little show I put on earlier? I didn't think anyone could see into my yard. The night seemed so pleasant. I don't know what came over me. I'm really not in the habit of going outside stark naked."

"I didn't see anything," said Nell, hoping Harrah couldn't hear the panic in her voice. "I don't know what you're talking about."

"Oh. I could have sworn I saw you looking down at me from that little side window."

"No. Now I really must get to bed. Good night, Mr. Harrah." Nell listened for departing footsteps, but none came.

"I think you did see me, Ms. Phillips. How long were you watching?" His voice sounded more tired than threatening. But maybe that's how monsters sound right before they attack. This was all new territory.

"Shut up, can't you just shut up and go?" This time no one could have missed the broken sob she spoke around.

"Aw hell," said Harrah. "That long. We need to talk."

"I called the police."

There was a long pause. "No, I don't think you did. They

277

would have been here by now. I think you're still in the 'am I nuts?' phase. Or worried anyone you call will think you are. Why don't you come out on the porch? It's weird talking through the door like this."

"Talking through a door is weird?" A bark of involuntary laughter escaped Nell's throat. "I don't think it even makes the scale tonight." She would call the police if he didn't leave soon. They could take her to whatever mental hospital was closest. Maybe she'd be safe there.

"I see your point. Listen, please. I'm not a monster. I'm just different. I'm no danger to you."

His words and the sheer stress of the situation snapped Nell's careening feelings into focused anger. "Bullshit," she said.

"What?"

Nell gritted her teeth. She attached the chain, pushed the door open a few inches and glared out at George Harrah. "I said bullshit."

He wore clothes now at least. The tan trousers and sweater vest made him seem more like an English professor than something from a horror story, but Nell knew better. "I saw what you are, or what you become. But even if you were just some guy from down the street, you're standing on my porch refusing to leave. Telling me, you're not going to hurt me. I've seen this shit on the news. I know how it ends."

Then George Harrah did something unexpected. He blushed from the top of his bald head to the collar of his blue, button-down shirt. "I'm . . . I'm." His mouth hung open for a moment. "I'm so sorry. You're right, of course. I'm going back to my house." He paused in mid-turn, raising his hands open-palmed toward Nell. "I like it here, Ms. Phillips. I like my house, the neighborhood. I don't want to leave." There were tears in the tall man's eyes.

"Go home, Mr. Harrah."

Harrah nodded. "Goodnight, Ms. Phillips."

Nell watched him walk back to his house and go inside. Then she stuffed towels under all the doors on the first floor. After those hardly adequate protections, she made herself tea, sat in the kitchen, and thought. It was a very long night.

Nell's head snapped up, springing from sleep to panicked alertness. She yanked her stiff legs from the kitchen tiles, seeing a floor seething with worms until she'd blinked the dream visions from her eyes. "I'm alive," she said. "That's something at least." Her laptop lay open on the counter. A magnified image of a Lumbricus Terrestris filled the screen. She shuddered. It turned out earthworms didn't have teeth after all. Somehow the fact didn't make her feel any better.

She waited until 10:00. It was a Saturday and people were out now. Mrs. Henderson mowing her front lawn, kids riding by on their bikes. Nell walked over to Mr. Harrah's house and knocked on the door. She wore long sleeves despite the summer heat, and her twill trousers were tucked into knee-high boots. The clothes made her feel safer somehow.

Harrah answered her knock so fast she suspected he'd been waiting for her.

"Ms. Phillips," he said. "Thank you."

"For what?"

"I'm just glad it's you. Not the police or some reporter."

"It's early yet," Nell said. "Torches and pitchforks look better at night."

"I'm hoping that's a joke."

"Only a little. I'm in a tough position here, Mr. Harrah."

Harrah nodded. "Do you want some tea?"

"No, just answers. And we talk out here on the porch."

"Of course."

They sat at the glass-topped patio table and stared at each other.

"What do you want to know?" he asked.

"What are you?"

"I grew up on a farm in Iowa."

"That's not what I asked."

"No," said Harrah. "But if you want to know about me. You're going to hear how we're alike, not just the worm stuff."

"Fine."

"I'm thirty-nine years old. We probably grew up playing the same games, eating frosted flakes for breakfast."

"And watching Captain Kangaroo, I get it. You're an all-American boy. But what else are you? Are there more of you?"

"I don't have any brothers or sisters. Reproduction is difficult for people like me. I was an accident. It was only my father and me growing up."

"Are you going to kill me?"

"Jesus. I may not be human, but I'm not a werewolf. No claws or fangs. It's just, on a pretty regular basis, I need to transform into my other state."

"Worms."

"Yes, sort of. Certainly, like worms. I don't lose myself. I'm still me when I change. There's just a lot of . . . me."

"You don't talk about this much, do you?"

"Of course not. And no one really explained it to me either. My father was more a 'do as I do' sort of guy. He'd rather I'd never left the farm. Bottom line is, I'm a thinking, feeling person just like you. I run a lawn and garden service. I pay taxes. Watch the Super Bowl every year. I'm not a monster. I'm just different. And I don't want to be some government lab experiment. Or be burned as a witch. And if you spread around what you saw, that's going to happen. So, tell me now, so I can pack my very human Ford pick-up and start over somewhere else."

Nell stared at him for a long moment. She actually felt a little sorry for him. *How did I become the bad guy here?* she thought.

280

"Well?"

"You own a lawn service? Isn't that sort of cheating?" Nell chuckled. It was all too ridiculous.

Harrah sat frozen for a moment then a reluctant grin spread across his face. "Well, I like to think I'm working to my strengths."

Nell laughed in earnest. When she'd finished and wiped her eyes, she still hadn't made up her mind about George Harrah. But for the life of her, she couldn't feel afraid of the man. "This might be horribly naive on my part, but I'm not ready to drive you out of your home." Nell stood and moved to the steps." And, I have more questions."

"Of course," said Harrah.

Halfway to her yard, Nell remembered the frantic phone call to Ted the night before. "Uh-oh." She called again that night. Got his voice mail. "Ted, it's Nell. I wanted to apologize for my call last night. Turns out it was only a nightmare." As she spoke, Nell looked out the window at the wooden fence surrounding Harrah's backyard. Wondering if he was there and if he was himself. "I feel so silly. Sorry to have bothered you. Say hi to Kelli" She cut the connection. "Say hi to Kelli?" she repeated and shook her head. "What the hell is wrong with me?"

On Sunday afternoon there was a knock on the door. Nell thought it might be her neighbor until a key turned in the lock. She snatched open the door to reveal her ex-husband, Ted, in the doorway. "You aren't supposed to have a key," she said.

"Well, hello to you too. I kept a copy in case of emergencies. Like when my wife calls in the middle of the night about monsters."

Ted's blonde hair swept straight back now instead of parting at the side. Blue jeans replaced the business casual khakis he'd always favored. He looked fit and tan. Kelli must be the outdoorsy type.

"I want that key," Nell said.

"Fine. And I want an explanation. And maybe a thank you for driving out here to make sure you're okay." He slid the house key along the ring as he spoke until it came off in his hand.

"I called you back. It was only a nightmare."

"So, my wife is hallucinating naked neighbors who turn into worms. Oh no, nothing to worry about there."

"That's the second time you called me your wife. It's ex-wife, Ted. Or did the whole divorce thing slip your mind? How does Kelli feel about you checking up on me?"

"It's Kerri. And she can think whatever she damn well pleases. A man has responsibilities."

There was anger in Ted's voice and not toward her. Trouble in paradise maybe, not that Nell cared. She almost told him where he could stick his responsibilities. But instead began to feel guilty. Ted had that effect on her. No matter how much of an asshole he acted like, he believed he was being noble. In a twisted, selfish way he cared.

"Let's not fight." Nell walked out and sat on the porch steps. Patting a spot beside her. Ted joined her. "I'm really all right," she said.

"Not a monster then?"

Nell sighed. "George is a very nice man."

"George is it? Are you dating?"

Nell's shoulders slumped. She bit her lip and counted to five before answering. "You don't get to ask me that, Ted. Thanks for coming out, but you should go now."

He stood. "Fine. I think about you, Nell. You know that? We had some good times."

"Leave the key. Ted."

Ted opened his hand, and the house key fell on the step.

Over the next few weeks, Nell had more conversations with George Harrah. On his porch or sometimes her own. At first, they were almost interrogations.

"What does changing feel like?"

"It hurts actually, quite a bit in fact. But after, when I'm no longer singular, it feels . . . amazingly freeing."

As weeks turned into months, the conversations changed. They talked less about George's condition and more about everyday life. How Nell's office politics were going. The odd customers George dealt with in his lawn business. And about Ted.

Nell told George about her calls after she'd witnessed his transformation. And about Ted's visit. "He seemed more jealous than concerned about my wellbeing. I think dreaming of a man turning into worms struck him as a bit Freudian." Texts came after. Ted "checking in." Asking about the mortgage or house repairs. Letting her know he still thought about her while at the same time telling her what to do. A bully's idea of sweet-talk. "He even called once, drunk I think, complaining about his girlfriend. I hung up on him."

On a Thursday night, while drinking tea on Nell's porch swing, George brought up his own social life. "I dated quite a bit when I was younger. Regular women. Like you. Well, you know, not able to change. I grew quite attached a few times, but I always broke things off in the end. Didn't seem fair, them not knowing and all." He said it all in a rush staring at the floor.

"Oh," said Nell. And was surprised to find herself blushing.

Their first date was at a local Italian restaurant. They drank wine and laughed a lot. George ordered the risotto much to Nell's relief. The idea of him sucking pasta into his mouth would have been too much like his transformation in reverse. *I'm on a date with a monster*, she thought. *And I'm having a very good time.* She kissed him in the driveway before they parted. A small kiss, quick and almost dainty. But the memory of it warmed her for hours. It was well past midnight when the knock on the door came.

She'd been reading on the couch. Too pleased to go to bed despite the lateness of the hour. *Don't ruin it, George,* she thought. *I'm taking this slow.* But she smiled as she approached the door and her stomach filled with a warm excitement.

Ted stood on the porch. Dark half-moons hung beneath his eyes, and his tan seemed sallow under the porch light's yellow glare. In his skinny jeans, Nell's ex-husband looked like the poster child for mid-life crisis. "I've done it. I've cast her off, Nell."

"Are you drunk?" it was a rhetorical question. Bourbon soaked his words.

"You're not listening to me. It's over. I'm coming home."

"Kelli's thrown you out?"

"Kerri," Ted said. "And we've parted ways. Differences of opinion."

"You mean she had one?"

Ted flinched as if Nell's words were a blow. "I'm not here to talk about Kerri," he said raising his voice. "I realized it that night you called. You need someone to take care of you. And to be honest, I need someone to take care of." He made the words sound like an accusation and a plea at the same time.

"I don't want to be taken care of, Ted. The call was a mistake." Without thinking, she shot a quick worried glance at George's house. "And I rang back. I told you it was only a nightmare. George is . . . harmless."

"George. You are seeing him, aren't you? It's understandable of course. You're fragile, Nell. You need someone with a firm hand in your life." Ted nodded, and there was something distant in his voice as if he spoke not to Nell, but himself. "What he doesn't understand is it's me you need. Not some nudist."

"You leave right now, Ted, or I swear you'll spend the night in jail."

Ted ignored her. "You stay here. I'm going to have a little talk

284

with your George. He needs to understand the lay of the land." Ted walked across the yard toward George's porch.

"Leave him alone. You're not in your right mind!" Nell ran toward the back of George's house. She tried the gate entrance, but it was locked. If George was asleep in bed, fine. The police could handle Ted. But what if he was changing? She yelled and slammed her open palm against the wood. "George! My ex-husband is here! He's acting crazy!" The sound of running feet came from the front yard. Ted slammed his shoulder into the gate right beside her. Nell screamed in surprise.

She grabbed Ted's arm, and he gave her a shove that sent her reeling. He slammed into the entrance again, grunting with the impact.

"Stop it," Nell yelled.

On the third try, wood splintered, and the gate burst inward.

Inside, George Harrah knelt naked in the grass. Half his head and most of his right arm had already changed. Worms slithered down his torso to the ground.

"Jesus Christ," Ted said. He turned to Nell, a condescending smile stretching across his face. "He's done something to you, Nell. Bewitched you somehow, but I'll sort it out." Cordwood lay stacked against the fence's interior. A hatchet jutted up from a thick log. Ted snatched it up and marched toward George. Nell scrambled to her feet and ran after him.

With no hesitation Ted crossed the yard and swung the hatchet at George's rapidly changing head. Worms showered onto the grass.

"Leave him alone," Nell shouted.

"It's all right, Nell. I'm here now," Ted said, rearing back for another blow.

George lifted his one solid arm. The hatchet bit deep into the still human flesh, blood poured down.

He'd be screaming, she thought, *if his head were still there, he'd be screaming.*

285

Worms swarmed over Ted's shoes and up his pants leg, but he took no notice. He swung the hatchet again. George's arm cartwheeled through the air, a trail of blood and worms streaming out behind it.

The sight of George's sheared off arm broke Nell's paralysis. She stepped to the woodpile and picked up a log as thick as her forearm. Crossing to Ted, Nell swung the log like a baseball bat, striking him in the ribs with a *thunk*.

Ted grunted, but his smile didn't falter. "You need me, Nell. Everything's going to be fine now."

Nell braced herself and swung again. This time with all the rage of fifteen years of bad marriage behind the blow. The log slammed into the side of Ted's head leaving a two-inch dent behind. Blood filled the dent, turning Ted's blonde hair a muddy red.

Ted froze, dropped the hatchet, then fell to his knees. Worms crawled up his sides.

"Just wanted to take care of you," he said. The words came out soft and dripping blood. Then wriggling shapes filled Ted's mouth, and he collapsed to the ground, disappearing under the writhing mass of George's worms. A few minutes later, both Ted and the worms were gone, leaving only dark, turned earth.

Well, not all gone, Nell thought. A few yards away, where George's arm had landed, a smaller pile of worms still crawled on the surface. *Why didn't they go with the rest?* The worms' movements slowed, and they began to knit back together. What they formed was not an arm.

"Oh my God," said Nell.

The tiny shape took a hitching breath and began to cry. The baby that had been George's arm looked only a few weeks old. Nell remembered George's words on the day she'd first confronted him. *Reproduction is hard on my kind. I was an accident.*

When George emerged from the earth again, Nell sat on the

deck, holding the tiny red-haired newborn. George walked past the two of them to the clothes he'd left folded neatly on an Adirondack chair and dressed. He had two arms again, but Nell thought he stood a few inches shorter.

"There are things you didn't tell me."

George didn't speak.

"It's a girl," Nell said and shifted the child on to her shoulder. "For a while, things were sort of undecided down there. Then she changed." She stared down into the baby's huge blue eyes and couldn't help but smile a little. "The red hair is new too."

George knelt in front of the chair and patted the child on the leg. "We imprint on the first person we see. Sex, the hair, the eyes, she's going to look like you. Not exactly, but close. I'm glad. Can you watch her a little while longer? I need to pack."

"What?"

"I killed your husband, Nell."

"Ted was deranged and attacked you with a hatchet. Besides, I killed him." Nell again saw the deep bloody dent in her ex husband's temple. "I killed him." She shook her head in disbelief. "You just disposed of the body. What—where exactly did you?" Did you bury him?

"I didn't eat him if that's what you're thinking. He's someplace far away and very deep. I can move fast when I need to. No one's going to find him. But the police don't always need a body." His hand went from the child to Nell's hand. "I can't stay, Nell. There's bound to be inquiries. We, the baby and I, can disappear. You'll be safe."

"Don't make decisions for me," Nell said. "I hate when people who do that." She didn't feel guilty. Maybe that would come, along with grief for a man she'd once loved, but right now she only felt determined. "You grew your arm back. How?"

"It's only a matter of shifting things about."

287

"Could you look like someone else if you shifted enough? Ted for example. Even the hair?"

George considered it. "I probably couldn't fool his wife, but in general, yes."

Later that night, Ted was caught on tape buying coffee at a gas station near his home. Authorities discovered his sporty hybrid a week later, parked on the shore of Lake Erie. Ted's clothes lay folded on a large stone at the water's edge.

"His girlfriend left him," a kindly policeman told Nell. "His coworkers said he'd been acting erratically ever since. We followed his footsteps to the water's edge. There was no note. Sometimes they just don't leave notes."

A year later, George pulled Nell's Honda on to highway 86 west. "You sure about this?" he asked." He'd seemed leery of the trip when Nell suggested it, but she thought he'd also been pleased.

Nell looked back at Lilly, asleep in her car seat. "Yes. I'm sure. Your dad should meet his granddaughter and me for that matter. Maybe, I can even get him to tell me the story of how you were born?"

"I told you he doesn't like to talk about it. It's considered impolite to ask about our accidents of birth."

Nell groaned.

"Okay fine. But only so you don't spend the whole trip interrogating Dad. I am the son of a loving if slightly clumsy father and the hay baler he bumped into. That's the whole story. Happy?"

Nell leaned over and kissed George on the neck. "I am," she said. "I really am. Although . . . "

"What?"

"Wouldn't it be nice if Lilly had a little brother?" Nell squeezed George's arm. "Does your dad still own that baler?"

THE GIANT'S
TABLE

Mary SanGiovanni

CREATURES OF THE NIGHT

IN HAVERSHAM, NEW JERSEY, west of the hospital and a couple miles into the forests which have reclaimed the land from the crumbling old highway, there is a large stone dolmen in a clearing three miles in. They call it the Giant's Table; four gray and weathered megaliths nine feet tall and as wide as oak trees support a massive stone slab about seventeen feet in length by nine across, a veritable dinner table for the gods. One could almost imagine enormous tankards of ale and dragon flank steaks on pewter plates the size of well covers up there. Of course, no one in Haversham has ever seen the top—no one currently living, that is—although idle theories about what may still be up there run rampant, especially around Halloween.

Once, Billy and Kyle Anderson attached a GoPro camera to a drone and flew it up to the top to get pictures, looking to get answers and assure their legendry and coolness at Haversham Middle School for all time. Billy has always claimed they lost the drone, that it's rusting and rotting somewhere on top of that slab where it crashed and broke and got stuck. He won't budge on that story, no matter what anyone says to him. Kyle, who'd be about 23 now, hangs with the barflies at Remmy's Tavern and while he can hold his beer, when he's had Tequila, he'll sometimes talk about what the GoPro camera showed them of the top of that dolmen. He doesn't make much sense, but the story is consistent, and Ida Fischer's husband, Bob, swears that the boy believes every word of it, crazy as it sounds. Bob'll admit Kyle isn't quite right in the head, but he strongly believes that's because of what Kyle thinks that camera happened to catch up there years ago.

The county college over in Wexton offers a local history class

291

which covers a bit of the place's past, though that is as much speculation as the contents atop the dolmen's slab. The popular theory is that the indigenous people of the area built it as some kind of altar to the gods, but there are carvings like runes along the megaliths that seem to contradict that. For one, the indigenous tribes that had settled in Haversham had no written language, nor is it believed that they had the tools to carve such complex three-dimensional symbols from so thick a stone. For another thing, the carbon-dating geologists once did on the dolmens suggests both it and its runes are of an age that predates both those indigenous tribes and the birth of written language itself. As to what the runes mean, linguists argue over most of the various translations, except for a small area of common ground regarding the mention of moons and stars and awaiting an alignment of both. The significance of the alignment is in contested territory, however, and is generally assumed to be some celestial event from eons ago.

Nowadays, though, it's a local landmark, a cool, fun place to explore, to make up stories about or to sit and meditate on nature. It's one of those spots far enough outside of town where people who fear they have no future can find solitude in a place that has no known, definitive past. Teens go there sometimes to party or make out. You can almost always find glittering green and brown bits of old beer bottles, the occasional used condom, sometimes even a random shoe. Lone artists hike the three miles to sketch it or to paint it at sunset. A local coven of Wiccans and their hippy hangers-on gathers there on the solstices to commune with nature and the spirits who guard it.

Most of the time, it sits quiet and undisturbed in its clearing in the woods as time patiently wears away its past and reshapes its purpose.

In the 124 years that Haversham has been an established township, there have only ever been six disappearances in the area of the dolmens—certainly not like the statistics of people gone missing in Nilhollow further southeast, or even in Zarephath out on the western border. Three had been runaways subsequently found alive and unharmed. The skeletal remains of two were found at the bottom of a cliff on the northwestern side of the forest and determined accidental deaths. The last, a 46-year-old housewife from Wexton, is still considered an open missing persons case, but likely a tragic displacement of a woman suffering from early onset dementia.

Until the week of October 14th, the dolmens had never made anyone disappear—not until the moons and stars in a different sky, on the other side of what Billy and Kyle Anderson saw, finally aligned.

Brock Culley was a budding psychopath. At only eleven years old, he had already killed a dog, two stray cats, his pet hamster, a bird, six chipmunks, and countless bugs and spiders. He liked to cut them up once they were dead. It was their insides that fascinated him. Seeing the blood and the way the guts squished around between his fingers stirred him down there in his boxers in a way that pleased him. He didn't feel guilt over much, but understood he was expected to feel at least a little bad about wetting the bed or setting fire to his sister's dolls and his brother's curtains. He probably would have been expected to feel bad about what he did to the animals, but he did it in private. They lived and died in his own private world, in his secret domain in the back woods behind his house, where no one ever came and no one ever bothered him. No one could try to make him feel guilty about that.

He was in a grumpy mood as he followed the meandering

dirt path toward his fort. It was little more than a wooden shack his dad had built with his older brother years before. Now that Tim was fifteen, he was "too cool" for it and his father had forgotten it was even there, so Brock had appropriated it for himself. He kept his special prizes there in a shoebox he had taken from his mother's closet. It made him feel good to go through that box when he was having a bad day, like today. He could turn over the skulls and the smooth white bones and teeth and he could remember.

His feet crunched the leaves as the path slipped under a canopy of yellows and reds. He was deeper in the forest now, close to the dolmens. That was his landmark—he turned right at the dolmens, off the path toward the fort. He'd never paid that much attention to it, never saw what the big fuss was about. It was just a pile of big, dumb rocks. Who cared?

That afternoon, though, he would have sworn he heard them humming. He frowned as he approached the nearest leg of rock, and put his ear to it. It was vibrating, all right—he could feel it against his earlobe—but the humming wasn't like that of a machine. It wasn't quite a humming like people made, either, although there was the suggestion of a voice in it.

He pulled away. Had it always hummed? Maybe he'd never noticed before. He shrugged. Humming or not, it was still just a dumb pile of rocks, and he was about to turn toward the fort when he heard someone call his name.

Brock looked around, surprised, scanning in between the trees for the source of the voice. He saw no one.

"Hey! Up here, Brock!" It was a little girl's voice, and it was coming from somewhere up above him. He didn't see anyone sitting in the comfortable Ys of the trees, no one at eleven-year-old tree-climbing height.

"Up here, you dummy!" the voice called again, and this time, when he looked up toward the topmost slab of rock above him, he saw a small face peering over the side.

It was that bitch, Jenny. And she was waving to him. Jenny, who had called him a freak and a cannibal in class, even though the dumb bitch didn't really know what a cannibal was. She'd heard him tell Luis Rodriguez that he'd killed a chipmunk and if the boy wanted to come over and see, Brock could show him the skull. Before Luis could answer, Jenny, who had been eavesdropping, started shouting it all over the playground. He'd wanted to kill her just then. He'd wanted to see what *her* insides felt like to squish between his fingers, and his resulting half-erection had embarrassed him more than Jenny's teasing. He'd run off and hid until recess was over, and had spent the rest of the day imagining cutting her all around the mouth and in the stomach.

"Wha—what are you doing up there?" he asked.

"Just playing. Want to come up?"

"How'd you even get up there?" he asked, as if somehow, she were trying to pull one over on him. "No one can get up there."

"I did. Want me to show you?"

He did but he wasn't about to let her know that. "I'm busy."

"With your skulls?" she asked with a small smile. From way up there, her pigtails hung over the side like two frozen waterfalls, chocolate waterfalls, around that teasing smile.

Brock scowled at her. "Fuck you, Jenny," he said, savoring the grown-up word. He thought it all the time—that word and other words—but seldom got to say it without getting smacked in the mouth.

She didn't seem surprised. In fact, she didn't react at all to the grown-up word, and it made Brock want to see her fall from up there and break her bones and splatter a little. Instead, she smiled. "Can I see them?"

Brock blinked in surprise. She couldn't possibly mean that . . .

could she? Girls didn't like icky, squishy things. They liked their puppies and kitties and bunnies all warm and whole and breathing.

"What?"

"Can I see them? Your bones, I mean. I want to see. That's why I'm here."

"Uh . . . I guess so." He started walking and a moment later, he heard the small leaf-crunching of footsteps behind him. He turned around.

Jenny smiled at him.

"How did you get down so fast?" he asked suspiciously. He couldn't shake the feeling that she was somehow playing an elaborate practical joke on him, that at any moment, his brother or those assholes from school who liked to shove him into walls, would come out from behind the trees and start laughing at him.

Or worse, that in letting her see his collection, she'd rat him out to a grown-up.

He'd half-made up his mind to hit her in the head with a rock before he even got her to the fort.

She didn't answer his question. Instead, she said, "Before we go, let me show you something. Something over there." She pointed back at the dolmens.

He frowned. "What?"

She giggled, and for a moment, he thought a strange light flickered in her eyes. "It's my secret—like your bones fort. It's cool."

If she showed him something as secret as his bones collection, then he'd have something on her if she ever tried to tell on him. If it was good enough, he might even be able to get her to do things for him, things like the older kids got girls to do for them, in exchange for not telling on her.

"Okay. Show me."

She clapped her hands excitedly and gestured for him to

follow, then led him to a shadowy spot where the scrub brush met the rock on a gentle incline. The shrub looked like it might be big enough for an animal carcass to be rotting away in there, although in sniffing the passing breeze, he couldn't smell any rot.

He was so preoccupied with what might be buried in the shrubbery that he didn't notice the distorted shadow on the ground, a shadow that might pass for person-shaped if you squinted and looked at it from a certain angle. He didn't see the shadow and so he didn't see that it was unattached to either his or Jenny's feet. He didn't notice that Jenny herself had no shadow at all, nor did he see the detached one bend upward off the ground and into the air, reforming into a kind of oval about his height.

"So what's this really cool thing you wanted to show me?" he asked, trying to sound casual. At his age, casual was not one of the tones he'd mastered, at least, not like innocent. He could fake innocent very well when he needed to, but sometimes emotions—excitement and anger, mostly—crept in when his self-preservation wasn't on the line.

"The tiny black hole," Jenny said. "The one that used to be on top of the dolmens. It's down here now."

Finally, Brock turned his attention to her. He started to ask "What hole?" but saw the shadow before both words had escaped him. Instead, he asked, "What *is* that?"

"That's the hole, silly."

Brock glanced at her and then back at the shadow-hole. He was genuinely impressed. He'd never seen anything like it before. "What does it do?"

"It shows you things. Tells you things. Sometimes it comes down from up there and it eats people, and then shits out what's left on the other side for the beasts to feed on."

To anyone else, her words might have raised an alarm in the mind. To Brock, though, they just added to the delicious strangeness of the thing before him. "You're weird," he said, but he smiled a genuine smile when he said it. "What else does it do?"

"I told you—when the stars on moons on the other side align, it feeds."

"On what?" he asked, turning to her.

She grinned, and he realized with a stirring in his gut that he did not like that grin. It was one of his grins. "Little boys."

"Bullshit," he said, enjoying the taste of another grown-up word.

"You're right," she said, putting her own Jenny-grin back on. "It's just a tiny black hole—not even strong enough to suck in grass and pebbles. Go ahead and put your hand into it. It's cold, and it tickles a little. See?" She stuck her own hand in and giggled, then drew it back out. For a moment, her fingers glittered but the effect dissipated.

When he hesitated, she shoved his shoulder. "Go on, try it! What are you afraid of?"

Brock glowered at her and despite the unease in his stomach, he stuck his hand in.

She was right. It was cold but not unpleasantly so, and it seemed to fizz all around him—that's how it felt, like a thousand tiny bubbles bouncing around against his skin. He wiggled his fingers and smiled.

"Cool?" she asked, gauging his approval.

"Cool," he agreed, and went to pull his hand back.

It wouldn't budge. Something on the other side, something he couldn't quite feel as anything other than bubbles, held him fast.

"I'm stuck," he said.

"Pull harder," she said, but she didn't sound so much like Jenny.

Brock turned to her and saw she was dissolving into a kind

of black mist, a series of corded tendrils of smoke coming unbundled. Those freed tendrils were feeding back into the tiny black hole, and before Brock could react to what he was seeing, the pain started.

First, his fingertips felt like they were on fire. This was followed by a series of pops from inside his fingertips outward which he was aware that on some level meant his fingertips exploded. The burning was intense, neither hot nor cold but concentrated pain that moved like plasma up the skinny stalks of his fingers and onto his hand.

He screamed, a short, clipped bark of horror. Then the tendrils that had been pretending to be Jenny reached out from the tiny black hole and yanked him through.

Before anyone had even noticed that Brock Culley had gone missing, the tiny black hole had managed to eat a rabbit, a few squirrels, one bird, and part of a fox. Brock would have been impressed if he had seen it, and even more delighted with the growing collection of viscera around the shrubbery near the hole. As it was, nothing of Brock was left on this side of the hole to see it.

Later that afternoon, the thing pretending to be a shadow, a little girl, animal prey, and a tiny black hole had managed to lure two joggers and a hunter into his dimension-straddling maw, leaving behind a running shoe and a rifle along with the back half of a fox and an assortment of unpalatable bones and organs. The sun in this world would be going down in a few hours, and that meant the moon and stars in the other world would be moving out of position. If it was to get its fill of meat, it needed search parties and concerned townsfolk. They were a reasonable expectation, given the child it had devoured.

It swirled and pulsed. It hummed an ancient song from a people long ago dead. It patiently waited.

Calla Jessup had never been a jogger like her husband. She understood that he got some kind of adrenaline rush from the endorphins, and although she appreciated his passion and even tried—unsuccessfully, due to unrelenting shin splints—to share it with him, running was not fun to her. Running was a necessary solution to the problem of someone chasing you with a chainsaw. Running in the woods had always struck Calla as a potentially dangerous thing, but Ryan loved it. He ran twice a day—once early in the morning before work, and once to wrap up the evening after supper.

When on October 14th, he went out for an early afternoon run, taking advantage of his day off and what sunlight was still left, she hadn't thought much of it. When he failed to return four hours later, then she began to worry. She put on her sneakers, grabbed a flashlight and her cell phone, and went out to look for him.

She knew he liked the jogging trails in the Haversham woods and in particular, the blue trail, so she started there. It led past the old dolmen, which Calla had never much cared for. There was something about the air of the place, a kind of hollowness, as if that area really wasn't entirely there, not wholly part of the woods around it.

Overhead, the orange glow of sunset was turning blue, inching toward darkness. Already, the woods around her were silhouetted, the dolmen looming from between the oaks and maples and pines. She shuddered and would have hurried right past it if not for the shoe.

Calla was, as her mother often put it, oblivious to the little details of daily life. She never remembered the names of streets or people's spouses, children, or pets. She forgot anniversaries and birthdays, and where she parked the car. Hell, she didn't even know what kind of car most of her friends drove. She didn't register decorative changes or new haircuts at all. And she never would have recognized Ryan's running shoe, except that she had gotten him that pair for his birthday last month. She'd picked them out especially for him—white, with black and blue trim. He'd said they were perfect, that he loved them, and she'd beamed with pleasure. He'd certainly broken those shoes in over the next few weeks, but when she saw them where he usually kicked them off by the back door, they always made her smile. They made her think of the man she loved doing something he enjoyed, and that made her happy.

Seeing one of them speckled with something which, in the twilight, looked black, made her scared.

She crept over to it—crept, because that seemed like the best approach even though she was alone on the trail. The spot where the shoe lay was near an oblong of shadow even blacker than the dark around it, and she couldn't quite shake the feeling that something predatory was or had recently been there.

When she got close enough to examine the shoe, she saw that the dark specks were blood, and her heart sank. "Ryan?" she called, at first tentatively, and then a little louder. "Ryan? Where are you, baby?"

There was no answer. She tried not to imagine him hurt somewhere in the gathering gloom of shrubbery, his ankle or leg broken, his sweaty face pale, unable to reply.

She shined the flashlight around the area slowly, scanning it for more blood, for movement, for any sign of Ryan.

"Hello?" she called and felt vulnerable doing it, naked somehow. "Ryan, are you here? Ryan!"

301

When he stepped out from behind one of the massive legs of the dolmen, she jumped, uttering a startled cry. He grinned at her as her hand flew to her chest to calm her heart.

"You scared the shit out of me. Jesus, baby, are you okay?" she asked, jogging over to him to give him a hug. He felt cold beneath her touch and smelled like old things left in the dirt, but she chalked that up to his sweat from the run. The temperature had been steadily dropping since the sun had begun to set; it was expected to be in the low fifties for the night, so his cooling sweat seemed the most logical answer there, too.

"I'm fine," Ryan said. "I'm sorry to make you come out looking for me. I fell and hit my head on a rock," he said, pointing toward the back of his head. "Knocked me out for a bit. So I sat a while and then finished my run."

She pulled back from his embrace. He was wearing running pants and a gray t-shirt. There was a brownish smear on the rib area, as if he'd touched the wetness on the back of his head, saw it was blood and wiped his fingers on his shirt. She shined the light at his chest to illuminate his face without blinding him. His eyes looked okay, but she was no doctor. Maybe the pupils were a bit big, but night was coming on.

"Let me see," she said.

"Huh?"

"Your head. Let me see your head."

He shrugged and turned around. Sure enough, there was a small spot just above the base of his skull where blood had clotted his shaggy brown hair. She reached out and touched it gently and he winced.

"Does it hurt a lot?"

"A little," he replied, turning around with a grin. "I'm okay. Really."

She thought about that a moment, sizing him up again in a girlfriend sort of way, and said, "You're missing a shoe."

"Am I?"

They both looked at his feet. One sock, filthy with dirt, sheathed his left foot. The sneaker she had bought for him he wore on the right.

"Huh," he said thoughtfully. "I guess I am."

"How'd your shoe come off?"

He ignored her question and said, "Hey, before we head home, I want to show you something." He took her arm and began leading her beneath the dolmen, but she resisted.

"Wait, wait. Show me what?"

His eyes sparkled in the dark. "You'll see. It's a surprise. It's really cool."

She let him lead her closer to the place where his shoe lay, but stopped short when she saw movement in that dark spot.

Ryan gestured broadly, a magician's *"Ta da!"* kind of motion. "See? It's cool, isn't it?"

"What am I looking at?"

He laughed. "I . . . I don't know. That dark spot there, that kind of has those oil slick colors swirling in it. It's like a miniature black hole. I've been feeding little twigs and rocks into it and Calla— Calla, I swear this—they just disappear! It's the weirdest thing."

"When did you find this?"

"What? Oh, after. After I finished my run. I came back here to rest again—I was feeling a little dizzy, probably from dehydration and my head or whatever—and I found this. It was easier to see of course, when there was still daylight, but I think it's starting to glow a little, around the edges."

He was right about that. A faint blue glow now delineated an oval shape about four feet high and maybe two across. It was big, bigger than it had looked from the trail.

"I don't like it, Ryan. Come on, let's go."

"Aw, come on, Calla! Don't you think this is cool? Aren't you the least bit curious.?"

303

"No," she said firmly. "You're hurt, and I'm getting cold. It's dark. I want to go home."

"Just come here for a second. Just try it. Try putting this leaf in it—"

"No!" she said more forcefully this time. "I want to leave. Let's go, Ryan."

"Now Calla, we can't just yet."

She could see him without the flashlight now, in the blue glow of the thing. It cast an eerie, late-night-TV sort of hue on him which made him look haggard, almost threatening.

"Because I'm still hungry, and this is the last chance I'll have to eat for a long time."

"What are you talking about? There's nothing to eat here. If you're hungry, let's hit a diner or –"

"There's you."

Taken aback, she watched his expression in the blue glow. He wasn't making the goofy-grin face that he did when he was joking with her. He looked very serious. In fact, he looked almost unfamiliar to her, like she was looking at a dummy wearing Ryan's skin, trying to mimic his expressions and failing.

"Are you joking?"

"No," he said. "I need you, Calla." He held out a hand to her.

"Are you coming on to me? Here? Now?"

Anger knit his features together. "Time is running out!"

"Time for what?"

"Oh, just shut up!" he shouted at her, and she reddened with surprise and hurt. "Just shut the fuck up, you bitch. Your incessant questions are driving me crazy."

She opened her mouth to say something, but then closed it. Ryan, she saw, was bleeding into the miniature black hole, meddling with it, feeding it so it could surge outward to her with misty black tendrils. The sight was so strange it sucked the air from her lungs. She couldn't talk. She couldn't scream.

She could run, though. She stumbled backward and turned to bolt out of there, back down the blue trail toward her car. Instead, she pitched forward and fell flat on her stomach. The ground beneath her was as hard as it was cold, and impact forced out what little air was left in her lungs. As she gasped to bring it back in, she rolled over and saw one of those tendrils from that black hole had wrapped around her ankle. She kicked violently to try to shake it off, but it yanked her toward the hole.

"Stop!' she yelled. "Let me go."

It pulled again and she slid across the dirt, kicking violently. Her arms flailing, she clawed at the ground around her. Her hand closed on a large rock and she heaved it toward the hole. It sailed into the rippling black and disappeared. For a moment, the tendril loosened its grip and she scuttled backward away from it.

A moment later, it spit out the rock, pitted and smoking, and the tendril reached for her again.

With a shout, she scrambled away. She could feel it clawing at her foot. She imagined it taking one of her shoes, a new mate for Ryan's discarded one, and for one terrible moment, she thought she would break into hysterical giggling.

The tendril ate through the denim of her pants leg and a moment later, she felt her calf burning. She screamed, pawing at the dirt in an effort to pull away from that horrible burning. Just then, another tendril wrapped around her other thigh, and she felt herself losing ground as she slid back toward the hole.

Two more tendrils snaked toward her. One wrapped around her waist and the other around her forearm, drawing her closer. She could see into the hole now, beyond the black. There were galaxies inside it, swirling and crashing into each other, a churning chaos of stars exploding and debris swirling into planets and moons. She struggled against it, but she was losing ground fast. The edge of the hole — was it a mouth? A stomach? —

305

was only a foot or so away now, and her fingernails dragged the dirt. She was so close that she could hear the roar of the universe beyond, and mingled with it, a million whispering voices. A cold wind blew, chilling her.

She closed her eyes, waiting. Her calf burned and her fingers hurt.

Suddenly, there was a horrible wailing, and a myriad of voices cried out at once over the sound. By the time she had opened her eyes, the galaxy was gone. The black hole and its halo of blue light were gone. She was alone—scuffed, bleeding and breathing hard, but she was alone.

When she had caught her breath, she ran all the way home.

The moons and stars had moved out of position. All around the dolmen, the trees quivered.

Atop the stone slab, the black hole winked and flickered in and out of this world. It was hungry and it was angry, but it had not survived so long without learning to be patient. It would hibernate as it had in the past, and wait for the next alignment.

And it would let the spawn gestate, for a time. When they were ready, they would leave the Giant's Table and spread out through the forest, moving toward Haversham proper. There were plenty to feed on there, and the moons and stars on the other side moved quickly enough through their orbits . . .

THE LAST THING YOU WANT TO BE

Jeff Strand

CREATURES OF THE NIGHT

"SIR, I'M GOING to need you to step out of the—"

I blew the cop away.

Correction. I would have blown the cop away if I'd had access to my bigger, more powerful guns, which were under a blanket on the back seat. So I just shot him in the forehead with a pistol. Not as messy and thus not as much fun, but the end result was the same: one less cop trying to muck around in my business.

For the pedantic among you who think it should be one "fewer" cop, what I'm saying is that there was *less* of him. Heh heh. And for those of you insisting that my joke still doesn't make sense from a grammar perspective, I just murdered a cop in broad daylight. What makes you think you're safe?

To be fair to the unfortunate police officer, he was simply doing his job. His job was to catch bad guys, and I'm a bad guy, so I couldn't really bear him any ill will. It's not accurate to say that I'd left a trail of dead bodies between Nevada and Louisiana, but I'd left a few of them along the way. One in each state, at least. Maybe that does count as a trail.

You may think there's going to be some sort of twist where I reveal that I only kill pedophiles or vampires or something like that. Nope. I'm a total thrill-killer. I'm not trying to cleanse sin from the world or silence voices in my head or anything that might cause you to think, "Well, I don't agree with his actions, but I can on some level empathize with his plight." I kill because, if I may take on the persona of an uptight British prick for a moment, it's a jolly good time. I love the sound of screams. It doesn't get me hard but it does make me happy.

My victims were mostly women, because I don't like women very much. If my misogyny offends you, then take your virtue-signaling social justice warrior snowflake ass someplace else. I've got a story to tell, and you're not my target audience.

So anyway, yeah, I shot the cop because if it were up to him, I wouldn't be able to kill any more women. And that would make me frown.

I love to take risks, but I try not to be stupid about it. Therefore, instead of leaving the cop to rot by the side of the road, I dragged his dead butt down into the ditch. He wouldn't have actually rotted—somebody would've seen him or run over him relatively soon, but it would be better for me if he were found the next morning instead of a few minutes after I'd murdered him.

Some people might be uncomfortable dragging a dead cop into a swampy ditch at midnight. Harder to see gators in the darkness. Me, I kind of liked the idea that I might accidentally step on a gator and have to fight it with a hunting knife to keep it from biting my leg off. Which is not to say that I purposely put myself in situations where I could be mangled by wildlife; I'm just saying that when I had to drag a cop into a ditch out of necessity, the extra element of danger was exciting to me.

Do I sound deranged? I hope so.

My mother once called me "a cartoonish parody of an evil person." I wanted to stab her for it, to prove her right, but I was only six. And she'd installed a lock on the silverware drawer.

Does that sound like something I made up? Am I a liar as well as a psychopath? *You* be the judge!

(The truth: After a very unfortunate incident when I was a child, she did indeed lock up anything I could use as a weapon between the ages of six and thirteen. I also wasn't allowed any more pets. She did call me a cartoonish parody of an evil person, but not until I was seventeen. I didn't stab her because I didn't want to do anything that might invalidate her life insurance policy. As of now, she's alive and well.)

You may be wondering why the cop pulled me over in the

first place. Was I dragging a dead pedestrian behind the vehicle? Did I have a severed head mounted on the dashboard? Did I take a swig from a flask of whiskey just as he passed me?

Nah. I was speeding. Not recklessly. A few miles above the limit that would've been perfectly okay any other time, but not when driving past a hard-assed small town cop who needed to make his quota for the month. I'm not very good at high-speed chases, so I decided to pull over, smile, politely hand over my (fake) driver's license, registration, and proof of insurance. If it went smoothly, I'd stick to the posted speed limit for the rest of Louisiana. If he heard noise coming from the trunk, I'd shoot him in the face.

You know how that turned out, but I'm going to repeat it, simply because I enjoyed it so much.

"Sir, I'm going to need you to step out of the—"

I blew the cop away.

Got him right in the nose. Few body parts do well when a bullet hits them at close range, but your nose is particularly susceptible to destruction. I wish I'd recorded it so I could watch the video over and over. In slow motion. In reverse, so it was like the splattery gore was sucked back into his face to form a regular Jewish-style nose. Maybe even in sped-up motion, though it happened so quick that a sped-up version would be over in a blink.

Anyway, I dragged the cop away (you already knew that, but I'll be as redundant as I damn well please in my own narrative) and then got back in my environmentally friendly vehicle (I'm not a complete monster) and drove a couple more hours. Then I decided to stop to make sure the bound woman in my trunk wasn't dead.

She probably wasn't. She'd only been in there for about six hours. Not enough to dehydrate or starve to death, and though she had duct tape over her mouth her nose was clear, so there was no reason she should have suffocated. The only way she should be dead is if she'd bonked her head when I hit one of the many bumps I'd encountered on various crappy roads. Barring a fatal brain injury, she should be okay.

I found a small convenience store that looked like it hadn't been open for business in many, many years. Some of the graffiti on the boarded up windows was a couple of election cycles out of date. I don't know the swamp equivalent of a tumbleweed, but I expected one to roll past my car as I drove behind the building and turned off the engine. It probably wasn't safe to check on her here—the entire building could come crashing down if I sneezed, removing my car.

I got my hunting knife out of the glove compartment, got out of the car, walked over to the trunk, and knocked on the lid. "You dead?" I asked.

No answer. She was either dead or pretending to be dead in a clever attempt to catch me by surprise.

"If you don't answer, I'm going to shoot through the lid," I informed her. This was a bluff. I wouldn't damage my car like that. But if *I* were locked in a trunk by a psychopathic killer and that psychopathic killer threatened to shoot through the trunk, I'd assume he was telling the truth. I wasn't expecting a coherent response through the duct tape, but she could say something muffled or kick something like she had when the cop pulled me over.

She made a muffled noise. I grinned.

"I'm going to open the trunk now," I told her. "Don't try anything."

I was just being amusing. No way could she try anything. Her arms were taped behind her back (which I'm sure was extremely uncomfortable during the long ride) and her feet were taped together at the ankles. I'd been generous with the tape; no cost cutting measures there. I obviously wasn't going to throw open the trunk and then just stand there in prime position to get kicked in the chest, but with just the bare minimum of caution on my part, I knew she'd pose no threat.

I opened the trunk. She did not try to kick me in the chest.

She lay on her side. Her hair was all messed up and filthy (I didn't do a good job cleaning the trunk before inserting a victim into it), as were her clothes. Light pink sweatpants and a dark pink sweatshirt—I'd kidnapped her while she was jogging. Her face was stained with tears. She gazed at me in terror.

It wasn't the same woman.

She was in my trunk, and she was wearing the same clothes, and she had duct tape in all the right places, but the woman I'd kidnapped had red hair and freckles. This woman was a blonde. And a different face, at least the part that wasn't covered with tape.

"What the—?" I said. I stopped because I was too shocked to finish the sentence, not because I had any aversion to saying the word "fuck."

She tightened herself into the fetal position.

Was I mistaken? I couldn't be. I had a very clear memory of the jogger. The woman in my trunk had bland good looks—still hot, but boring. The jogger had quirky good looks, like she'd be in a sitcom where she was a total klutz who messed everything up but the male viewers would still desperately want to bang her. She wasn't the first woman I'd ever locked in my trunk, but she was the only one of this particular cross-country killing spree.

This was not flawed recall. This was something very strange.

I couldn't interrogate the woman with her mouth taped up, so there was going to be some trust involved here. I held up the hunting knife and slowly slid it out of its leather sheath. "I'm going to take off the tape," I told her. "If you scream, I will use this to poke a dozen tiny holes into your lungs so that you choke to death on your own blood. Do I need to explain what a terrible way that is to die?"

313

She shook her head.

I'd wrapped the duct tape around her head a couple of times, so trying to unwind the whole thing would be too much trouble. Instead, I slipped the tip of the knife under the edge, right next to her mouth, and cut a straight line down. Having the knife so close to her face would be wonderfully intimidating.

"Stop trembling," I said. "I don't want to cut you." ("I don't want to cut you" was a lie.)

She kept trembling, but I worked carefully and all she got was a small nick. Then I tore the tape from her mouth, eliciting a wince of pain, and cut away the part that had been over her lips.

"Hi," I said.

She didn't answer.

"I'm Mike." (Not my real name.) "I'm a serial killer. What the hell happened to the woman I kidnapped?"

She looked surprised by my question. It was, I suppose, an odd question. But though I'm insane, I know the parameters of my insanity, and they do not include hallucinating shit like this. The woman I'd kidnapped was not the same woman who was in my trunk right now, and I wanted to know what was going on.

"Answer me," I said, waving the knife in the vicinity of her right eyeball.

"I don't know what you're talking about!"

"Yes, you do! I stuffed a redheaded jogger in here a few hours ago, and you're not her. I've stopped the car three times since I kidnapped her; once to fill it with gas, once to kill a cop, and now. I was right next to the car the whole time I was at the gas station, and it was in my sight the whole time I hid the dead cop. So what happened to her?"

"Listen to yourself," said the woman. "If you never let the car out of your sight, how could she get out? It doesn't make any sense! What was she wearing?"

"The same thing you are."

"Are you saying that somebody broke into your trunk, took her out, and replaced her with me, wearing the same clothes and tied up in the same way?"

"I never said that you were tied up in the same way."

"You didn't say anything about it when you cut away the tape."

"I think you just gave away that you know something."

She frantically shook her head. "I don't know anything. I don't understand what you think *could* have happened! I was jogging through Wilson Springs Park, you jumped out at me, you shoved a wet cloth against my face, and I woke up in here!"

The woman was correct about that part. But I absolutely was not imagining this. I was not questioning my sanity (in this particular regard). This was not the same woman.

I held the tip of the knife half an inch from her eye. "Talk. Now. Or I'll get sprayed in the face with eye jelly."

"I'm a shape shifter," she said.

"You're what?"

"I can change form. I did it to try to get out of the duct tape, but I can't really change my body size or shape, so it didn't do any good. I tried a bunch of different options, and when you opened the trunk I couldn't remember what I'd been when you grabbed me."

That sounded absolutely batshit crazy, but there wasn't an answer to this that *wasn't*, so I nodded and moved the knife away from her eye. "Thank you," I said. "That's all I wanted to know."

"You're . . . welcome?"

"Prove it. Change back."

She immediately transformed back into the quirky looking redhead. I'm not proud to say that I jumped back and let out a yelp. Though I'm sure it was less of a yelp than you would have let out under these circumstances.

"Please don't kill me," she said.

"Are you kidding? I've got a shapeshifting chick in my trunk and you think I'd kill her? I'm sure there are lots of great things I could do with you."

She nodded. "There are. Lots."

"Kinky things."

"Yes! Very kinky!"

"Do tell." I hadn't raped any of my victims on this particular trip, but such a thing wasn't entirely out of my realm of experience.

"I can change while we're having sex," she said. "It's like you can have one girl after another. I can't change my body that much, but I can make my boobs grow a little in your hand, and with my face I can even do requests. Any celebrity you've ever wanted to be with, I can look like her."

"Make yourself look like Marilyn Monroe," I said.

She did.

I very nearly crapped my pants. I could have any woman I wanted, all with one woman! Sure, I'd have to go elsewhere for my fat chick fetish, but if I locked the jogger in my basement (I'd have to get a house with a basement) I could fulfill every celebrity fantasy I'd ever had!

As a reasonably cautious psychopath, I knew I should wait to get her someplace more private before we really got into it. But I couldn't help but grope Marilyn's breasts. While I squeezed them, she leaned up to kiss me. I returned the kiss, figuring I could punch her in the stomach if she tried to bite me.

I suddenly got very dizzy. I lost my balance and fell to the ground.

It took her a few tries, but she sat up and peered over the edge of the trunk. "I forgot to tell you. I can also change other people. And until you get used to the process it's really hard to control your body."

I wanted to call her a bitch, but I couldn't get my mouth to move.

I had to watch, unable to do anything but flop around a little, as she got out of the trunk, landing on the ground with a painful looking thump. She managed to get to where I'd dropped my knife, and after a lot of effort she wedged it under a tire, then scraped her wrists against it until she'd cut through the tape. The whole process took at least an hour, and I wasn't getting any better with my motor functions.

With her hands free, it was easy for her to cut away the tape binding her feet.

She rubbed her legs to help get the circulation back, then, with some effort but less than it had taken to get the knife into place, she got me into the trunk and slammed the lid.

I felt like she might not treat me with kindness.

That is, I *feel* like she might not treat me with kindness. I'm still in the trunk. I think I've been here for a couple of days. I'm making up stories to keep my mind occupied. Nobody will ever hear them, I'm sure, but at least the distraction is keeping me within the previously established parameters of my insanity.

The trunk lid opens.

She jabs me in the arm with a hypodermic needle.

Suddenly I'm sitting in the passenger seat of a car. We're parked outside of a restaurant. The woman is wearing different clothes but she still looks like the quirky redhead.

"Hi," she says.

I try to see myself in the rear-view mirror. She tilts it to help me out. I don't look all that much different—like I could be my own brother.

"I've been resting up," she says. "Changing myself is no problem, not anymore, but changing somebody else is pretty exhausting. I'll need a lot of energy. Did you know that I can change you into somebody that already exists, almost like I transported your mind into them? Of course you didn't. But I can. And I've been waiting for the perfect specimen."

"Who?"

She points to the restaurant window. A heavyset man sits in a booth, his face covered with orange sauce, eating Buffalo wings. A very large pile of bones is on a plate next to him.

"He's eating inferno wings. He'd eaten at least two dozen of them when I walked up and kissed him, and he hasn't stopped. I can still feel them burning my lips."

I can't figure out her angle. This seems pretty bad, but not *vengeance* bad.

She notices my confusion and smiles. "I don't have to change you into a complete person. I can change you into part of a person."

Suddenly, I understand.

"That's right," she says. "You're about to become his asshole. Enjoy your evening."

She kisses me.

ONE THOUSAND WORDS ON A TOMBSTONE

Josh Malerman

BULLY JACK

Here lies Bully Jack,
as that's how he announced himself
upon emerging from a brand new toy chest,
opened by Evan Holmes on his eighth birthday.

Corrupt creature
who told young Holmes he would forever covet
what Holmes desired.
Whether Holmes asked for it or not.

Abhorred cruelty
that betrayed his fondness for boxes
numerous times through the years,
vanishing for days only to be discovered
in the cornmeal, the pantry, a shipment of furs.

JOSH MALERMAN

Hateful being,
responsible for the death of six,
the first being young Ralph Pict,
found in the school yard mid-winter,
the snow having hid him for ten days,
this all following a fantasy
belonging to Evan Holmes
of revenge upon Pict for punching.
But it was fantasy alone.

Loathed non-living,
hiding behind the icebox as Mother Holmes
scolded young Evan for things needing scolding,
Bully Jack waiting, perhaps,
for another fantasy to appear
in then eleven year old Holmes's head,
a vision of murdering his own mother
for the sake of revenge
for justifiable punishment doled.

Detestable man,

if man he be,

at every gathering, every date, Holmes's teen years,

Bully Jack hiding in the trees,

but not hid enough for Holmes to miss him.

Conniving trickster

who always dressed well, deceptive, dressed well enough,

smiled, and always waved to Holmes

the first time Holmes saw him that day, every day;

Bully Jack waving from the corner

of Holmes's childhood bedroom,

then from the corner of classrooms at university,

then from behind the coat rack of Holmes's

own psychiatric office on First Street.

Hateful fiend

that saw every trick coming, every attempt Holmes made

to rid himself of Bully Jack,

the man who had first appeared sprung from the toy chest,

a present gone terribly wrong.

Insidious complainer
who asked Holmes regularly why he feared him so,
why Holmes wasn't grateful for the deeds,
like when he murdered a rival psychiatrist on Miffin Street,
that being the second death at the hands of Bully Jack.

Worrisome letch
who took to Theresa Ray as wholly as Bully Jack,
who often arrived at the lady's house before Holmes,
who often could be found lounging in her study,
reading books held upside down,
or was heard snickering beneath her couch and bed.

Execrable hellion
who hid in a present from Holmes to Ray
one Christmas morning,
Holmes having came downstairs before Ray,
there to close an open window, too cold,
only to sense something amiss
amongst the boxes beneath the tree;
Holmes having rescued Ray from a life of Bully Jack
everywhere she looked, she being so close to becoming
the next person to open a box with him in it.

Wicked barbarian!
Who feigned carving meat behind Allan Whorl,
a patient of Evan Holmes,
as Whorl described painful memories
and proved problematic for the doctor,
the doctor unsure how to proceed,
but Bully Jack knew how
and told Holmes in pantomime, mid-session,
sharpening imaginary knives
with a smile as stretched and thin
as Holmes's patience with Whorl.

Savage!
Who took from this world Allan Whorl
as the troubled young man
attempted to cross First Street,
he, Holmes, watching the patient
from his office window,
the doctor able to see Bully Jack give the shove
that sent Whorl beneath horses hooves
in the middle of the street,
this being the third death at the hands of Bully Jack.

King Imp
who stood in the corner of the delivery room
as Theresa Ray gave birth to twins,
Harold and Henry Holmes,
the boys wailing as new mother attempted to soothe,
as new father believed they cried
because they saw him, too,
Bully Jack, so awful to look at, lurking in the room,
the very first room they ever entered.

Wretched maggot
who hid in a box of books belonging to the boys,
schoolbooks, the twins aged ten,
and who hid once, too, in the lesser used toy chest,
a place Evan Holmes checked regularly
over the years, the months, the weeks,
lifting the lid to peek and more than once being caught
by Theresa who came to refer to this behavior
as proof of Holmes's irrational fear of hiding bugs.

Accursed damnation
who smothered Theresa Ray Holmes in her sleep
as Evan Holmes drank in Lichter's Pub on Hampton Street,
attempting to drink off monetary strains
and an argument he'd had with Theresa that night;
but this vision was in fantasy alone
and should have stayed put in fantasy alone!

Awful thing!
Sleeping in the Holmes bed,
taking the side Theresa slept upon for so long,
Holmes waking to find Bully Jack looking back at him,
tucked up to the chin, smiling thinly,
just us in bed now, just us, my Evan Holmes.

Horrid actuality,
being found in the stories of a patient aged sixty,
Miss Geraldine Lang, who professed to Doctor Holmes
a fear of boxes for the eyes she saw peering
out of boxes in her home, boxes in store windows,
boxes on the backs of delivery coaches in town;
he Bully Jack tracking Miss Lang, getting closer, closer,
until Holmes couldn't help but imagine
her drowned in her own tub, silencing her tales of tracking,
exactly as she was found days later.

Unforgivable animation,
for stealing into the window
of Harold and Henry Holmes's university dorm,
putting an end to the bloodletting of money by their father
who saw patient after patient to pay for their schooling,
but whose deaths (fifth and sixth by Bully Jack)
should have remained fantasy and stayed fantasy alone!

Here lies Bully Jack
whose fondness for boxes led him to this one, here,
as Evan Holmes searched the town, the country,
heard word of a ghoul in Marksville,
tracked the beast here, to this box,
Bully Jack lying on his back
and smiling up at Evan Holmes,
the doctor who thought fast to close the lid,
secure the lid, then cover the lid in dirt,
leaving the rotten reality to suffer darkness and solitude
until someone else should set him free again.

Engraved by Evan Holmes, aged ninety-one.

ABOUT THE AUTHORS

Mark Cassell lives on the south coast of England with his wife and a number of animals, and is the author of the bestselling supernatural novel *The Shadow Fabric*. Primarily a horror writer, his steampunk, dark fantasy, and sci-fi stories have featured in many reputable anthologies. His jobs have included baker, laboratory technician, driving instructor, and actor. As a familiar face on the UK convention scene, Mark sells his books as well as his photographic art. For more about his work, please visit www.markcassell.co.uk.

Richard Chizmar is the author of *Gwendy's Button Box* (with Stephen King) and *A Long December*, which was nominated for numerous awards. His fiction has appeared in dozens of publications, including *Ellery Queen's Mystery Magazine*, and multiple editions of *The Year's 25 Finest Crime and Mystery Stories*. He has won two World Fantasy awards, four International Horror Guild awards, and the HWA's Board of Trustee's award. His third short story collection, *A Long December*, was recently published to starred reviews in both Kirkus and Booklist, and was featured in Entertainment Weekly. Chizmar has appeared at numerous conferences as a writing instructor, guest speaker, panelist, and guest of honor. Please visit the author's website at RichardChizmar.com.

Tim Curran is the author of the novels *Skin Medicine, Hive, Dead Sea, Resurrection, Hag Night, Skull Moon, The Devil Next Door, Clownflesh,* and *Biohazard.* His short stories have been collected in *Bone Marrow Stew* and *Zombie Pulp.* His novellas include *The Underdwelling, The Corpse King, Puppet Graveyard, Worm,* and *Terror Cell.* His short stories have appeared in such magazines as, *Splatterpunks, Book of Dark Wisdom,* and *Inhuman,* as well as anthologies such as *Ride the Star Wind, Eulogies III,* and *October Dreams II.* His fiction has been translated into German, Japanese, Spanish, Russian, and Italian. You can find him on Facebook.

Ray Garton is the author of the classic vampire bestseller *Live Girls,* as well as *Scissors, Sex and Violence in Hollywood, Ravenous,* and dozens of other novels, novellas, tie-ins, and story collections. He has been writing in the horror and suspense genres for more than 30 years and was the recipient of the Grand Master of Horror Award in 2006. He lives in northern California with his wife Dawn where he is at work on a new novel.

Eddie Generous is the author of several books, including *Radio Run, Great Big Teeth, Camp Summit, Trouble at Camp Still Waters,* and more. He is the founder/editor/publisher/artist behind Unnerving and Unnerving Magazine, and the host of the Unnerving Podcast. He lives on the Pacific Coast of Canada with his wife and their cat overlords.

Kev Harrison is a British author of horror and dark fiction living in Lisbon, Portugal. His folk horror novelette, *Cinders of a Blind Man Who Could See* is available now from Demain Publishing, while his work has also appeared in the acclaimed *Lost Films* anthology from Perpetual Motion Machine Publishing among others. His debut novella, *The Balance*, will be released in 2019 by Lycan Valley Press. You can find out more at www.KevHarrisonFiction.com.

Curtis M. Lawson is an author of unapologetically weird and transgressive fiction, dark poetry, and graphic novels. His work ranges from technicolor pulp adventures to bleak cosmic horror and includes *Those Who Go Forth into the Empty Place of Gods, Black Pantheons*, and *It's a Bad, Bad, Bad, Bad World*. Curtis lives in Salem, MA where he hosts the Wyrd Live Horror reading series.

Andrew Lennon is the author of *Every Twisted Thought* and other books in the horror and thriller genres. He has been featured in various bestselling anthologies, and is becoming a recognized name in the horror and thriller writing community. Andrew is a happily married man living in the North West of England with his wife Hazel & their children.

Adam Light resides in northeast Florida with his beautiful wife and daughter, and their two dogs, Walker and Aspen. He haunts a cubicle by day, writes horror stories at night, and rarely sleeps. *Toes Up: Horror to Die For* is his debut collection of short horror and weird fiction, and his work has been featured in *Doorbells at Dusk, Dead Roses: Five Dark Tales of Twisted Love* and the popular *Bad Apples* Halloween anthology series.

Evans Light is a writer of horror and suspense, and is the author of *Screamscapes: Tales of Terror, Arboreatum, Don't Need No Water* and more. He is editor of the well-received *Doorbells at Dusk* anthology, and is co-creator of the *Bad Apples* Halloween anthology series and *Dead Roses: Five Dark Tales of Twisted Love*. He lives in Charlotte, North Carolina, surrounded by thousands of vintage horror paperbacks, and is the proud father of fine sons and the lucky husband of a beautiful wife.

Chad Lutzke has written for *Famous Monsters of Filmland, Rue Morgue, Cemetery Dance,* and *Scream* magazine. He's had a few dozen stories published, and some of his books include: *Of Foster Homes & Flies, Wallflower, Stirring the Sheets, Skullface Boy, The Same Deep Water as You, The Neon Owl* and *Out Behind the Barn* (co-written with John Boden). Lutzke's work has been praised by authors Jack Ketchum, Stephen Graham Jones, James Newman, Cemetery Dance, and his own mother. He can be found lurking the internet at www.chadlutzke.com.

Josh Malerman is the New York Times Best Selling author of *Bird Box, Unbury Carol, Inspection,* and *A House at the Bottom of a Lake*. He's also one of two singer/songwriters for the Detroit band The High Strung, whose song "The Luck You Got" can be heard as the theme song for the Showtime show *Shameless*.

Mason Morgan was born and will die in Texas. Currently, he is an active member of the Horror Writer's Association and is at work on his debut collection. Previously, he has been published in *Deadlights Magazine, Two Hawks Quarterly,* and served as the opinion editor for his alma mater, Texas A&M University. He, too, once feared the toilet.

Christopher Motz was born in 1980 and lives in small-town Pennsylvania with his wife and step-daughter. He's an avid music fan, collector of classic vinyl, and musician. Since 2016, he has released six novels and two novellas as well as having several of his short stories appear in horror anthologies.

Frank Oreto is an editor and writer of weird fiction living in Pittsburgh Pennsylvania. When not writing new stories, he spends his time cooking up elaborate meals for his wife and perpetually hungry children. You can follow his exploits both literary and culinary on Twitter *@FrankOreto*.

Glenn Rolfe is an author from the haunted woods of New England. He studied Creative Writing at Southern New Hampshire University, and continues his education in the world of horror by devouring the novels of Stephen King, Brian Keene, Ronald Malfi, and many others. He and his wife, Meghan, have three children, Ruby, Ramona, and Axl. He is grateful to be loved despite his weirdness. He is the author of *The Window*, *Becoming*, *Blood and Rain*, *The Haunted Halls*, *Chasing Ghosts*, *Boom Town*, *Abram's Bridge*, *Things We Fear*, and the forthcoming works, *Follow Me Down* and *Until Summer Comes Around*.

Kristopher Rufty lives in North Carolina with his three children and pets. He's written numerous books, including *Anathema*, *The Vampire of Plainfield*, *Jagger*, *The Lurkers*, *The Skin Show*, *Pillowface*, and more. He can be found on Facebook and Twitter.

Mary SanGiovanni is an award-winning American horror and thriller writer of over a dozen novels, including *The Hollower* trilogy, *Thrall*, *Chaos*, The Kathy Ryan series and others, as well as numerous novellas, short stories and non-fiction. She has a Masters degree in Writing Popular Fiction from Seton Hill University, Pittsburgh, and is currently a member of The Authors Guild, The International Thriller Writers and Penn Writers. She is a co-host on the popular podcast *The Horror Show with Brian Keene*, and hosts her own podcast, *Cosmic Shenanigans*. She offers talks and workshops on writing around the country. Born and raised in New Jersey, she currently resides in Pennsylvania.

Jeff Strand is the Bram Stoker Award-nominated author of over 40 books, including *Pressure*, *Dweller*, *My Pretties*, and *Sick House*. He's primarily known for mixing horror with humor, though he also writes non-humorous horror and non-horrific humor. He lives in Atlanta, Georgia, and you can visit his website at www.JeffStrand.com.

Mikal Trimm has sold over 50 short stories and 100 poems to numerous venues including *Postscripts*, *Strange Horizons*, *Realms of Fantasy*, and *Ellery Queen's Mystery Magazine*. Admittedly, it took a lot of blackmail.

Gregor Xane is the author of *Six Dead Spots*, *Taboogasm*, *The Hanover Block*, and the forthcoming *Brides of Hanover Block*. His work has been featured in *Stupefying Stories*, *Dead Roses*, *Doorbells at Dusk*, and the popular Halloween anthology series, *Bad Apples*. He lives inside a suburban home in southwestern Ohio, and he's never seen his neighbors.

CARVE YOUR PUMPKINS AND TURN ON THE PORCH LIGHT.

Halloween frights begin
with the sound of...

DOORBELLS AT DUSK.

Brand-new Halloween tales from modern masters
& rising stars of dark fiction, horror and suspense.

**These are the thrills you crave,
in a collection that's pure Halloween.**

Featuring stories by:

Josh Malerman, Jason Parent, Thomas Vaughn

Evans Light, Chad Lutzke, Curtis M. Lawson

Gregor Xane, Amber Fallon, Charles Gramlich,

Adam Light, Joanna Koch, Lisa Lepovetsky

Ian Welke, Sean Eads & Joshua Viola

Available Now
from CORPUS PRESS

MORE FROM THE EDITORS

ANDREW LENNON

EVANS LIGHT

WANT MORE?

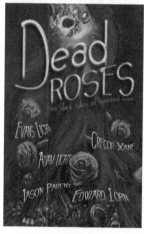

HORROR AND WEIRD FICTION AT
CORPUSPRESS.COM

CPSIA information can be obtained
at www.ICGtesting.com
Printed in the USA
FSHW012046160719
60094FS